'Have you dec____ trusted?'

Janeta's lips tre_____ ___ ____ ____ awkwardly, 'I cannot be sure of anything in this
frightening world outside my convent walls,
but I am at your mercy, sire, and I have
prayed to the Virgin for her protection. So
far you have proved trustworthy.'

Instantly the laughter left Bertrand's eyes and
his voice was far more serious. 'I assure you
that your innocence is your own protection,
demoiselle. I am no saint, but I never yet
broke my knightly vows and pressed unwelcome attention on any lady.'

Joanna Makepeace taught as head of English in a comprehensive school, before leaving full-time work to write. She lives in Leicester with her mother and a Jack Russell terrier called Dickon, and has written over thirty books under different pseudonyms. She loves the old romantic historical films, which she finds more exciting and relaxing than the newer ones.

Recent titles by the same author:

CROWN HOSTAGE
CORINNA'S CAUSE
RELUCTANT REBEL
BATTLEFIELD OF HEARTS
THE SPANISH PRIZE

THE DEVIL'S MARK

Joanna Makepeace

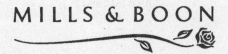

MILLS & BOON

MILLS & BOON, the Rose Device and LEGACY OF LOVE are trademarks of the publisher.
Harlequin Mills & Boon Limited,
Eton House, 18–24 Paradise Road, Richmond, Surrey TW9 1SR
This edition published by arrangement with
Harlequin Enterprises B.V.

© Joanna Makepeace 1995

ISBN 0 263 79084 3

Set in 10 on 11 pt Linotron Times
04-9506-87861

Typeset in Great Britain by CentraCet, Cambridge
Printed in Great Britain by
BPC Paperbacks Ltd

CHAPTER ONE

IT WAS Sister Boniface who came to tell Janeta that
her father had arrived and was asking to see her. The
kindly nun's round red face revealed her concern. It
was over three years since Sir Hugh Cobham had
presented himself at the convent, and as far as she was
aware no message had been delivered to his daughter
during that time. She could not help engaging in sinful
curiosity about the reason which brought him here
now. Janeta was nineteen, long past the age to take
her first vows into the noviciate; it was likely that Sir
Hugh had come finally to give his formal consent,
though it had been generally accepted that the child
would become a bride of Christ since she had first
come here to be educated, soon after her tenth
birthday.

Janeta lowered her head submissively as she had
been trained.

'Thank you, Sister. Will you give me a few moments
to compose myself before I come to Reverend
Mother's parlour?'

Sister Boniface nodded, smiling. 'Smooth your
gown, child. You will want your father to see you
looking your best. It may be the last time you see him
for several more years.' She bustled off, closing the
heavy door of the dortour, and Janeta sank down on
her hard little bed, one hand thrust tight against her
fast-beating heart.

So—he had come. She had hardly dared to believe
that he would answer her anguished little note, delivered for her by the carter who passed through

Winchester and on to the coast. The abbess had graciously agreed to her sending her request, so there had been no need for subterfuge. It was so very important that he should listen quietly to what she had to say. It had been so long since she had seen him that she could scarcely remember exactly how he looked. Even before he had placed her here he had rarely condescended to come to the manor nursery, and her recollection of her father was of a tall, big man, with a hard, unyielding countenance, who barked brief orders to her nurse, regarded her charge frowningly and quickly left.

Janeta had never once dared to gainsay him; indeed, she had scarcely uttered more than a few words to him. Now she must gather her courage to explain how she felt, and she must remain determined, however he stormed or frowned her down. She drew a hard breath, rose and smoothed down her rough grey homespun gown, and put up a hand to assure herself that her barbette was tight and her fillet and coarse white veil decorously straight.

The nuns were busy in cloisters, gardens and kitchens, for it was well past Prime and their office in chapel was done for at least another hour. The girls in their charge were with the mistress of the novices at their embroidery, and it was from her chamber that Janeta had been summoned and taken to the dortour to ensure that she was composed and seemly to receive her father. She allowed herself the luxury of running lightly down the day stair and out into the cloister, where she received only a gentle chiding glance from old Sister Mary, who was seated on her stool near the door, warmly wrapped, her beads clasped in rheumaticky hands. The old nun was too aged now to work in the garden, and her eyesight was too dim to sew, so she was allowed to bask in what wintry sun there was this December day of 1237, until one of the younger nuns escorted her to chapel for Terce.

Janeta moderated her step and went more slowly across the green to the abbess's parlour. Sister Agatha let her in, scolding gently.

'Here you are at last. You have been a long time. Reverend Mother was about to send me to find you.' She glanced briefly over Janeta, assessing her appearance, and gave a little bird-like nod of approval. 'Your father is waiting. Somewhat impatiently, I'm bound to say.'

She knocked on the parlour door and, at the mellifluous tones of the abbess bidding them enter, stood back to let Janeta in.

The abbess was seated in her high-backed chair and she inclined her head as Janeta paused in the doorway, curtsying deferentially.

'Come in, Janeta. As you see, your father is here and wishes to speak with you. I have been telling him how well you have progressed in your studies and what beautiful work you have done on our latest altar-cloth. I wish to inspect the kitchen before Terce, and I know you would wish to be alone with him, so I will leave you together. Sister Agatha will bring ale and bread and meat if you call.'

She turned to her male visitor, smiling, and he came from the window and bowed, stepping back respectfully as she swept through the door with a soughing of black draperies. The abbess was a stately figure, still scarcely more than in her fortieth year, well-born and with the gracious, aristocratic airs of her ancestors. For all her haughty manners she was a fair mistress, respected by all her nuns and the novices and children in her charge, who held her in awe but were unafraid in her presence. Janeta curtsied again, and then turned uncertainly to face her father.

He towered over her, a majestic figure in riding clothes, his heavy-hooded mantle thrust back now in the warmth of the parlour. Janeta ventured a swift glance at his unsmiling face. He had changed little. His long lips were held in a hard line over a square, unyielding chin; brown eyes, opaque like marble, regarded her darkly over his heavy, fleshy nose. One hand was thrust into his gilded leather belt, the other upon his hip, and he stood, feet astride, as if ready to give judgement on some errant serf on the manor. She saw now that there was some greying of the short, dark hair at his temples, and realised with a slight jolt that he was older than she had imagined him in her thoughts.

'Well?'

His simple opening remark was uncompromising, and she gave a little start of alarm. It would not be easy trying to convince him. She swallowed hard, then faced him bravely, her chin out-thrust, her grey eyes searching his face for some sign of concern for her welfare or pleasure at seeing her again after so long.

'I am sorry, Father, that I had to bring you out of your way, but I felt I had to see you.'

'So you said in your message. I'm waiting to know why.'

She hesitated. 'The nuns are expecting me to take my vows into the noviciate.'

'Yes?'

Her body tensed, but she forced herself not to flinch from facing him and continued to look into his dark eyes directly.

'I cannot do it, Father.'

His face darkened ominously and his eyes narrowed in anger and astonishment.

'I don't understand. I thought you were happy here.'

'I am. The nuns have been very good to me.' She

did not add that she had received from them the understanding and affection she had not received from him or from her older brother, who had not once come to see her since she had been brought here.

'Then I see no reason. . . It was understood from the beginning——'

She cut into his diatribe. 'I have no vocation.'

'Nonsense. Many young girls must have doubts when about to take such a step, but this convent is your home. You are secure here. Mind me well, Janeta, there can be no future for you outside these walls.'

She blanched, staring at him pleadingly. 'Father, I must try and make you understand. My nature is not——' she sought desperately for the right words '—fitting for such a life of pious contemplation.' She hesitated again, looking a little beyond him. 'Lately I have experienced feelings—violent emotions—quite outside the knowledge of the nuns. I could not take a vow of obedience. Poverty I can accept—I have known no existence other than this since my nurse died— chastity I would accept—if—if I fully faced the need for that promise—but I cannot obey without question. It is not in me. I lose my temper too easily and—it can be quite frightening. I have seen the older nuns turn quite pale when I am in one of my rages. Reverend Mother has been kind—and forgiving—but what was acceptable in a child is not to be borne from one who is now a woman grown. We are asked to pledge ourselves to unquestioned obedience. I know I could not live in that way. I must not take the veil. Allow me to come home, Father. At least give me a chance to know what I shall miss in the world. Perhaps then I should be more willing to contemplate the life of the *religieuse*.'

She waited for his answer, and when she turned back to him she saw that he was choking on his own fury.

'That is quite out of the question. At the moment I am actively engaged in arranging a match for Ralph. There can be no place for you at home. There is sufficient gold to furnish you with the small dowry needed for your final entrance here—but I could not find enough to get you a husband.'

She stared at him blankly, and he continued in callous, brutal tones, 'Face facts, girl. What man would contemplate marriage with a girl scarred with the devil's own mark, even if the dowry was plentiful, which it isn't? And you are now almost past marriageable age. This temper of yours is further proof of what we have always feared—that only here, within the holy precincts of sanctified ground, will you be safe. Reverend Mother knows the truth, and is prepared to protect you. If I were to die, Ralph would be totally unwilling to have you live on the manor a penniless dependant. It would not be fair to his bride. In time there would be talk, questions as to the reasons why a husband was not provided. No, Janeta, it is impossible. Here I brought you, and here you will stay. Make up your mind to accept your destiny, and be glad the nuns are willing to have you—in spite of everything.'

Her eyes widened in pain, and she placed one hand defensively upon her left breast. She had carried this burden since she had been old enough to understand. Few knew her secret, even within the community— each hard little bed within the pupil's dortour was furnished with curtains, shielding it from the others. The abbess was aware of the ugly mark which marred the whiteness of Janeta's youthful body, and the infirmarian, who had tended her during the minor childish illnesses she had suffered since her arrival here, and dear Sister Boniface, who was her mentor and her confidante. Not one of them had remarked upon the significance of the wine-coloured stain which crept from her left breast upwards along her shoulder, and stopped short of showing itself to the world at large upon her throat. She had tried to avoid looking at it herself on the occasions when she removed her chemise in the curtained privacy of her bed-space.

There were no mirrors within the convent and she had long forgotten exactly how she appeared to strangers. She knew she was of medium height, dark, with grey-blue eyes, but not one of her companions had said she was either pretty or plain. Vanity was frowned upon and the girls, wary of bringing down the wrath of the mistress of postulants, kept their opinions on the appearance of others to themselves. Janeta had soon become aware that her position in the nunnery was different from theirs. They had come here to be educated and to return to the world; she was known to be destined to assume the habit. If they pitied her, they did not tell her so, and it was only lately that she had begun to envy them the adventure life offered outside these sheltering walls.

Now her father's harsh words reinforced her dimly understood longings. The others would marry, have children, rule their own households. None of these blessings could be hers. She was set apart. She shivered as she recalled the superstitious terror in her nurse's eyes and the way the woman had crossed herself and made the sign against the evil eye whenever Janeta's child's body was revealed to her during bathing or dressing. Now her father had put those fears into words. It was not simply that she was plain or crippled, but the fact that she was marked by the ancient enemy of man prevented her from sharing the simple, homely pleasures her companions would know.

She swallowed. Here, she could keep secret that fearful disfigurement, her wimple would hide it from the world, but to a husband she would be forced to reveal it in all its stark ugliness, and no amount of inducement could make her acceptable to masculine eyes.

She said quietly, 'I understand. I had not thought out exactly—how things would be. Tell my brother I will pray for his happiness.' The final words were whispered, and even that dour, unapproachable man who had sired her winced away from the pain in them.

He said awkwardly, 'I shall pray for you too, daughter. Speak to Reverend Mother. She will advise you how to search for consolation in the profession of your faith. I am sure that—eventually—you will see the wisdom of what I propose and gain some measure of peace.'

She nodded, her tongue suddenly cleaving to the roof of her mouth. She would not plead further. There was nothing more she could say to him. For the first time she realised how her birth had wounded him. Ralph was strong and hale, a son to be proud of—and then had come this girl-child, marked so cruelly for whom there could be no hope of an advantageous marriage which might further his ambitions.

He came close and tilted up her chin with one finger. 'God bless you, daughter.' His embarrassment had hardened the tone of his voice again. 'When you are ready to take your final vows inform us, and Ralph and I will visit you again.'

She was not to see him before that, then, during the long years of the noviciate. He was abandoning her and she could find no further arguments, nor could she hold him with her longer. She curtsied, received his dutiful kiss of kinship, and watched him walk from the room without a backward glance. She waited, bleakly, to hear his hurrying mailed feet on the stair, the ring of his spur against one of the risers, then she walked blindly to the window to stare out, unseeing, over the herb-garden.

Reverend Mother returned soon after. She spoke briskly, did not enquire as to what had occurred during the visit, and dismissed Janeta firmly, though her brown eyes were moist with pity as the girl curtsied and withdrew from her private parlour. She sighed. Like Janeta, she had had no choice about entering the cloistered life, being the third daughter of an impoverished, noble household, but she had accepted her fate cheerfully and found true consolation in her faith. She was not at all sure that the same could be expected of Janeta Cobham.

Janeta retrieved her embroidery from the chest where the silks and costly materials were stored in the nuns' common parlour and went to sit a little apart from the other girls. Her eyes were misting with tears and she was afraid of marring the white silk of the new altar-cloth with tear-stains transferred from her fingers, and finally she placed the work down on her knee. Usually she enjoyed the intricate stitching, and was the most skilled of all the girls, habitually chosen to work on the finest of materials, but today she received no pleasure from concentration on the piece in hand. The bleakness of her future stretched ahead with frightening finality and she could not bear the thought.

Alice Smallthorpe, her nearest companion in age, came to sit on the stool beside her.

'I hear your father visited.'

Janeta nodded. She was still too close to tears to speak, and Alice regarded her thoughtfully.

'I hope there was not bad news. You have a brother—he isn't ill?'

Janeta shook her head and forced an answer.

'No. Ralph is soon to be wed.'

'Ah.' Alice gazed dreamily across the width of the parlour. Next Easter she was to be married. Arrangements had already been made. She would leave the convent to return home for the Christmas feasting and, as yet, was unsure whether she was pleased or sorry. Like Janeta, she had been enclosed in this safe little cocoon for some years and the announcement that she was to wed a man some ten years her senior, and on whom she had never set eyes, had both excited and alarmed her. She turned back to her companion and eyed her closely.

'Is it—is it that you too would like to be wed?' she said awkwardly, in a sudden rush. Nothing had ever been said about Janeta. It had always been assumed that she would take the veil, and now Alice wondered if Janeta's fears were as real and terrifying as her own.

Janeta stared woodenly ahead. 'My father has no intention of finding a match for me. He—hasn't the means. . .' Her words trailed off. She could not reveal to this curious girl the reason why her request to return home had been so summarily dismissed.

'So—so you will stay here?'

'No.' The single word was thrust out vehemently. 'No, I will not. If I have to beg in the streets, I will not take my vows.'

Alice stared open-mouthed as Janeta snatched up her work and fled from the parlour, the disapproving eyes of the mistress of the novices following her undignified running steps.

After a sleepless night, in which Janeta went over and over in her mind the alternatives stretching before her and found no solution to her hopeless situation, she rose at the sound of the bell and went with the other girls to the refectory. All the time she was eating silently she was aware of Alice's avidly curious gaze, and felt anger welling up within her. Stubbornly she told herself that she would stick to the answer she had given Alice. Whatever happened, she would not allow herself to be immured here for the rest of her life. There must be some way of providing for herself, despite her father's determination not to do so.

She worked industriously in the herb-garden, hoping that hard, physical labour would dull the ache in her heart, but she was still troubled when she made her way back to the cloister, intending to return to the parlour and continue her work on the altar-cloth.

She stopped abruptly as jeering voices cut across the peace of the enclosure. Sister Mary was, as usual, seated on her stool near the convent door. Before her stood two of the younger pupils, both waving aloft the rough blankets in which the infirmarian had shrouded her elderly charge against the winter morning. Sister Mary rose and tried to totter forward in order to retrieve them, or so Janeta thought. The girls teasingly stepped back, each laughing towards the other and holding out their trophies invitingly.

Sister Mary gave a distressed little cry and tried again to move towards them, but her rheumaticky limbs were stiff and her balance uncertain. She teetered awkwardly, and only with an effort managed to stay upright. Janeta sprang towards the old lady, put a supporting arm round her shoulders, and led her back to her seat. The two girls, thoroughly alarmed now at the possible tragic result of their thoughtlessness, stood transfixed. Janeta lowered Sister Mary, soothing her gently as she saw weak tears squeezing under her blue-veined eyelids.

'It's quite all right, Sister. You know you mustn't try to walk without help. Sister Catherine would scold you.'

The younger of the two girls came hesitatingly

forward with the pilfered blankets, and Janeta snatched them from her and tucked them securely round the elderly nun's form.

'I'm—I'm sorry, Sister. We meant no harm.' The girl gulped uncertainly. She had only recently arrived at the convent with her older companion. The two found the routine of the place stultifying and were constantly seeking ways of entertaining themselves. Frequently they played tricks upon their companions, who took the sport good-humouredly. Janeta had had pranks played upon her and taken no heed, but she was incensed by their stupid, foolish cruelty towards an old lady who was helpless to retaliate.

She gestured the younger girl back and, with a roar of fury, launched herself upon the other, Ursula Nollys.

'Have you no sense at all?' Her fingers dug into Ursula's shoulders and she was shaking the frightened girl as a terrier might shake a rat. 'Can you not see she is unsafe on her feet? What if she had fallen? A broken bone at her age might have meant her death, and it is bitingly cold today. You have been a torment to the younger girls for weeks now, and it will stop. Do you hear me? It will stop!' Each final word was accompanied by a shake and Ursula was rigid with fear. Her barbette and veil had been displaced by the violence of the attack and her fair hair streamed down her back in disarray. Janeta was so incensed that she did not hear the frightened crying of the second girl until a gentle, authoritative voice bade her give way, and she released Ursula so violently that the girl stumbled backwards and fell, giving a final terrified yell of pain and fear.

Sister Boniface took Janeta by the arms and held her very close.

'Janeta, what are you doing?'

The red rage she felt behind her eyes began to clear,

and Janeta became aware of the two younger girls crying, clasping each other tightly together as Ursula was helped to her feet. Janeta forced herself to stop shaking with a determined effort. As Sister Boniface released her she put a trembling hand to her forehead.

'I—I—I was so angry. They were teasing Sister Mary. I—I couldn't allow them to. . .' Her voice trailed off as she fully realised the enormity of her attack on Ursula. Her breath was still coming in ugly quick pants and she put the other hand to her breast as if to calm herself mentally. Her face puckered and she burst into tears, rushing into Sister Boniface's motherly arms and sobbing against her ample bosom as if her heart would break.

'Oh, Sister, I am so—sorry. They meant no—harm. I know it was all foolishness but—but—oh, why do I do this? I just can't help it. Something inside me snaps and—and. . .'

Sister Boniface was gently patting her back. 'There, there, child. I know you have been in great distress lately, and have been unable to come to me and tell me what is wrong. We all know you can very quickly lose your temper, but over this last year you have tried so hard, and succeeded in holding it in check. Now—recently—it has been to the fore again. Hush, Janeta, no harm is done. You will alarm poor Sister Mary. The girls have gone now.'

She led the sobbing girl into the building and hastened with her to the lavatorium, where she waited while Janeta washed her face and tidied her own barbette and veil. She turned at last, controlled, to her mentor.

'Reverend Mother must be informed and I must be disciplined,' she said quietly. 'Sister, I am growing alarmed by the increase in violence I display. It comes without warning. Am I truly the daughter of the devil, as my father believes? If so, there is no place for me here, no place for me anywhere.' Her eyes were brimming with tears and her lips trembling, but she had herself under control now, and the shaking of her limbs was evidence of her own sense of outrage at what might have happened, rather than a further display of ungovernable temper.

Sister Boniface shook her head reprovingly. 'Of course you are no spawn of the devil. If you were so, would you be so frightened or so contrite? You were righteously angry, as I might well have been if I had come upon those two, cruelly teasing a helpless old lady. You simply let your control slip.' She gave a heavy sigh. 'I think it is a sign that all is not well in your heart, Janeta. You are terribly unhappy. Only God in his wisdom can give you the courage you need to fight this. Go to the chapel, child, and pray for guidance. I will find Ursula and see she suffered no hurt from the fall. Don't be afraid. I will see Reverend Mother, and,' she added grimly, 'I doubt that either of those two young minxes will have complaints against you to offer. If so, I will see to it that the score is set right.'

Impulsively Janeta bent and kissed the work-worn hands and curtsied before she set off, as bidden, to the chapel.

She stretched herself out, arms wide in penitence, before the altar, her lips moving in a prayer to St Catherine, the patron saint of all virgins, to give her guidance. How long she remained there in the silent, dim-lit chapel, the stone-flagged floor icy cold beneath her, she could not tell, but at last she rose stiffly to sit back upon her heels, her hands clasped as she looked up beseechingly towards the altar crucifix. Finally, sighing, she rose and turned to leave the chapel, then gave a little start as she saw that she was no longer alone. Alice Smallthorpe was kneeling in one of the choir stalls. She too rose as she saw Janeta about to leave, and the two girls padded silently out of the chapel and down the corridor into the cloisters, instinctively moving towards a corner away from another group of nuns and postulants taking their exercise before supper in the refectory.

Alice said timidly, 'I could see you were greatly disturbed. After what you said about not taking your vows the other day, I thought. . .' Her voice trailed off and she gazed steadfastly ahead as they walked together, moderating their pace each to the other, since it was far too cold to stand or sit, yet needing to be some distance from their companions and, in some silent way, communicating a need for comfort.

Janeta turned towards Alice sharply. They had never been close, yet now she sensed the other girl's unhappiness was as great as her own.

'What is it, Alice? I thought it was settled that you would leave us soon to marry. Surely that is what you desire?'

'I don't know.' The answer was almost a frightened wail. 'I am not really very pretty. My younger sister is much more attractive than I, and—perhaps—I had thought I would be spared. . .'

'Would you have preferred to remain here?' Janeta said wonderingly. Here was Alice wanting in vain the life that Janeta thought was being forced upon her.

Alice shook her head despairingly. 'I haven't seen Will, my betrothed. He is a widower. His wife died in childbed and——' she drew a shuddering breath '—I am terrified that such a fate will overtake me. I lost an older sister so, and my mother and aunt. I shall never forget the birth of my mother's last child. Her screams rang through the house for days.' She turned to face Janeta now, and tears were welling up in her eyes.

'Here the nuns have no such peril to face. It would be quiet here—and safe.'

'Have you spoken of this to your father?'

'No, no,' Alice said hurriedly. 'He would not understand, let alone listen. The marriage is arranged. He is pleased by the settlement and I must be content. You want to leave, Janeta. Is it that you want marriage? Aren't you afraid of bearing children and—and——' Her cheeks reddened in acute embarrassment '—what —what will happen in the marriage-bed?'

Janeta paused in her walk, her expression thoughtful. 'I had not thought of all that.' She realised, startled, that she had not. She had wished to leave the convent because it had begun to mean a curtailment of her liberty. Now she understood that if a husband had been found for her, as Alice's had been, it might well have meant a different kind of imprisonment. What she required was freedom, and even as she recognised the need she realised the impossibility of achieving it.

'Not all women die in childbirth,' she said consolingly. 'Your mother had several children in safety, and one of the women who stayed at the guest-house last year told me she had had twelve children. You are young and strong, Alice. You must not fear without cause. You said your Will is ten years older than you— twenty-eight, a comparatively young man. You may be extremely happy together, and you will have a household of your own. . .'

'That is what you want, a life of your own?'

'Yes.'

'And your father is adamant that you must stay here?'

'He is. He has his reasons. He is not entirely a hard man. It is just that he cannot see the possibility of marriage for me.' Janeta smiled wistfully. 'I want what you are so anxious to reject. Life can be very cruel sometimes. Were you praying for guidance in the chapel?'

'For courage,' agreed Alice. She smiled suddenly. 'I think you have given me some comfort at least. You are right. I am strong. Perhaps I shall give Will many healthy children and he will love me.'

'I shall pray that he will do so.'

'I wish I could help you.' Alice sounded doubtful. 'If I knew Will better perhaps I could persuade him to allow me to take you into our household. . .'

'That is not very likely.' Janeta smiled.

Alice turned to her impulsively. 'If you cannot return home and you are determined to leave here, you must find a way of providing for yourself.'

Janeta inclined her head. 'It was for that I was praying, for some glimmer of light, and also for help in controlling my tempers.' She laughed suddenly again, a trifle bitterly. 'As a servant I would not last long with such a failing.'

'But you are so skilful a seamstress,' Alice interposed eagerly. 'I think many households would welcome you. My aunt has an elderly dependant who works for her, has lived with the family for years, and lately married my uncle's steward. She does exquisite embroidery, but even so is not as skilled as you are. It would be one way out for you, Janeta.'

Janeta stood stock-still in wonder. 'I think,' she said slowly, 'we each received an answer to our prayers in chapel, Alice. You have given me hope. In Winchester there must be some household who would employ me as a seamstress and maid. Better that life by far, hard as it might be, than remaining here to wither and die before I know any freedom of spirit.'

'But would Reverend Mother let you go without your father's consent?' Alice's voice betrayed sudden doubt.

'No,' Janeta said bluntly. 'She will not. But now I have hope, I'll find a way.'

During the evening meal Janeta was glad of the imposed silence, for she had a great deal of time to think. Alice had spoken the truth indeed, for Janeta was sure that her father had insisted that his daughter be closely watched. Though St Catherine's was not an enclosed order, it was rare for the nuns to leave it. The abbess did, of course, go on expeditions to other convents, and frequently to view the work on the convent lands. Her nuns, should they need to walk abroad, always did so in pairs. The postulants did not leave the convent, and the girls receiving education there, as Janeta was, never without their parents or visiting kin. It would not be easy to escape from the enclosure. The portress kept strict watch on the gate and Janeta's absence, should she manage it, would soon be noted and a report made to the abbess, who would set a search in motion. Janeta gritted her teeth in impotent fury. Now she had seen a possible way of escape from this seemingly sterile life she must make it soon, for pressure would soon be put upon her to enter the noviciate.

The December chill abated somewhat over the following days and the nuns were able to resume some final tidying up in the herb-garden. A watery sun lightened the sky and Sister Mary was glad to assume her seat outside again. Janeta was sent one day to examine the apples laid out in rows under the roof to keep throughout the winter, and after she had removed the rotten fruit and ensured that all was well with the rest she sat on the scrubbed wooden floor of the loft, her skirts kirtled high, and dreamed for a few blessed moments of the privacy of life in the town. It would soon be the holy season of Christmas and she remembered, longingly, the twelve days of rejoicing that the household had enjoyed on the manor. The Yule log had been hauled into the hall and boughs of greenery nailed to the walls and tucked behind tapestries. There had been laughter and music and feasting and dancing. Here, the Holy Christ Mass was celebrated lovingly, but without that noisy abandonment she recalled but had not fully understood. Reverend Mother abominated some of the Christmas customs, declaring them to be pagan, but the nuns enjoyed extra delicacies and had permission to spend more time talking and communicating pleasantly in the common parlour than was usually allowed.

Janeta's thoughts flew to her own family. Possibly Ralph's betrothed would be brought to the manor by her parents and there would be special festivities to mark his official betrothal. Would the girl be fearful, as Alice was? Perhaps, as Alice had tearfully professed, Janeta might be fortunate to escape the ills which threatened womankind. Yet, she thought fiercely, those fears must be put aside if she was to face the excitement and challenge of life outside these protective walls. She had chosen freedom, with all the perils it might entail, and she would not shrink from seizing it if the opportunity was to offer itself.

It was to come sooner than she could have dared to hope.

Reverend Mother was faced with a dilemma, and unaccountably chose Alice and Janeta to solve it for her. She received tidings that the Bishop was to visit the house and had got little warning. Reverend Mother kept faithfully to the rule of St Benedict but for one small infringement: she possessed a small Italian greyhound, on whom she lavished much love and pampering. The keeping of pets was forbidden by the rule, with all such attachments to worldly things, and

Mother was loath to allow the Bishop to know her weakness. Her pet must be kept far from the convent buildings during the visit. Her nuns loved and admired her—many of them bestowed pampering on the affectionate little creature—and they were willing enough to fall in with her attempt to keep the dog's presence secret. They would not betray her, she knew. She sent for her two eldest pupils.

They rose from dutiful curtsies. Reverend Mother was clearly in something of a dither.

'I want you girls to do something for me—and keep quiet about it,' she implored, looking anxiously into their curious young faces. 'Can I trust you?'

'Of course, Reverend Mother,' they chorused dutifully.

'I want you to take Tip away from the convent for a few hours. You will keep a close hold on him at all times?'

They assured her that they would.

'You are such sensible girls, I can trust you to keep close to the convent lands and not stray into the village. The peasants here can be trusted, but I am not sure of the villagers so near to the ale-house.' She gave a little shudder of distaste. 'The Bishop will wish to interview my nuns, so I cannot release one to accompany you.' She gave a hearty sigh. 'I cannot understand why it is forbidden to keep my lovable little dog. I'm sure Our Lord would love him as I do, as he loved all vulnerable creatures, yet I know the bishop will not approve and will order me to discard him.'

Janeta said comfortingly, 'I'm sure Our Lord would, Reverend Mother, and your affection for Tip cannot be regarded as a sin. He will be safe with us. You can be sure of it.'

'Then go and wrap up warmly. It is quite mild for December, but you will need to remain outdoors for some time and it may get colder as the sun sets. The portress has her orders to allow you out and re-admit you both after the bishop and his retinue have left. Take shelter in one of the barns if you get too cold.'

Her eyes were already straying to the door, for she could hear the scurrying of feet outside in the corridor as the nuns rushed to make sure all was correct and in readiness for the illustrious visitor. The abbess called her pet to her and smothered him with kisses.

'Take him quickly, then. Food will be provided for all three of you and is waiting in the kitchens.'

Janeta took the soft leather leash the abbess held out to her and drew the little dog out of the parlour.

'Stay out of sight in an angle of the cloister,' she instructed Alice, handing over the leash. 'I will go and fetch cloaks for us and the food.'

Alice gave an answering grin of impish delight for the hours of freedom ahead and ran off, the little dog loping excitedly after her.

Janeta was relieved to find the dortour deserted. She riffled through the two small travelling-chests which stood near to her bed and Alice's to find the woollen hooded cloaks that the postulants and pupils wore on colder days when walking in the garden and cloister.

Janeta had few possessions of her own. Every garment she had brought with her she had grown out of and she had been provided with no money, for she simply had never had need of any. Her mother had possessed few jewels, and as a child Janeta had not been given what there were. She supposed that her mother's jewels would now be given to Ralph's bride, or sent to the convent to be sold as part of her entry dower. She was reluctant to take convent clothing, but she needed her cloak. She had been allowed to keep one small reliquary, a present for her mother from her father on her wedding-day, and she slid the gold chain over her head, tucking the reliquary, containing a sliver of St Andrew's cross, beneath the neck of her gown. She could not bear the thought of parting with it, but she faced the grim fact that it might be necessary to sell it if she did not immediately find some refuge in Winchester. Then she hastened to the kitchens, to find that bread, cheese, onions and cold bacon had been packed for them to carry in a clean kerchief.

Before rejoining Alice, Janeta slipped hurriedly into the chapel and knelt before the altar, murmuring a plea to the Virgin and to St Catherine to forgive her if she was causing anxiety to the good nuns who had so lovingly cared for her, and to grant her their protection in the hardships she faced.

Alice was laughing at the dog's antics as he rolled on his back to be tickled and did not appear to notice that Janeta seemed in any way agitated. She slipped on the cloak offered and glanced approvingly at the obviously well-filled kerchief of food.

'Oh, Janeta, how wonderful it will be to be free of the mistress of novices just for a day.' She made a face. 'Who knows whether I will ever be allowed such freedom from household tasks again? I know I shall be surrounded by chattering women, as much in my new home as here, and I wonder if I shall be allowed complete control over them.'

Janeta smiled in answer. She was not about to spoil Alice's day by speaking of her intentions just yet. They took the dog for a romp in the small wood just outside the enclave, and from its shelter saw the arrival of the bishop's retinue. As the wind got up and the temperature fell they found the grange barn and ate some of their provisions, laughing as the dog greedily consumed his share and begged for more. Alice's face was flushed with pleasure and she turned, with a little start of surprise, to find Janeta eyeing her gravely.

'You know I must take this opportunity, Alice. It
may be weeks, months even, before another comes. I
won't leave you until it is almost time for you to
return.'

Alice looked anxious. 'Janeta—I know what you
were planning and—and I encouraged you—but—but
you must know how dangerous what you propose could
be. Suppose you do not find a household willing to
take you? Where would you go? And at this time of
the year it will turn so cold. It's much colder now than
it has been for the last few days. . .'

'I know. I have considered all you've just said. If I
wait I might well find the pressures on me too great.'
Janeta absently stroked the little greyhound's soft fur.
'The Holy Season makes people more kindly, I think,
and there will be extra tasks—gowns torn during the
horseplay—I think it is the best and only time.' She bit
her lip uncertainly. 'If I cannot find work in some
household, why, then I must look for other opportunities—a tavern or cookshop. We have both been
well-educated in the kitchens and I have been well-
trained in herblore.'

'A tavern?' Alice breathed, horrified. 'Janeta, you
cannot mean that.'

Janeta took her friend's hand and squeezed it hard.
'I must, Alice. Do you understand?'

They looked into each other's eyes for moments,
then Alice gave a little nervous laugh.

'Yes, of course you must, and why am I frightening
you with all my portents of woe? Things will go well
with you; I'm sure they will. And you must go now. If
you wait till late afternoon it will be almost dark, and
you should be well on your way by then. Will you
make for Winchester? It is full six or seven miles, I
think.'

Janeta hesitated. 'I think it best if you are not sure

which direction I shall take. You will be questioned and pressure will be put on you to tell what you know. I would not have you lie, Alice.'

Again Alice nodded, after a brief pause for thought. 'Have you coin?'

'No, but I have a small jewel I must offer for sale if I need it. I hate to take my convent clothes, but I'm sure my father will agree to pay the nuns.' She shuddered. 'I could not bear to face the cold without my cloak, and, in any case, I have no gown of my own I can wear now.'

Alice still had a tight grip on her hands. 'When my father comes to take me home I will persuade him to make right any debt you may have incurred, though I think the sisters will be more concerned about you than the habit and cloak. If—if the worst comes to the worst, go to our manor. I'm sure my father will find you a place. . .'

Janeta pulled a wry face. 'He would return me to my father,' she said grimly.

'I suppose he would.' Alice bit her lip. 'I wish I could have helped you more. The Virgin guard you, Janeta.' She thrust the kerchief into Janeta's hand. 'There is still a little food remaining. If you had told me earlier, I could have gone without. As for him,' she said affectionately, ruffling the dog's neck fur, 'he is just a greedy-guts, and will well do without until he is returned to the abbess's care. A little fasting will do him good.'

There were tears in her eyes as she hugged Janeta. 'Go now. I shall stay here until I hear the sounds of departure, and then I shall wait a little longer. The longer I delay my return, the longer before I am questioned. Reverend Mother will be so glad to see the back of the Bishop and have Tip safely returned that she will think of nothing else until you are missed and there is a hue and cry for you. I shall say we became separated and that I have no idea where you might have gone. It will be the simple truth.'

Janeta withdrew herself from her friend's embrace. Now the time had come for parting she found that her mouth was very dry. She murmured a choked little 'goodbye' and slipped through the barn door. The wind caught her cloak and set it billowing, and she knew a moment of panic, then she set off at a run through the wood. Once clear of it she turned for one final glimpse at the cluster of buildings which had been her home for so long, her eyes blurred with tears. From here she could imagine the square shape of the cloister, hidden from her now by the enclave's high grey wall. Above was the squat square tower of the chapel, and beyond, the low, snug lines of the domiciliary buildings, with their infirmary and outlying huts for the garden spades and hoes and the room for the drying of herbs. It was all very dear and she caught back a sob, then resolutely turned away and began to head for the village which she knew lay on the Winchester road.

CHAPTER TWO

BERTRAND D'AUBIGNY reined in his destrier for the second time that afternoon and dismounted to examine the left forefoot of his sumpter mule. The poor beast had gone lame early that morning and it had taken Bertrand some time to discover the cause; a small thorn, almost undistinguishable to the naked eye, lodged under the front of the hoof. He had managed to extract it but the foot was still sore and he had been careful not to push the creature too hard. The light would soon be going and he had hoped to find his old camping spot before dark fell completely. He would rest his horses and be in Winchester tomorrow.

The mule sidled nervously as he whistled encouragingly between his teeth and assured himself that all was still well with her. Yes, he would lead her on now slowly, and there should be no more delays. He wanted to establish himself comfortably in the town before it became overcrowded with members of the King's retinue from London. After Christmas there would be the customary tournament and an opportunity to refill his meagre purse. Morris had been generous, according to his lights, but Bertrand would not be able to afford a lodging at one of the town's best inns, and while he could accept a measure of discomfort himself he was not prepared to subject Saladin to any degree of neglect. He would closely question the stable-lads at the lesser inns before making his choice. Saladin's well-being was vital to his chance of success in the jousts. The destrier had cost a king's ransom, or so Morris had disdainfully declared, but was worth the outlay of every silver penny.

He remounted Saladin and continued at a relatively slow pace, leading the sumpter mule, loaded with his spare suit of chain-mail, weapons and helmet, besides the saddle-bags containing his few possessions. He had left Stoke Charity, where he had watered his horses, some six miles back, and the old, deserted village he sought was some four miles ahead.

The road appeared deserted, the few villeins he encountered long gone from the field strips, huddling for warmth under their shabby hooded cotes. He looked up at the sky; it was clear; there would certainly be a hard frost tonight, and it was essential that he get shelter from the driving wind. If it dropped there might well be snow in the morning. He pulled his own hooded mantle well around him and prayed he would not find himself benighted upon this lonely stretch of road.

He had not allowed himself to dwell upon the finality of leaving the manor. There could be no future there for him and, since his father's death, tensions had tightened between himself and Morris. He had always known his fortunes lay apart from his home manor and now, at twenty-three years of age, he had at last decided that he would not return. The consequences of his not doing so could be far-reaching and disastrous.

Morris had been surprised by his apparently precipitate decision, but could not entirely disguise the fact that he would be relieved to see his younger brother finally depart. Had his mother lived, there would have been more of a struggle to bring himself to go, Bertrand considered. He gave a slight sigh of regret. He loved the old grey manor-house in Northampton shire, and he knew every villein who worked the land there, but he must set his thoughts now on forging a place for himself, either as a mercenary or upon the tournament circuit. The late great William the Marshall had shown how that could be accomplished. Born a younger son, he had risen to the highest prominence in the land. While Bertrand did not aspire to such heights he was optimistic about his prospects, and refused to allow himself to become depressed over the events of the last months. Morris would soon bring his bride to the manor and there was an end to the old life.

He was lost in his thoughts and swore savagely as a shrill scream broke the silence. A bird rose up before his destrier's hoofs and sent the beast into a sudden rearing panic. Bertrand kept his seat with difficulty, and managed to restrain his plunging mount, but the sumpter mule tore loose from its lead-rein and set off at a stumbling pace back the way she had come. Bertrand simmered with rage as he realised she could soon injure the foot he had been so carefully nursing. He would frighten her further if he set off in pursuit mounted on Saladin so he dismounted, running his hand gently down the beautiful black neck to soothe his favourite. The great horse was trembling but was excellently trained, and would remain where he was until his master's return.

Bertrand's mailed feet sounded hard on the rutted icy road as he set off at a run, whistling for the mule to stand still. He found her soon enough, her head hanging, her chest heaving and her thick grey coat wet with sweat, clearly frightened almost out of her wits. It was the work of moments to calm her and begin to lead her back to the waiting courser.

He was about to remount when he remembered the scream and stood, one foot poised in the stirrup, frowning. In his hasty attempt to assure the safety of his two mounts he had set aside his first conviction that the scream had been human, not the cry of some small creature caught by a predator. He turned towards the ditch from which the bird had risen in frenzied flight and stalked to the side of the road.

A hooded figure was trying to scramble clear of the mud and water which lay in the bottom of the ditch. Bertrand stood for a moment, hands on hips, staring, until he realised that the figure was female and clearly hurt, for she was whimpering in pain.

Quickly he stepped nearer, and reached out a hand to help. The hooded head turned at his approach and, in panic, the girl almost fell backwards full into the ditch again.

'Take my hand,' he called sharply. 'What are you waiting for?'

Hesitantly his hard male hand was grasped by a small muddied one, and the woman was soon pulled clear of the ditch and on to the harder firm ground of the road.

'What in the name of all the saints happened to you?' Bertrand snapped. 'Screaming out like that you frightened and nearly maimed my horse. He's valuable property, and had you done so I'd have had some of the worth of it out of your hide.'

'I am not valuable, I suppose,' she snapped back at him. 'I couldn't help it. I was scrambling over the field strip towards the road when some creature startled me and, not seeing the ditch ahead, I fell in.'

He had at first assumed her to be some female serf, working the land and late home, but now, by her speech and manner, he recognised his mistake.

'Why are you out unescorted so late?' He retorted with a further question.

The hood had slipped back and he glimpsed a mane of dishevelled dark hair, which she pushed back with an impatient hand. She was young, he judged, little more than a child, and he recalled her whimper of pain as he saw her lips tighten again, as if to withhold another cry.

'Here,' he said, 'you're hurt. Lean against me while I see what is wrong with that foot.'

'I wouldn't dream of doing so,' she said hastily, and hopped a short distance from him, but the effort cost her dear and she gave a little hiss of pain again.

'Don't be a foolish child,' he admonished. 'I shan't harm you and you'll not be able to walk far on that.'

She had managed to find an old Roman milestone and sank thankfully on to it, feeling the fast-swelling right foot anxiously.

He gave a little cluck of annoyance and purposefully walked over to her. Settling down on his haunches before her, he firmly pushed aside her hand and began to examine the injured foot gently.

'I think you twisted it when you slipped into the ditch.' His touch was feather-light, as it would have been if he had been examining a horse or hound, and his care not to alarm her further was just as meticulous. 'There are no bones broken but it should be bound, and you must not walk on it for a while.'

'But I must,' she blurted out, then caught back further comment as he looked questioningly back at her. He was a big man, a knight, like as not, for she saw he wore chain-mail over his cote and had a serviceable sword strapped at his side. She could not discern much of his features or his colouring, for the light was going fast now, but he was a young man, definitely, and she flinched from the possible danger of coming across him here on this deserted strip of road. He had been angry at first and now was appearing helpful, but life in the nunnery had taught her a distrust of all men, save her own kin, and she shrank from the strong though gentle feel of his fingers upon her stockinged ankle.

'Where are you going?' he demanded. 'I must carry you on my courser and restore you to your family.' By now he had decided she was the daughter of some local landowner, out alone about some foolish prank which had brought her to this idiotic disaster. What were her kinfolk about to leave so vulnerable a young girl without careful watch on her? Weren't they aware of the perils which could beset her on the open road without groom or servant?

She shook her head angrily. 'That, sire, is no business of yours.'

He stood up abruptly, his lips tightening in irritation.

'You cannot remain here. It is late and unlikely that anyone else will ride this way. Do they know at home where you went? Will they come looking for you?'

'I hardly think so,' she said drily, 'since they are not aware that I am travelling.'

It was as he thought, some stupid childish trick—and dangerous.

'Then I must take you home.'

'No, that is impossible,' she said evenly. 'My home is very far away. I—was hoping to get to Winchester.'

'Winchester? That is at least sixteen miles. You couldn't walk it by nightfall if you had *not* injured your foot.'

She looked alarmed. 'Oh, but I thought—I thought it was only two or three miles away.'

'Then you must have been walking in the wrong direction,' he said grimly.

He was now beginning to realise that the girl was unsure of her way, so she did not live near by. How then had she come to be on this stretch of the road? It was a mystery, and it was far too late and growing far too cold to go into the ramifications now.

'There is a nunnery near by,' he announced. 'I'll take you there. They'll be glad to take you into their guest-house, and you can decide what to do in the morning. You will get help there for your injured foot.'

'No.' Her horror at that suggestion was patently evident, and he stopped in his movement back towards the horse to look back at her, frowning.

He made up his mind suddenly. 'You can't stay here all night. There may well be snow before morning and you'll freeze. You had best come with me. No,' he said firmly as he saw her about to argue again, 'I'll not leave you here. I'll carry you by force if I must, but come with me to find some shelter from this biting wind you will.'

Janeta felt that familiar frightening rage begin to well up within her and she took firm hold of herself. This would not do. This man was bigger and stronger than she was. If she went into a sudden tantrum he might very well carry her by force, as he had threatened, back to St Catherine's. She was still very frightened, but so far he had shown her no discourtesy and she had to trust him, for a while at least, until she was well and truly far away from the nunnery.

'Do you want me to carry you?' He faced her, one hand on hip, eyebrows raised interrogatively. 'Or will you take my arm and hop towards my mount?'

She swallowed awkwardly. 'I think—I can manage if you help me.'

He put a supporting arm round her shoulders and she struggled up from the milestone, and with his assistance half walked, half stumbled towards the two patient mounts.

Without more ado he swung her up and mounted himself behind. She tried not to shrink away as his arm tightened around her waist, drawing her close to him, then he had taken the lead-rein of the mule in his other hand and was urging his courser forward with the skilled pressure of his knees.

She shivered suddenly and he pulled his woollen mantle around her. He was right; she was beginning to feel numb with cold and the jarring pain of her injured foot as he rode made her only too anxious to have this short ride ended, so much so that she was sick at heart and cared little, at this juncture, where he was taking her.

The sun had almost completely westered before he gave a little murmur of recognition and began to urge his destrier off the road and towards a cluster of half-ruined buildings which she could only just distinguish in the deepening gloom.

Once near one of them, he drew rein and dismounted, speaking soothingly to his horses, and reached up to lift her down. Her body slid along the length of his strongly muscled form and she gave only the slightest little gasp of pain as he lowered her to her feet and, momentarily, she was forced to put weight upon her bad foot.

'Steady.' He put up a supporting hand again and she was able to lean on him as he conducted her sure-footedly to a tumbledown hut to their right. 'This is the best of the bunch. It is some time since I came here but I think there will be enough of the roof in place to give us some shelter if it does decide to snow.'

She found herself inside the hut and he motioned her to sink down on to a little pile of dead grass and bracken against the far wall.

She shied away from him instinctively. 'I don't understand. Where are we? What is this place?'

It was even gloomier in here and she had the greatest difficulty in judging his expression. His back was against the doorway, limned in outline against all that was left of the light. She was shut in alone with this man—a total stranger.

He turned away and moved towards the open doorway.

'Don't be afraid. I know this place well, have stayed here on one or two journeys. No one will disturb us.'

His words were not reassuring, and she scrambled back against the support of the crumbling wattle and mud wall.

'But—but where is it? Why is everything so tumbledown. . .?'

He shrugged. 'I don't know. As you can see, it's an old deserted village. It appears the people who lived here didn't even want what building material was here. Frightened of the place, I suppose. Who knows what happened?'

She gasped with a sudden terror. 'Deserted? Then perhaps it was plague-stricken. . .'

Again he shrugged. 'I suppose that is possible. I found no human remains, but in all events there appears to be no hint of contagion. As I said, I have stayed here a few times and haven't been affected. In this cold the sickness will be in abeyance anyway. Actually, I think it more likely that the village was raided during the civil wars between King Stephen and the Empress Matilda. There were terrible happenings back then, and little to check the perpetrators. Probably the villagers stolidly buried their dead, started over again on a new site, and left the memories of the horrors behind.' He gave an ironic half-laugh. 'I have had no visits from ghostly victims.'

She winced inwardly at the grim jest and gazed round the shadowed place fearfully. As he had said, it afforded some shelter from the biting wind and most of the roof was intact. Her foot was aching again, and as he left her alone she was conscious that her gown and cloak were soaked at the hem and badly splashed where she had stumbled ankle-deep into the icy waters of the ditch. The cloth clung to her unpleasantly, chilly and dank.

She could hear him outside, encouraging the horses into the shelter of the barn adjoining their hut. He was some time gonè and she wondered if he was feeding them with some hay he carried on the sumpter. They needed watering too. Perhaps he knew of some spring close by, or a stream.

Despite her relief at his reappearance, for she still felt a superstitious dread of the place, she could not help a little frightened cry as he came in again and threw a bundle of clothing in her direction.

'You are soaked to the skin. You'll catch your death. Get your wet clothes off and put on this under-tunic of mine.'

'No!' she cried, appalled. 'Not here. What—what are you thinking of? I—I—can't. . .'

'Of course you can,' he returned cheerfully. 'I won't look.' He chuckled low in his throat. 'I never go where I'm not invited.'

It was a calculated insult, she felt, perversely, but she was inclined to believe him. She scrambled towards the back of the hut while he turned his back again and left, probably to fetch something else from the saddle-bags. Hastily she undressed, fearful of his quick return. Fortunately the convent garb was simple to handle. She had never been used to the services of a maid and was able to discard her gown and chemise, rub her cold, damp body down with her cloak, and then don the homespun sleeveless under-tunic he had provided. He was a tall man and it was far too long for her, but he had also thoughtfully presented her with a length of rope, and she bound it round her waist as a makeshift girdle, tucking into it the excess cloth.

A sudden plop behind her made her turn instantly,

wincing at the sudden, thoughtless jar on her foot again, to find a short woollen cloak at her feet.

'Thank you.' She mumbled an embarrassed and somewhat ungrateful acceptance, put it on and sat down again, still defensive, against the rough wall, facing him.

He crossed to her side, smiling to see that she had at last obeyed him and was more comfortable. In the half-light he saw that her dark mass of hair was tumbling round her shoulders.

'Now,' he said encouragingly, 'let me have another look at that ankle.'

He was determined, though she winced away from his touch more from embarrassment than fear of the pain he would deal out. She saw now that he was carrying a wooden drinking-cup and a length of torn cloth.

'Allow me to tie this tightly round the ankle to give some support.' There was icy cold water in the cup so her guess had been correct. He had gone to find some spring or stream. She had seen the infirmarian deal with such injuries many times and sat back gratefully while he soaked the cloth and tied it tightly round her ankle. The compress, she knew, would lessen the swelling and give the limb support. It would have helped if she had had some witch-hazel lotion to bring out the bruising, but the compress would have to suffice.

Awkwardly she thanked him again. 'I am giving you a great deal of trouble.'

He shrugged, stood up, and went back towards the doorway. She could just glimpse the horse and mule through the gap in the wall which connected the ruined hut with the adjoining barn. She smiled a trifle wryly. He had said his mounts were very valuable to him. He would not risk losing one, but keep them close at all times.

He did not approach her again for some time and she sat back, appreciating the relief from the chill wind, huddling within the rough comfort of the borrowed cloak. She was glad to keep some measure of distance between herself and her rescuer despite his kindly efforts to help. She watched idly as he brought large stones from somewhere outside and arranged them in a circle beneath the smoke-gap in the hut roof to form a rough hearth. There was still a quantity of dry bracken inside the hut and she wondered if it had lain there since his last visit. He fetched tinder and flint from the capacious saddle bag and coaxed a tiny spurt of flame, then fed it with small twigs from outside. She was comforted by the orange glow, small as it was, and watched anxiously when he rose and left her again in case it died on him completely. She let out a litle relieved breath when he returned with branches and brushwood.

He gave a little grunt as the damp wood gave out pungent blue smoke, which escaped through the smoke-gap, but his efforts bore fruit, and at last he managed to get a reasonable fire going.

He called to her imperatively as he once more searched in the bag.

'Come and sit near the fire.'

She shook her head nervously and, hearing no answer and sensing no move towards him, he turned back to her again in one swift, fluid movement.

'I said come to the fire and eat something.'

'Oh, no,' she murmured huskily, 'you have done too much for me already. I could not deprive you of the small amount of food you carry.'

He had come close and was towering over her,

holding out his hand imperiously so that she could grasp it and rise to her feet.

'Certainly you must share it with me. I do not intend to go to my bed still hungry, and I could not eat in your presence while you sat without.'

Reluctantly she took his hand and rose, then came to sit by the small smoky fire while he seated himself cross-legged opposite.

'That's better. It's frugal fare; rye bread, cheese and some salted pork from the last tavern I stayed at. It was all they had and, truth to tell, all I could afford, but it will serve.' He handed her a wine-skin. 'Ale, but I find it more refreshing than wine when I am on the move.'

She drank gratefully and handed back the skin. 'Thank you. I was very thirsty.'

He drank and broke the bread, handing her a portion with a hunk of cheese and a small quantity of the salt meat. She hesitated for a moment, reluctant still to deprive him of food, since he had admitted he was on short commons, but she was ravenous after her struggle through the woodland and ice-rutted fields.

The warmth of the fire played on her chilled form and she began to feel better. He had spread out her damp gown and chemise near the hearth so it would dry more quickly. Her face flamed at the thought that this stranger had handled her under-garment, and instinctively her hand went up to touch the ugly mark hidden beneath his tunic. She knew the light in this place had been too dim for him to glimpse the betraying mark, but close contact with anyone, let alone this uncompromising stranger, made her fear that her secret would be revealed, and added to her natural discomfort at being partially unclad and alone with this man.

She looked up to find him watching her curiously,

and she flushed again and hoped he would put the rosy glow which swept down her throat and flooded her cheeks down to the warmth of the fire.

He said suddenly, 'I am Bertrand D'Aubigny, on my way to Winchester. I am at your service, demoiselle.'

Warily she stared back at him, then she said hesitantly, 'I—I am Janeta Cobham. My father has a manor in Berkshire. . .'

His eyebrows rose. 'You are far from your home, demoiselle. Where can I lodge you tomorrow for safety?'

She bit her lip doubtfully. 'I—I would be grateful if you would see me as far as Winchester, since it will not be out of your way, sire.'

He was silent for moments, as if considering, then he enquired, 'You have kin in Winchester?'

It would have been simpler to deceive him and claim that it was so, but, unaccountably, she found she could not do it. She said in a sudden rush, 'I—I might as well confess, since you saw my reluctance to return to St Catherine's, that I ran away from there only this morning.'

Again he waited before acknowledging her explanation, and she said hurriedly, 'You need not fear that you are assisting a runaway nun. I have taken no vows. I have been educated at the nunnery, but—but. . .'

'You have been pressured to take vows?' His voice was calm, without hint of either disapproval or sympathy.

'Yes.' The single word was a released pent-up breath.

'Could you not appeal to your father to take you home?'

'I have done so. He refused categorically.'

'Ah.'

Her voice carried a half-ashamed note. 'He—he does

not think there would be a chance of finding a suitable husband for me.'

'He doubts that?' There was a trace of suppressed humour now in his voice, and she felt somewhat affronted.

'He is not wealthy,' she said, lifting her chin defensively. 'There would be insufficient money to provide a sizeable dowry.'

'That I understand,' he grinned. 'I am in a similar position. My elder brother holds our manor and he is to court a wife shortly. He informs me that I must now provide for myself.'

'It is for that reason you are travelling to Winchester?'

'Aye. I hope to further my prospects in the Christmas jousting.'

'But the Church disapproves of tournaments and the King forbids his barons to take part, or so I heard,' she said hastily as his lips curled in a smile of wry amusement at her forthrightness.

'So, they still have you in thrall at the nunnery. You carry their strictures in your heart.'

She was abashed by her own frankness, which amounted to downright rudeness, and to this man who had been so willing to help her.

'I——' she floundered. 'I merely thought that the jousts were dangerous and—it is a mortal sin to risk one's life without just cause.'

'My cause is just enough,' he said wryly. 'If I don't get money I starve. It's the tournament circuit for me, or life as a mercenary.'

'But you could lose your immortal soul!' she exclaimed, and he laughed, a short, faintly bitter laugh.

'Aye, *routiers* are excommunicated. A merciful way for Mother Church to behave towards men who have

no other course but to take to arms, to put food in
their scrips and clothes on their backs.'

'Sire,' she said formally, 'you must think me ungra-
cious indeed to find fault with your plans. Your needs
are your own business, as my plans are mine. Please
excuse my foolishness. As you said, the nuns have
taught me well, perhaps too well for the necessary
finding of my own place in the world.'

He nodded. 'I have been considering that. I take it
you intend to look for service?'

'Yes, I thought as a seamstress or maid.'

His lips twitched. 'I do not think that idea is very
realistic.'

'Why not? The nuns taught me well. I sew exquisitely, or so I have been assured, and I know herblore
and——'

'I was not criticising your lack of skill or experience.'

'I do not understand. Why should I not be
considered?'

She felt him look her over carefully, in a deliberate
scrutiny, and he said evasively, 'You are very young,
demoiselle. I think many noble ladies or merchants'
wives might wish to take someone much older into
their households. However, it may not be impossible.
Have you no other kinfolk whom you might sue for
assistance?'

'I know of none. I have been at the nunnery since I
was ten years old. I know my mother was an only
child, and that my father's brother's wife died recently
and he remarried. I hardly think his young wife—for I
am informed she is some twenty years his junior—
would wish to acquire me as a dependant.'

His lips twitched again and she felt he might break
into a grin. 'No, I am inclined to agree with you there.'

She sighed. 'If needs must, I will apply to some
tavern. . .'

'I think not,' he said decisively, then, as she stared at him wonderingly, added, 'I'm sure we can do better for you than that. Certainly I will take you with me to Winchester. Once there I think it safer if we allow people to think we are kin—cousins, perhaps.'

'But. . .'

'It is a trifle unusual for a young lady such as yourself to be travelling unescorted. It might be thought——' He shrugged eloquently. 'I assure you it will be safer this way. I can then do the searching for employment for you.'

She blinked unhappily. 'I put you to far too much trouble.'

He laughed. 'Nonsense, and while we are together in Winchester you can perhaps see me perform at the jousts, and I can reassure you that I am unlikely to be killed in defiance of the strictures of Mother Church and like to lose my immortal soul.'

'You are making fun of me, sire, and I deserve it.'

'No, demoiselle. It is simply that the nuns have kept you from the knowledge of the world.'

He turned slightly from her to mend the fire with more brushwood. It flared up and illuminated his features so that Janeta was able to take the opportunity of regarding him fully for the first time.

She had already noted that he was tall and well-made, finely muscled, obviously an experienced fighting man. Perhaps she could assume he was right when he told her he was well capable of holding his own in mock-combat and on campaign. Now she saw that he was pleasantly featured, his eyes well-spaced and deeply set, his nose slightly too large for his good-humoured face. His lips were long and she had seen how easily he could break into laughter. Even in the firelight she was still not absolutely sure of his colouring. He looked to have fair or light brown hair, cut short and curling into his neckline, and she thought his eyes were light brown too, for they shone golden in the firelight. He had laughter-lines at the corners of his eyes and deeply indented ones from his nostrils to the corners of his mouth. He was clean-shaven, and she was unsure whether this was fashionable nowadays, for she had seen few men over her years at the nunnery save the serfs who worked on the convent land and the elderly reeve who had charge of them. He had a long drooping moustache and small goatee beard, but she concluded that that style had gone from fashion many years ago.

As if aware of her scrutiny he turned back to her, and she flushed dully. There was a large dimple in his square chin and his golden eyes twinkled.

'Have you decided if I am to be trusted?'

Her lips trembled and she said awkwardly, 'I cannot be sure of anything in this frightening world outside my convent walls, but I am at your mercy, sire, and I have prayed to the Virgin for her protection. So far you have proved trustworthy.'

Instantly the laughter left his eyes and his voice was far more serious.

'I assure you that your innocence is your own protection, demoiselle. I am no saint, but I never yet broke my knightly vows and pressed unwelcome attention on any lady.'

He rose to his feet in the graceful manner she had noted before and stood regarding her steadily, his thumbs pushed into his sword-belt.

'I think you should try to get some sleep now. It has already begun to snow and we may well have a hard journey tomorrow for those last few miles.'

She turned anxiously towards the adjoining barn-space, where the horses were tethered, and saw one or two flakes drifting in through the gaps in the crumbling wattle of the wall. She shivered and scrambled to her feet, understanding now how necessary it had been for him to find shelter for them through the night.

He was already shaking up the dried-bracken bed near the far wall and she went to it. He smiled, nodded, and went back to the fire. She slipped to her knees, drawing the cloak tightly round her, then watched him nervously, but he had turned his back to her now and appeared to be doing something once more to the sulkily burning fire. With a little sigh she wriggled into a sleeping posture and turned her back to the wall. It was still deadly cold in the hut, away from the meagre heat of the fire, but she did not dare to think what conditions would have been like for her in the open field in damp clothing and with an injured foot. Closing her eyes and folding her hands in prayer, she appealed once more to the Virgin to keep her safe through the night and to forgive her for her sin in disobeying her father and alarming Reverend Mother, then she tried to compose herself for sleep. She was still trembling, half with fear and half with excitement, but she froze as he approached her makeshift couch again.

'There's nothing to fear,' he soothed. 'I think you need even more protection from this cold. This might stink of horse but it will give added warmth.'

He wrapped one of the horse-blankets round her, and her eyes pricked with sudden tears of gratitude and her throat closed up, so that she was unable to utter a satisfactory reply. As she turned from him again he stood for a moment, looking down at her huddled form.

She was such an innocent! And so beautiful, with no knowledge of her own vulnerability! Blessed God, how would she fare in this world of sin and intrigue without a protector? And yet, in his circumstances, he could not encumber himself with a child.

She moved only slightly and the blanket slipped back so that he had a sudden glimpse of the swell of her breast against the rough homespun cloth of his under-tunic. Was she a child? Certainly she seemed to be so, but he could not ask her openly about her age. Did she really think any sensible woman would take such a lovely creature into her household and run the risk of losing her husband's heart to her? His own heart had been stirred when her hood had first slipped back from her flower-like face on the road. Had she not been so young and at his mercy he might well have satisfied his unrequited longings within her arms.

Now that he had seen her more closely he was deeply puzzled by her comment that her father had not tried to find a suitable husband for her. Why? Even without a substantial dowry there must be many well-endowed men who would wish to wed her. She had accepted her father's word so simply. Had she not seen her loveliness reflected in a mirror somewhere in the manor, and had no man or woman told her the truth about herself? No, of course not. She had been immured in the nunnery since childhood. There would have been no mirrors there, and the nuns would have been determined to crush every vestige of vanity in their charge, but they must have been aware of it. She was so small, like some faery creature, slim and exquisitely built, with those wide grey-blue eyes with that disturbing outer dark rim about the pupils, that high-bridged, aristocratic nose and full, sensuous mouth, and that heavy mass of hair whose colour defied description. At first he had thought it dark as night, but in the firelight it had taken on a subtle copper glow.

He turned abruptly, stirred too greatly for his own

peace of mind. What in God's name was he to do with her? She trusted him completely and he could not begin to think where he could place her for her own safety.

CHAPTER THREE

JANETA woke with a start to find a cold white light filling the hut. She shivered and pulled the rough horse-blanket more closely round her. There was no mistaking that gleaming whiteness. Sir Bertrand had been right in his forecast of last night. It was snowing. If the drifts were bad, how were they to get to Winchester?

She sat up reluctantly, putting aside the cloak and blanket, feeling the bitter chill on her shrinking flesh. Even the dank feel of the nunnery stone walls and stair as they had gone in procession to matins had not prepared her for this frightening absence of sound, and the harsh crispness of a winter morning without any relieving heat.

She looked round anxiously for her rescuer but she was alone in the hut, and she could hear no evidence of his presence with the horses. Her gown, cloak and veil lay neatly folded near her. The fire had long ago died and she felt a moment's blind panic. He had abandoned her!

Common sense returned almost immediately and her practical self-sufficiency reasserted itself. More than likely he had gone to water the horses, as he had last night, and even if he had decided that she would prove to be an insufferable burden and left her to make her own way she would manage. After all, she was no worse off than she had been last night. She uttered a swift prayer of thanks that he had come upon her and made sure she had shelter. Had he not done so, she surely would have perished. She pulled off the garments he had loaned her and donned her own clothes.

51

They were sorely crumpled and not as clean as she would have wished, but they were dry, and still retained a modicum of warmth from their sojourn near the fire earlier. She was tying the cloak-strings when she heard him come into the adjoining hut, murmuring encouragingly to his horse. Her heart fluttered with a deep sense of relief. Already she had come to trust him and rely on him to see her safe to the town.

He nodded approvingly as he came in, shaking the snowflakes from his mantle.

'Ah, I see you are dressed and ready. I imagine you are aware that the weather has worsened. We'll make a hasty breakfast and get on our way before we find this narrow track impassable. I'd not have Saladin break a leg if the snow ices over.'

He picked up the discarded garments and pushed them into one of the saddle-bags, then produced more bread and cold bacon.

'I didn't try to rekindle the fire as we shall not be here long and everything is so damp.'

She nodded and munched gratefully at the food, following it up with a couple of swallows from the skin bottle of ale.

'Will it take long to get to Winchester?'

'Several hours, possibly longer if the going gets rough. Don't worry, I'll get you there. Did you sleep well?'

She flushed. 'Yes, very well, much better than I could have dared to hope. Sire, I don't know how I would have fared if you hadn't come along and offered to help. . .'

'I was merely fulfilling my knightly duty.' He was smiling teasingly, and had now finished his frugal meal and knelt down before her. 'Let me look at your ankle.'

She felt the blood flame again in her cheeks as he

gently examined her injured foot. Whatever would Reverend Mother have said had she known Janeta had allowed such an intimacy?

He rose to his feet. 'It seems less swollen. Try to stand and put your weight on it, but only for a moment.'

She was relieved to find the action much less painful than she had feared though she was still wary and unwilling to risk the pulses of pure agony which had resulted when she had tried to walk last night.

'It—it seems much easier.'

'Good. I'll help you to mount, and by tomorrow all should be well again.' He looked very intently into her face. 'You have really thought again about what you intend? Life will not be easy. If you have reconsidered, I could, even now, take you back to the nunnery and leave you at the gate.'

She shook her head decisively. 'There is no going back for me. If you will take me to Winchester I will be eternally grateful to you. After that you must leave me to find my own way.'

He frowned. 'We'll see about that. I'll try to find you honourable employment. If not—' he shrugged uneasily '—we'll have to think again. You realise there will be a hunt for you? Don't you think, when you are settled, you should try to get word to your father? I take it that at the nunnery they taught you to write?'

'Yes, I can write my letters and read too well enough. Can you?'

He chuckled. 'I can make shift, though scribing is not my favourite occupation. Our parish priest convinced my father that my brother and I should be able at least to see that our reeve and the clerks were not cheating us. Though,' he added thoughtfully, 'I should not let it be known too easily that you can do so. Mistresses are not too anxious to employ servant wenches who are more learned than themselves. If your father were to be assured of your safety, however, if you could contrive it, he would possibly make no further moves to press you to take your vows.'

'Glad to be rid of me, eh?' She spoke drily. 'You could well be right, sir knight, but I'll take no risks. He'll give up the chase soon enough, when he knows I am no longer his responsibility.'

He quickly resumed his final packing up. She had gone to the hut doorway and was watching the snow-flakes settling softly on to the silent track and fields. The world was so very beautiful—and desolate. More than ever she was grateful for his company in this frightening existence stretching ahead of her.

This time he lifted her to the croup and mounted before her. At his insistence she settled herself behind him and clasped him tightly round the waist. She had ridden little, though she could remember her small pony before she had left for the nunnery. Since then there had been no opportunities to ride. She thought, surprised, that she had felt little or no fear of the great horse last night, merely of her intimate closeness to the stranger. This morning she thought only of the dangers of the journey.

The snow had checked now and the flakes lay some two or three inches deep on the track. It was less cold than it had been in the night but she understood how precious the animal was to Sir Bertrand and watched their slow progress over the uneven surface anxiously. Should the destrier place his foot awkwardly, there could be serious damage to a leg, and this would ruin his master's hopes in the Christmas jousting. The mule ran steadily and confidently after a first show of reluctance.

Sir Bertrand called back to her where she sat pillion. 'Are you comfortable? Too cold?'

'No, now we're moving I feel fine.' Indeed she did feel a curious sense of exhilaration at this unaccustomed freedom of motion. His nearness gave body-warmth. In the convent touching was forbidden and she had not experienced such comforting closeness since her nurse had held her on her knee.

His attention was on the track ahead and he spoke to her very little. She did not mind that. She was able to give full rein to her admiration of the beauty of the hushed, blanketed landscape.

They had joined the main highway now and Sir Bertrand seemed less fearful of hidden ruts or hazards beneath the frozen surface. He was riding at a faster pace and they were almost upon the skirmish in the roadway ahead of them before they realised what was happening. There had been a bend in the road which hid the combatants from view, and the snow had muffled the sounds of iron blade on blade and the swift, desperate scuffling of feet.

With a muffled curse Sir Bertrand drew rein and, horrified, Janeta stared at the frantic struggle in front of her. There appeared to be four men engaged in battle, one fighting fiercely in what seemed to be a doomed attempt to fight off savage attacks from the other three. She gave a little gasp of mingled fear and pity as she saw the victim almost slip on the icy ground and go under the mailed feet of his opponents, then recover himself and force his way forward again, the wintry light flashing white fire on the blade of his longsword.

Sir Bertrand dismounted and swung her down, leading his two horses to the side of the road near the crumbling wall of a barn.

'Stay here. Don't move and don't touch Saladin. He's unused to any hand on his bridle-rein but mine and trained to kick and bite in combat. Keep hold of the mule's rein, though, or the stupid beast will charge off again. She's easily frightened.'

Janeta made no attempt to restrain him from joining the battle, knowing it would be useless. Already he was allying himself with the threatened traveller, and gave one shout of warning as he moved in close to him, side to side. Janeta held tightly to the mule's rein, her frightened eyes watching closely the progress of the fight.

The balance had altered now. There were two against three and Bertrand was fresh to the conflict. His companion was fighting doggedly and ever more fiercely, but his breath was coming hard, and Janeta thought this struggle had been going on for some time. She felt a rush of admiration for the man's fighting spirit against such odds. Obviously his attackers had thought it would be a simple matter to dispatch him. She could hear now the continued clash and ring of the blades, muttered curses as some blows found their marks, and the hard, panting breath of men beleaguered. Her own breath was coming fast as she feared for Bertrand. She had known him so short a time. Was she destined to see him butchered before her eyes? A great shudder ran through her at the thought, and yet it had not occurred to her to believe him foolish to join in. The man's knightly responsibility lay in coming to the aid of another, grossly outnumbered in combat, and he had not hesitated for a moment.

She narrowed her eyes against the weak sun, which was threatening to blind her, for a careful scrutiny of the combatants. The man to whose aid Bertrand had gone instantly was tall, taller than Bertrand, well-built, with a taut, muscular body, and from a distance she judged his age to be some ten or twelve years older than her companion. He was certainly no peasant or merchant, for he travelled in mail and handled his sword like a man accustomed to hard fighting. She could not tell if his clothing was of good quality, but he was a knight, clearly. His horse stood obediently still, as Bertrand's Saladin did, some distance off, waiting for further command from his master.

The other men wore mail too, and were obviously experienced swordsmen, for they fought as determinedly as their two opponents, but Janeta could see now that they were not so skilled, despite the fact that there were still three against two. Bertrand and his comrade in arms were steadily pressing their advantage and the three attackers were falling back under the onslaught. A horse whickered somewhere in the bushes to their right, and Janeta thought the three must have been hidden in that thicket to ambush the strange knight as he had ridden along earlier. This was no chance attempt at robbery of an unknown, then. The aim was to kill their victim, and Bertrand had come to his rescue in good time.

There was a sudden scream and one man fell, the other two trampling him down mercilessly beneath their feet. One of the others gave a hoarse shout of command to retreat and the two remaining on their feet turned and ran for the thicket. Bertrand made to follow, and then turned to his companion as the man staggered and fumbled groggily at his sword-arm.

'Let them go.' The man's Norman French was more accented than that of most Normans now living in England, and Janeta judged that he was one of the King's Poitevin favourites, now so prevalent and popular at Court with the young Henry. Was that, then, the reason for this cowardly and unprincipled attack on a hapless traveller?

Bertrand gazed after the two fleeing attackers, shrugged, and returned his attention to their injured victim. He called to Janeta.

'Bring the mule over here, demoiselle. I have some linen and unguents in my saddle-bags.' He gave a contemptuous glance at the fallen man, who was scrambling uncertainly to his feet and attempting to run, crabwise, after his companions. Bertrand raised his sword threateningly, while the tall man looked on with a grim smile. The attacker gave a frightened cry, quickened his pace and managed to reach the thicket safely. They could hear him scrambling about desperately in the undergrowth in an attempt to find his mount. Probably the frantic flight of the other two had frightened the animal and he had broken free from tether. At all events neither Bertrand nor his companion made any effort to follow and deal out summary justice so Janeta joined the two men, looking behind anxiously in case Saladin should take fright and gallop off in pursuit. The great beast sidled nervously and gave a great snort of distress, but stood quietly at a further word of command from Sir Bertrand.

The strange knight was leaning tiredly against the crumbling wall and Sir Bertrand was feeling cautiously along the injured sword-arm. When his patient grunted, he paused and nodded.

'It doesn't feel as if anything is broken, sir. Can we manage to push up the sleeve of your hauberk so I can bandage the gash and staunch the bleeding?'

At Bertrand's direction Janeta rummaged in one of the saddle-bags and produced a small canvas sack containing strips of rough linen and a little pot of unguent. Clearly Sir Bertrand had provided for all eventualities in the coming tournament, and expected minor wounds and bruises at the very least. She carried the sack to the two and smeared unguent on to one of the clean strips. The ointment smelt of comfrey and tansy and Janeta approved its suitability. There was no water near by so she dampened another small piece of cloth in ale to wipe away the blood and assure herself that no snippet of thread or cloth from the knight's shirt had worked into the wound. This, she knew, could spell disaster for the chance of successful healing.

The man had pushed back his red woollen mantle, and the loose sleeves of the mail hauberk and the linen shirt beneath had been pushed clear so she could see the long gash along the forearm. The wound was not deep and would have no need to have its edges pulled close or even stitched, and the blow appeared to have glanced off the bone, so there was no great harm done. Again the knight grunted as Sir Bertrand stood back and allowed her to cleanse and bandage the wound. It was soon over and the knight drew down his sleeve, though clumsily, with his left hand.

'Thank you, demoiselle.' His voice was low-pitched and musical, and again she noted the slight accent that marked him out as a French or Norman outlander.

He smiled mirthlessly at Bertrand. 'You appear to travel well-prepared for combat and accidents.' His mobile lips twitched in faint amusement and his eyes went from his two helpers to Bertrand's mule and patient destrier. 'You live close, sire, and travel without groom or squire?'

Bertrand was sizing up the knight with equal care. He gave only a trace of an answering smile.

'As you do, my lord earl.'

The knight started, and his dark eyes narrowed. He had strong, finely drawn features, high cheekbones, and heavy, level black brows under which his brown eyes looked almost black. His jaw was square and determined and his long lips were held in a hard line. Janeta looked up at that dominant, high-bridged nose and knew immediately that this was no man to cross with impunity. One of the King's courtiers he might well be, from his manner of speech, but he was no foppish favourite. His method of handling himself in the fight had told her that.

He was staring down aggressively now at Bertrand. 'You know me?'

Bertrand's eyes went to he heraldic device on the man's green woollen tunic.

'Everyone knows that the silver lion rampant on a field of red is the device of Simon de Montfort, Earl of Leicester, my lord.'

The man's hard smile deepened. He turned his gaze to where Janeta stood awkwardly, still holding the pot of unguent. Noting his curious stare full on her, she moved hurriedly to replace the healer's sack in its saddle-bag on the mule.

The Earl said firmly, 'And you, young sire, are?'

'Sir Bertrand D'Aubigny. My brother holds a manor in Northampton shire, not far from your Leicester shire holdings my lord.'

'Then you are quite some way from home. You travel to Winchester?'

'Aye, my lord. I hope to try my luck in the tournament.'

The Earl chuckled as Bertrand's cheeks mottled with angry colour. He held up a hand, as if to ward off a proud retort. 'Do not bridle, sir knight. I know only too well what it is to be a younger son and to need to try one's fortune far from the family home. I was fortunate in having my claim judged fair by the good Earl of Chester and by His Grace the King. I think none the less highly of you, my friend. I noted how well you handled yourself back there in the fight, and am sure you will soon find yourself a master ready enough to take you into service.'

'I could find no man I would more readily serve than you, my lord earl.'

Again the Earl started, then he threw back his head

and laughed. 'It is in such a way that master and man find themselves and, in an instant, know they will rub along well together. Welcome to my service, Bertrand D'Aubigny. I need men I can trust about me, as you saw just now.'

'Doubtless my lord, you have your own reasons to be travelling without escort,' Bertrand said drily. 'I would not advise you to repeat the error. These are not safe days for men about the King, particularly men from France.'

The level dark brows rose at Bertrand's impertinent comment but the Earl shrugged slightly. His dark eyes twinkled. 'Will you introduce me to the lady who so carefully tended me? Your sister, perhaps?'

Bertrand was about to answer when Janeta hastily cut in.

'No, my lord. Sir Bertrand came to my aid on the road.' As Bertrand looked at her warningly she shook her head but slightly, and went on, 'I have no right to his protection and he has proved a gallant and courteous knight to me.' She lifted her chin defiantly. 'I— I—was fleeing from St Catherine's nunnery and he has agreed to take me in safety to Winchester.'

For some indefinable reason Janeta had known instantly that it would be injurious to Bertrand's hopes to lie to this man. It was imperative that she tell the truth and free him from any constraints, even if it meant the Earl thought badly of her.

He continued to eye her gravely, then he said quietly, 'I will not insult you by asking your reasons, demoiselle. I am sure they are real and necessary, but can you understand how hard it will be for you in the world? Have you taken vows?'

'No, no, sire,' she said, shocked. 'I would never turn my back on vows made before God's holy altar. I was placed by my father at the nunnery to be educated.

Now he wishes me to remain there, but I have no wish to comply.'

The long lips smiled understandingly. 'Then we must try to find you some safe place of refuge, demoiselle.'

As Bertrand was about to speak the Earl lifted his head and held up one hand to silence him. Clearly he had heard something the other two had not. Then Janeta caught the sound, very faint still and distant, but coming closer all the time; the click of horses' hoofs on the rutted road and a tinny sound she could not immediately identify. A procession of horsemen was approaching and the Earl gave a little decisive inclination of his chin in satisfaction. This, then, was what he was expecting, and probably the reason he had been on the road unescorted.

Bertrand glanced quickly at Janeta, and then back at the Earl. Simon de Montfort was pulling his mantle into place and straightening his helmet. Janeta was puzzled. For whom were these hasty preparations? Was the King riding this way? Surely not, for there would have been more elaborate arrangements, out-riders, men-at-arms, clearing the way for the royal entrance into the old capital of Winchester.

Bertrand said hesitantly, 'My lord, would you prefer me to withdraw? I could escort the demoiselle Janeta another way. . .'

'No, no, this meeting may well serve our purpose. Stand your ground, Sir Bertrand.'

The first horsemen were in sight now, rounding the bend in the road, mounted men-at-arms as Janeta had surmised, riding two by two. One was carrying a pennant bearing a device unknown to Janeta but obviously recognisable to the Earl. He moved forward to stand in the middle of the road with the intention of making his presence known. Janeta saw now that the sound which had puzzled her was explained, for the palfreys following the advance escort were splendidly caparisoned, their bridles ornamented by silver bells which tinkled delightfully in the frosty clear air.

Riding behind the three pairs of men-at-arms was a lady escorted by an older knight who, like the Earl, was clad in mail, helmeted and fully armed. He moved in closer to his charge as the apparent intruder appeared to halt the procession.

The lady laid a gloved hand on his arm to check any precipitately aggressive action.

'Steady, Sir John. If I am not mistaken, this is the Earl of Leicester.'

She leaned down in a welcoming gesture and the Earl went instantly to her side, and, taking her hand, turned it palm uppermost and kissed it.

'My lady, I had hoped to meet you on the road and offer to accompany you into the city. I heard you had left your manor at Odiham and intended to join your brother's Christmas court.'

She laughed merrily and Janeta realised she was quite young, possibly little older than she was, and clearly of noble birth and great importance, for men-at-arms brought up the rear also, and behind came wagons and sumpter mules laden down with baskets and chests. The lady intended to appear at Court attired in several costly changes of clothing, obviously. Janeta stared open-mouthed. She herself had never possessed more than one complete change of apparel in her whole life. The lady's palfrey sidled and she put a controlling hand on her bridle-rein.

Janeta knew little of current fashion but she could see that the lady was dressed exquisitely in a heavy woollen gown of deepest blue, and over it her scarlet mantle was embroidered in bands round the neck and hem and lined with squirrel fur. She wore barbette and veil of finest linen, held in place by a golden fillet, and

Janeta caught the glisten of gold and gems beneath the mantle.

Sir Bertrand moved in close and murmured softly in Janeta's ear, 'The Dowager Countess of Pembroke, the King's youngest sister, the Lady Eleanor.'

He drew her back against the wall, as it was clear to them both that the Princess and the Earl were exchanging confidences. Even the elderly knight whose charge she was had drawn apart, though Janeta saw that the man kept a watchful eye upon Eleanor. So, also, did a lady riding slightly behind her in attendance. The woman was perhaps some ten years older than the Princess. Though she rode proudly and was clearly someone of importance she wore plain homespun garments, and kept her eyes modestly lowered when they were not fixed intently upon the Countess.

Eleanor's laughter rang out and a frown crossed the older woman's face which Janeta could not fail to notice. The Countess was still leaning close to the Earl and her fingers dug lightly into the flesh of his sword-arm. Instinctively he gave a hastily caught back gasp of pain, and instantly, Eleanor straightened in the saddle and one hand crept to her heart.

'My lord, you are injured.'

He laughed joyously. 'My lady, it is nothing. I was set upon on this road barely an hour ago. I was alone and would have fared badly had not this stout fellow come quickly to my assistance. There were four of them and between us we beat them off. One's sword managed to pierce the gap between my shirt and hauberk-sleeve and left a long, shallow gash. It is painful and will stiffen by morning but it is not serious, I do assure you.'

The Countess's blue eyes looked hurriedly round for Bertrand, who, at the Earl's prompting, came forward and bowed low.

'You have my gratitude, sir,' the Countess said earnestly, 'and that of His Grace the King, for the Earl of Leicester has proved himself of inestimable worth at my brother's side, both in service and counsel. If some harm had come to him we would have been devastated.' She turned back to the Earl. 'You should not have been riding unattended. That was foolishly rash. The roads are infested by footpads and they hunt in packs. It seems I must be grateful that providence brought this man to your side in time. There must be some way in which I can reward him. . .'

'There is no need, my lady. Sir Bertrand d'Aubigny tells me he is in search of some landed baron to whom he might attach himself in service. I am only too willing to take him into my household. He has already proved his ability.'

She gave a deep, relieved breath. 'Then we can be certain you will have a stout arm on which to rely in sore need, my lord.'

The Earl now turned towards Janeta, who had been left standing awkwardly by herself.

'There is one way you could help, if you would, my lady.'

'You have only to ask, my lord.'

'Sir Bertrand has made himself responsible for the well-being of this lady, the demoiselle Janeta. She also seeks service in some worthy household. Like Sir Bertrand, she came readily to my assistance after the attackers had fled, and proved a very gentle and competent nurse. It would relieve Sir Bertrand's mind and mine if you could offer to take her into your service.'

'Come here, girl.' The Countess's voice was kindly but imperious. Janeta approached timidly and curtsied low.

'What is your name and why are you seeking a place

now? Have you been dismissed from your former employment? Are you serf-bound or free?'

Janeta hesitated. What could she say? Dared she confess to the Countess her reason for fleeing St Catherine's? Yet those piercing blue eyes demanded the truth as, instinctively, she had known that the Earl of Leicester had. It would be useless to prevaricate. To be offered a place in the Countess's household would be more than she could have hoped, yet she dreaded the possibility of the Countess's decision to return her summarily to the convent, once she knew her identity. She drew a hard breath and explained diffidently. Throughout she felt the hard eyes of the Countess's companion upon her, judging and finding her wanting.

'And you are?' the Countess demanded at the close of this halting tale.

'Janeta Cobham, my lady. My father is Sir Hugh Cobham. We have a manor in Berkshire.'

'And he refuses to listen to your request to be free of the nunnery?'

'Yes, my lady. He—he has his reasons. . .'

The Countess considered. 'This is a delicate matter. Your father must be informed of your presence in my household.'

'But, my lady, he will demand that I be returned. . .'

'I do not think so.' The blue eyes flashed imperiously and Janeta began to realise the mettle of this lovely young widow. Princess she was—the daughter of the late King John—and the second most important lady in the realm, after Queen Eleanor of Provence, King Henry's wife, since her older sisters had long been given in state marriages.

The Countess continued. 'I cannot believe that after he has heard my decision to offer you a place in my household he would continue to press you into a life you believe would be wholly abhorrent to you. At all

events you must come with us into Winchester and
remain under my protection until your father can be
summoned.' She smiled warmly at Bertrand. 'You will
also be assured by sight of her there that the lady to
whom you have offered your protection will be safe
from harm.'

Though her companion frowned and the older knight
coughed disapprovingly at so precipitate a decision,
she was not to be gainsaid and the Earl, smiling
broadly, indicated that they should mount up immediately and join the Countess's company.

Janeta, mounted pillion behind Bertrand, clutched
wildly at his waist, feeling the hard links of mail
beneath his gambeson. She shivered as she thought of
what peril she had been in only a few short hours ago.
Her fortunes had altered dramatically so suddenly. She
had been delighted to receive an offer of service so
soon. Now she was not so sure. Her life had been so
sheltered, a safe, ordered routine within the sheltering
convent walls, and soon she was to be plunged into a
different world, among strange people—one of whom
she felt disapproved of her from the start—a frightening world of Court opulence totally unknown to her.
Of course she would be relegated to the servants'
quarters of the Countess's apartments. Probably she
would be required to sleep in a dormitory with other
girls——She gave a little shocked gasp at the thought.
Within the convent dormitory she had been enclosed
in her own small curtained space. Now there would be
other maids, avidly curious to question her, observe
her closely. How could she keep her secret, and if the
mark was discovered would the Countess turn her
away, repelled by the sight of that ugly, blood-red
stain, the sure sign that Janeta had been marked by
the devil from her birth?

As if he sensed her uneasy silence, Bertrand called

to her. They were riding slowly, setting an easy pace
for the ladies on their palfreys and jennets, and he did
not require so much close concentration on his mount.

'You are very quiet, Demoiselle Janeta. Aren't you
pleased by the way things have fallen out? This is ideal
for you. I told you, you could not have been left to
cope alone in the city. Life can be difficult for girls
without protectors. . .' His voice trailed off. He was
embarrassed by the need to warn her of dangers which,
in her sheltered existence, she might not have guessed
at. He frowned, gazing abstractedly at the road ahead
and the stolid backs of the two men-at-arms in front of
him. Naturally she must be feeling frightened. Life
would be very different for her in the intrigue-ridden
air of Court. Perhaps, after all, it would have been
easier for her if she had found work in some merchant's
home, and yet she was gently born, and likely she
would find Court life challenging and entertaining. His
thoughts flew to Roesia, soon to be Morris's bride. She
would have sold her soul for such an opportunity.

Janeta said softly, 'Thank you, I am not afraid.
Yet—yet I am trying to come to terms with what has
happened to me. It has come so suddenly, and I fear
my father will not so easily be turned from his purpose,
not even by the Princess's command.' She was silent
for a moment, then she asked, 'Who is the lady in
attendance on the Princess, the one wearing such plain
clothing, almost like—almost like a nun's habit?'

His voice drifted back to her. 'I don't know her.
Why?'

'She—she seemed to disapprove of me, especially
when she heard about the nunnery and—and. . .'

'And?'

'I was watching her. I do not think she approves of
the Earl either.'

It was his turn to ride silently for several moments, deep in thought.

At length he said reflectively, 'There are many at Court who are jealous of the Earl's sudden rise to prominence. It's said he has the ear of the King, and he *is* a foreigner.'

Janeta looked ahead to where the Earl rode proudly now at the Countess's right side. Her brows drew together in sudden doubt. Had her earlier thought been right? Had those men lain in ambush for the Earl? Their horses *had* been hidden in the thicket. If so, it seemed he had determined enemies, and those enemies would become Bertrand's too.

CHAPTER FOUR

THEY entered Winchester by the north gate and already the snow on the streets had turned to slush underfoot. Janeta peered curiously around her, fascinated by the bustle, noise and stink of the ancient capital. She had never been in a large town before and she stared, bewildered, at the huddle of timber and mud-daubed dwellings, so crowded together that the inhabitants could clasp hands by dint of leaning from facing upper windows. The Princess's procession was slowed now by the throng of people going about their business, although two of the men-at-arms went ahead to cry 'passage' and make way for her to reach the Old Palace, where her brother the King had taken up residence for the Christmas festivities and the traditional crown-wearing ceremony.

Janeta looked eagerly for sight of the great stone minster she had heard so much about, but saw only a glimpse of one of the towers and then they were nearing the palace itself. Her mouth became suddenly dry. She had no idea where Bertrand was to lodge and realised, with a sudden jolt, that these might be the last moments she would have in his company. Their acquaintance had been very short and yet she could not imagine herself coping without him in this strange new life.

The palace of the Saxon kings was a disappointment. At first glance it appeared to be a collection of timbered, thatched buildings, very like the squalid houses of the town. Accustomed to the solid stone of the convent, Janeta thought the palace lacked distinction.

The company rode through a gate into a courtyard crowded with grooms, ostlers and servants, redolent with the scents of horses, oil and hot metal, emanating from the huts of the armourers and smiths, combined with the pleasanter cooking smells from the kitchens— fresh-baked bread and roasting meat. Janeta's mouth watered as she recognised the fact that she was extremely hungry. The food she had shared with Bertrand had been scrappy, cold, and had progressively become stale.

He dismounted in front of her and reached up to lift her down. She had stiffened during the cold ride and stumbled against him awkwardly. He laughed as he set her firmly on her feet, supporting her with a hand round her waist.

'Steady. You are as unsure of your footing as I was the first time I set sail for Normandy.'

She withdrew from his hold, anxious that he should not realise how fearful she was of losing his company.

'Thank you, Sir Bertrand,' she said breathlessly. 'You have been untold kind to a stranger.'

'A stranger no longer.' He laughed down at her. 'Can we ever be that, now that we have broken bread together by our own hearth fire?'

It was a tacit reminder that she had slept within feet of him and her cheeks burned dull red at the memory.

As she did not answer he bent close to murmur in her ear, since the noise of shouting men-at-arms and grooms, the clatter of horses' hoofs on the ground as they were led to stabling, as well as the sound of the armourer's hammer and the shrill crying of hawks from the nearby mews, made it almost impossible to be heard.

'You must not be overawed. You will soon get used to all of this.' He indicated the general mayhem with an amused sweep of his arm. 'The Countess will be your protector, and I am glad that I shall no longer have to worry about you.'

She found herself almost shouting back at him. 'I am not your responsibility. I never was. Go your way, sir knight, with a glad heart that you are rid of a burden you did not chose to acquire.'

He read the anger in her voice, for he put both hands upon her shoulders and turned her to face him.

'You wrong me if you consider that I think so little of our short acquaintance. Of course I shall continue to be interested in your welfare. I don't know yet where I shall be lodged, but I shall be very close within the town, and I shall come soon to the palace to enquire after you. The Earl will see to it that I am not turned back.' A little doubtful frown crossed his brows. 'I hope the Countess will remember to contact your father — No,' he said hurriedly, placing a gentle finger on her lip to quell any possible remonstrance, 'he should be told where you are. Even under the Countess's protection, you need the added security of a father to guard your interests. Court can be a lonely and even dangerous place.'

She stared back at him questioningly, but he looked down at her, smiling, as the Earl came to his side.

'Well, D'Aubigny, we are to be lodged at the castle, so you must take leave of the demoiselle Janeta.' He bowed his head gravely at her and she curtsied in answer. 'Allow me to lead you to one of the Countess's ladies, who will arrange for your accommodation, little one. Don't be afraid; you will see both Sir Bertrand and myself frequently while we are in Winchester. I come often to wait on the King, and I'll have Sir Bertrand in attendance. Once you are settled and have made friends all will be well with you.'

Janeta swallowed hard. This was what she had longed for throughout those long, wearying days at St

Catherine's, yet now the prospect of life in this hectic company threatened to overwhelm her totally. She forced a smile and hardly had time to turn again for a last glimpse at Bertrand before the Earl led her towards the Countess, who was watching the unpacking of some of the sumpter mules.

The dark, forbidding woman, whose obvious disapproval had already alarmed Janeta, turned at the Earl's approach and surveyed his charge.

'You can leave the girl with me, my lord,' she said coldly. 'I will see to it that she is found a mattress in the girls' dormitory.'

The Earl relinquished Janeta's hand and turned uncertainly, as if he would crave a final word with the Countess, but she was striding forward impatiently to snap at one of the men who had almost dropped one of her precious wooden chests.

'Take care, man. Do not dare to let that fall. The contents are invaluable.'

The fellow instantly recollected himself and tugged a forelock, then the Countess turned to sigh at her companion.

'Oh, Cecily, so often you chide me for my want of patience, but sometimes, I swear, these foolish men would try a saint's. Ah, the little demoiselle. She can stay within my chamber tonight.' She glanced down at Janeta's sorely muddied and torn gown and cloak. 'She will need to be found some suitable apparel.'

Dame Cecily's bottom jaw dropped open in her astonishment.

'But, my lady, you do not know this girl. . .'

'Tush, Cecily, do you think she harbours a dagger within those sleeves, to thrust it into my breast? Besides, you will be near, as usual. She can sleep on a truckle in the outer chamber, close to me. I wish to question her more fully about her home and paren-

tage.' The beautiful blue eyes became strangely
dreamy. 'I know what it is to lack a mother's care, as
you know well. This child helped to render my lord
earl good service and she shall be rewarded for it.
Now, bring her in with me. Let us get quickly to my
apartments. I shall turn into a block of ice if I remain
out here much longer.'

Dame Cecily looked down at Janeta and the girl
read there a mixture of bewilderment, annoyance and
downright spite. The older woman gave her a sudden
push as she herded Janeta before her in the Countess's
wake.

Janeta was as amazed by the Countess's pronounce-
ment as Dame Cecily was. Why should she, an unim-
portant newcomer, be singled out for particular
treatment? Even within the convent, where humility
was considered the most important virtue, Janeta had
known jealousy among the nuns. She knew, unhappily,
that this would not make her popular with her companion attendants—and she had no skills in dealing
with the requirements of noble ladies.

The palace proved as rambling inside as she had
judged it to be, and they passed along a multitude of
corridors and through halls and rooms crowded with
people, jostling together for attention. Even in daylight
the palace was lit by brands set in sconces along the
walls, because it was so gloomy. They were preceded
by a page dressed, to Janeta's marvelling eyes, in
bright and gorgeous clothing.

The Countess's apartments were as noisy and
crowded as all the rest. Men struggled through the
doorways carrying unwieldy packages and wooden
chests, serving-women chided them loudly, despite
their perspiring efforts to please, dogs flew at the
ankles of the heavily laden newcomers and hampered
their progress and a falcon on a stand in one corner of

the solar fluttered its wings wildly and set up a shrill screeching.

The Countess stood in the midst of all this confusion and clapped her hands imperiously. At once all was quiet. The women dropped into curtsys, and the men laid down their burdens to await instructions as to where to bestow them.

'Cecily, please attend to all this. I must bathe and change into fresh clothing before descending to the great hall for supper. You——' she addressed an older woman close by '—arrange for my tub to be brought into my bedchamber and unpack the larger of the clothing chests. I shall wear the blue velvet gown tonight. I shall want another gown for this lady, who is to join my attendants. Find something suitable for her to wear to attend me in hall, and since she is slightly shorter than I it will require altering.' She turned and took Janeta's hand. 'Come, child, in here with me. We will see to your toilet and re-dress you before I greet my brother.'

Even more mystified, Janeta entered the Countess's bedchamber. Already the servants had unpacked clean linen sheets and fur coverlets for the bed. Janeta stared wonderingly at the painted walls with their bright hangings to keep out the chill draughts of winter. The rushes had been fresh-strewn and the aromatic scents of rosemary and lavender mingled with them and were stirred by their feet in passing. A man stumbled in with one of the clothing chests, guided by the older woman who appeared to be in charge of the serving-wenches. The Countess stripped off her heavy fur-lined mantle and threw it on to the bed. Tiredly she removed her barbette and veil and Janeta marvelled at the wealth of red-gold hair in two heavy plaits which reached well beyond her waist. How sad it was that such a beautiful woman should have been widowed so early! Eleanor smilingly indicated a joint-stool at the foot of the bed while she sank down on a chair with a leathern back.

'How good it is to be out of that bitter wind. Now, your name again?'

'Janeta, my lady. Janeta Cobham.'

'Ah, yes, I remember now, and straight from your education in St Catherine's convent.'

Janeta trembled as she sank obediently on to the stool and the Countess gave a silvery little laugh.

'Don't be afraid. I've no intention of returning you there. Now, while we wait for the tub to be brought, tell me everything about your meeting with Simon de Montfort.'

Janeta's grey eyes widened. There was little more to tell than she thought the Countess already knew but she repeated the story of the ambush and how Sir Bertrand D'Aubigny had plunged instantly into the fray and how the two men had vanquished their foes. The Countess listened as eagerly as if she were hearing some tale from the lips of a troubadour and, truth to tell, Janeta thought the encounter had savoured of the same romantic aura. Both men had fought with dash and courage and she could not but feel a glow of pride for Bertrand's part in the affair.

'The men had horses hidden in the wood, you say? You think they might well have been lying in wait for the Earl?' The question was sharply put.

Janeta wriggled uneasily on her stool. 'Sir Bertrand and I both thought that very possible, my lady.'

The Countess nodded her golden head and looked up hastily as a knock sounded on the door and, on her call to enter, two men struggled in, bearing a tall-sided heavy wooden tub which they placed at the foot of the bed with much gasping and grunting, then backed and withdrew. The older attendant ushered in two very young serving-girls laden with steaming ewers of water which they poured into the tub. Several more followed with hot and cold water and the attendant, pointedly staring at Janeta, who had still not dared to move from her stool until commanded to do so, began to arrange a contraption of wooden screens, overlaid with towels, around the tub. Still the Countess gave Janeta no instructions, and she waited while three more girls entered and helped the Countess to undress and step into the tub, her glorious hair piled high on her head with ivory combs. The older woman, whom Eleanor addressed as Martha, knelt to soap her mistress and wrap her in one of the towels as she stepped out again and ran, shivering and laughing, to the brazier placed near the window for safety, lest its fumes affect the inhabitants of the chamber adversely.

'Get into the tub, Janeta,' she called gaily. 'The water is still hot and Martha has laid out fresh clothes for you.' She wrinkled her nose disdainfully. 'Those you are wearing must be disposed of. They are sadly stained and not in the least becoming.'

Janeta was horrified by the suggestion that she should strip before these two women. She feared her secret would be revealed and the Countess repulsed by the sight of her ugly birthmark, but she could not disobey, and scrambled behind the rickety screens, hoping she would be well-hidden.

She was glad of the warmth of the scented water and the delight of feeling really clean once more. She could hear the Countess's laughing voice as she gossiped with Martha and thought the woman must be an old retainer, possibly the Countess's former wet-nurse. The two were intent on the Countess's toilet and took little notice of her as she scrambled out of the tub, a difficult feat without assistance, and draped herself hurriedly in another of the towels left on the screen-rack.

Martha called that a gown and chemise had been laid out for her on the chest and she went hastily to see for herself what had been chosen. The gown was of fine wool, dyed in a rich shade of saffron-yellow. Instantly Janeta felt it would complement her dark hair and donned the unfamiliar chemise and gown, fumbling awkwardly at the ornamental buttoning on the long, tight sleeves. Fortunately the gown was not as long as the Countess had feared and the girdle of softest brown leather adequately dealt with the excess material. Janeta was struggling with the unaccustomed back-lacing when Martha came, tut-tutting, to her side to assist her. She stood back to examine her critically, mouth pursed, but the Countess came in a rustle of soft blue velvet to voice her approval.

'That will do very well. Sir Bertrand will approve, I think. The apricot barbette and veiling, please, Martha.'

Janeta's heart leapt unaccountably. Was she to see Bertrand again so soon?

Martha brought the head-dress and veil and adjusted it for Janeta under the Countess's keen eye. She laughed as she handed Janeta an ivory-backed, keenly polished iron mirror from her travelling-chest.

'Here, look at yourself, child. I imagine you have had little opportunity to do so during those cloistered years.'

Janeta stared in wonder. She looked like a princess herself. The soft fine cloth clung to her bosom and the belt cinched in her small waist. Beneath that the full skirts swirled to the floor in soft folds. She examined her own features with a kind of detached curiosity. This was the face Bertrand had seen staring back at him over the hearth fire. Her face was oval, her features small and delicate but for her mouth, which was, to her critical eyes, somewhat over-large, the bottom lip too full for beauty. Her eyes were smoky blue-grey under frowning dark brows, and the circlet of padded apricot velvet, with its barbette and veil of a slightly lighter shade, hid most of her dark hair. In the uncertain light from the high lancet window she thought she detected a tinge of copper in her straight heavy locks, which echoed the red-gold splendour of the Countess's own.

Had Bertrand found her attractive? They all spoke of her as a child, belying her nineteen years. She gave a faint sigh. The years in the convent had blunted her development as a true woman; she understood that now. The Countess was little older than herself in true years, but life and marriage had matured her, so that there seemed almost a generation of understanding between her and Janeta.

'Well?' The Countess was smiling but impatient as she held out her hand for the mirror.

'I—I can hardly believe it is really me. You are so good to me, my lady, and I have yet to prove myself in service. . .'

'You will do that. I know it.' Eleanor brushed off Janeta's husky attempt at gratitude. 'Now, come, we must descend to the hall for supper. Is Lady Sandford ready?' she enquired of Martha.

'She was coming along the corridor as I came in with the clothing for the demoiselle Janeta,' the older woman answered.

'Cecily, come in.' The Countess's lovely blue eyes were dancing with amusement as her former governess entered and curtsied. 'Look at the transformation of our little novice. Is she not beautiful enough to prove a true ornament among my ladies?'

Lady Sandford was dressed similarly to the way Janeta had first seen her, in a dark blue gown of fine wool and a severe nun-like barbette and white veil.

She regarded the newcomer, eyebrows raised, mouth pursed. For a moment it looked as if she would make some objection, then she gave a thin smile and nodded.

'My lady, the girl looks—very charming. It is to be hoped your brother the King will approve your decision to take her into service. After all, her father. . .'

'Will be only too ready to approve when she realises she will have a better future with me. As for Henry——' the Countess gave a rueful shrug '—why should he object? I pleased him once mightily in my marriage; now my life and my household are my own.'

They made the bewildering journey back along the gloomy corridors to the great hall, preceded by another curly-headed page. Janeta walked beside Lady Sandford, uncomfortably aware that that dame thoroughly disapproved of her acceptance into the household.

The noise and confusion of the banqueting hall smote Janeta like a blow in the face. The long hall seemed crowded with people, and the smell of wine, rich food and humanity was breath-stopping. A steward came, brandishing his white wand of office, to lead them to the high table, where the Countess took her place under the canopy of state with the young King and Queen. Lady Sandford curtsied to the royal pair and, in a daze, Janeta heard herself being introduced. At Lady Sandford's prompting, she curtsied low and rose to find herself under the scrutiny of the richly dressed young man lolling back in his carved chair. Janeta saw, in a fleeting, shy glance, that he resembled his sister. His hair shone bright red-gold under his golden circlet. He was handsome, his features amiable and regular, marred only by the distinct droop of one eyelid. He nodded, smiling, and bent to explain his sister's decision to take Janeta into service to his young queen, whose understanding of the Norman French tongue spoken by these Northerners was still slightly incomplete. Janeta saw that she was small and exquisitely formed, her complexion creamy and the suggestion of hair peeping from her barbette black as night. This was the other Eleanor in Henry's life, his queen, Eleanor of Provence, and it was clear to all in the hall that he adored her.

The slight cessation of noise that had marked the Countess's entrance had ended and the talk and bustle resumed. In a daze of wonder Janeta allowed herself to be led down the length of the banqueting-table to where the Earl of Leicester sat. He stood up as the two approached. To her delight she glimpsed Bertrand, craning forward, further down towards the table's foot, well below the salt.

'My lord, the Countess requests that you take charge of the demoiselle Janeta during the feast and find her former companion,' said Dame Cecily. 'At the close of the festivities I would be grateful if she could be returned to the Countess's apartments.'

He bowed formally. 'Certainly, Lady Sandford. Allow me first to escort you to your own place.'

'I can find that for myself sir,' she replied frostily, and swept off towards the head of the table once more.

Simon de Montfort's dark eyes twinkled at Janeta. 'Then let me take you to Sir Bertrand, who, I am sure, will be delighted to share cup and trencher with you, demoiselle Janeta.'

Her fingers trembled in his grasp and he squeezed them reassuringly.

Bertrand was instantly at his side and holding out his hand to take Janeta's. She found herself seated at the long bench beside him, while the Earl bowed his head to her.

'You have become a very great lady indeed, demoiselle.'

She flushed darkly, feeling embarrassed by the stares of those near them at table and uncomfortable in her unaccustomed finery. The Earl left to resume his place and Bertrand grinned down at her, still keeping a tight grip on her cold fingers.

'The Earl is right. You look magnificent, a rival to the splendour of both the Queen and the Countess of Pembroke.'

'That might well be,' she said wryly, 'since my borrowed plumes are the Countess's own.'

'Then she is being kind to you?'

Janeta blinked thoughtfully. 'I cannot understand why she should give me marks of favour,' she said slowly. 'It is all very strange, and Lady Sandford has already shown her deep displeasure. I'm afraid I have made an enemy there.'

Bertrand followed her gaze to where Lady Cecily Sandford sat near the junction with the high table, a crow among so many gorgeously plumaged birds. She sat rigidly upright, disdainfully picking at the food her neighbour had thoughtfully placed upon her trencher.

Bertrand sighed. 'I hear she was once the Countess's governess and her constant companion since childhood. She, too, was widowed young, and apparently has never put aside her mourning-gowns. My informant told me she is a very pious lady, constantly at her devotions, so possibly she disapproves of your decision to leave the convent.'

'There will be many who do so,' Janeta agreed glumly.

'But I am not one of them.'

She glanced at him sharply, but already he was giving attention to her needs, catching the eye of an attendant page with a wine-jug to refill his cup, and himself leaning forward to pick up slices of venison in a rich wine sauce with his dagger for their shared trencher. He saluted her gravely as he offered her his cup, first wiping the rim carefully with one of the napkins provided. Their fingers touched again as, shyly, she bent to drink. She was actuely aware of the intimacy of the act, for she had never shared plate or cup with another being since her arrival at St Catherine's; close contact was frowned upon as displeasing to God, even between the young girls who had formed her companions.

His fingers were cool and firm and she smelled the odour of his wine-scented breath and the male tang of leather and armour-oil still clinging to his hands and body. He was used to bathing frequently, she was sure, for she had noticed no unpleasant stink of sweat or greasy dirt about his person, even when she had ridden so close to him. She knew, from the remembrances of her own father and brother and the men she had been close to on the demesne so many years ago, that this was unusual. Had he bathed in the icy stream on that chillingly cold morning before he had come back to her in the hut? Cleanliness had been instilled into all the girls at the convent and she was glad of his thoughtfulness.

The noise around her was confusing. At St Catherine's they had all eaten in silence, apart from the occasions when one of their number had read aloud a portion of the scriptures or a passage from the life of one of the saints. She found herself eating without realising exactly what, as course after course was brought in and removed. The food was so rich that she could take only a little, and she was afraid to drink too deeply from the wine-cup, but Bertrand, she saw, ate heartily, though she noted he was as abstimious in his drinking as she was.

'Are you truly settled at the castle?' she asked, leaning close to catch his answer above the clamour of talk and laughter around them.

'Yes, and I've found good stabling for Saladin and the mule. I share sleeping quarters with several men of the Earl's service and I am to take part in the Christmas tourney as part of his household.'

She felt a tremor of doubt and bit her lip. 'So you intend to ride in the tournament?'

'Aye, it is my reason for coming to Winchester.'

'But if you are now in the Earl's service you have not so great a need to risk your life and limbs for gain.'

His light brown eyes, golden in the glare from the torch set above them high on the wall, looked intently down at the prim set of her mouth.

'Still you disapprove of the tourney. It is but sport for the Christmas festivities. I need to prove to the Earl how skilled I am in the arts of war.'

'I know,' she said slowly. 'I understand, truly, but take care.'

'Ah, you are concerned for me?'

'Of course I am. You are my only friend at Court and I would not lose you so soon.'

He bent and took her hand again. 'I am honoured by your friendship, Demoiselle Janeta. I look to see you many times in the near future. I shall not foolishly jeopardise my chance of that.'

She bowed her head to hide the sudden smarting of tears that came to her eyes. Well she knew that this was only Court banter, but a warmth at his kindly words spread throughout her being. This meeting with him again and his consideration for her at the feast had cancelled out the coldness she had felt emanating from Lady Sandford in her obvious dislike of her. She was unsure of her welcome at the Countess's side tonight — for was not the favour of princesses often marred by just as easy fickleness?—but she was able to put aside her doubts for the moment and enjoy the delight of his company.

Janeta had mixed feelings when Lady Sandford presented herself and demanded that Janeta follow her to the Countess's apartments. The bawdy banter of the jesters, which had brought the hot blood to her cheeks, the boisterousness of the tumblers and acrobats, the constant laughter and chatter around her had brought on a headache, but she balked at being deprived of Bertrand's company and went somewhat unwillingly, though obediently, in her mentor's wake.

She found she had been incorrect in her assessment of the Lady Eleanor, who greeted her as warmly as ever and asked, with a little sly smile, if she had enjoyed her first taste of Court banquets. It was clear that Janeta had been observed in her talk with Bertrand. It was arranged that Janeta should sleep on a truckle-bed in the ante-room to Eleanor's chamber in the company of Martha, whom she discovered to have been the Countess's wet nurse. A brazier brought a welcome warmth to the chamber, and the bed was certainly no less comfortable than her cot in the dormitory at St Catherine's, but Janeta lay wakeful for hours. She was troubled about the coming tournament and could not rid her mind of her feelings about the attack on the Earl of Leicester on the Winchester road.

Next morning it seemed that the event was the current topic of conversation among all the Countess's ladies, with the exception of Lady Sandford, who kept a tight-lipped silence on the matter other than remarking tartly that such shows were directly opposed to the teachings of Holy Church. The younger ladies took no heed whatever. One pulled a face behind her back and laughingly said to Janeta, 'Take no notice of the old crow.'

A crow Lady Sandford certainly resembled, but Janeta could in no way deem her old. Though she had been governess to the Lady Eleanor, who was still in her twenties, Janeta thought there were but a few years between them in age, and they were still close companions.

She found her tasks in no way disagreeable or onerous. There were many hands to make light work of bathing and dressing the Countess and Eleanor, though imperious, did not appear too hard to please.

On the day following her arrival Janeta was summoned to her side.

'Do you ride, Janeta?'

Janeta was somewhat startled at the question. She had not expected it.

'I rode a pony as a child, my lady,' she confessed, 'but had no occasion to ride at the convent and am sadly out of practice.'

'Well, you will need to ride out with me in company with my other ladies, so we must see to it that you have some instruction, and quickly.'

A little bemused, Janeta could only nod in agreement.

'The grooms are all busy and cannot be relied upon. They are a motley company, drawn from so many households. You need someone you can trust. I shall send to the castle and request that the Earl of Leicester allow us the services of Sir Bertrand to ride out with you and impart confidence in your early attempts. You will soon be able to hawk and hunt with the best of us.'

Janeta stared at the Countess open-mouthed. It seemed that she was being constantly and deliberately thrown into Bertrand D'Aubigny's company, and, glad though she was of the opportunity to see him again, she could not quite understand the Countess's motives for such an interest in her welfare.

It seemed that Cecily Sandford shared her opinion. In the corridor later that afternoon, catching Janeta alone, she seized her arm and drew her imperatively close.

'It would be better for all concerned, demoiselle,' she hissed, 'if you were to find life unfulfilling here at Court, and profess a wish to return to your convent.'

The grip on her arm was painful, and angrily Janeta struggled free.

'I am sorry, my lady, that you have formed such a poor impression of me. I cannot believe that I deserve it but, indeed, I *do* like it here very much, and have no intention of returning to St Catherine's, whether at your wish or even that of the Countess. I shall do my best to please her in every way and I cannot understand why you should be at pains to rid yourself of me. I am nobody, have no particular skill to take the Countess's favour from you, and can in no way be deemed a threat to you.'

It was a bold and candid speech to one whose position in the household was secure and Janeta regretted her hasty words as soon as they were spoken.

Lady Sandford made to reply, then gritted her teeth, shook her head and made to walk away, but then she said, more gently, 'You do not understand. You are a threat to all our hopes—well, let that be. *You* cannot be held responsible.' She hastened off and Janeta stared after her helplessly, aware that the lady's voice had been muffled, as if by tears.

As bewildered as ever, Janeta resumed her journey to the Countess's chamber where she had been bidden to find a length of veiling.

The following day she was sent to the courtyard, accompanied by an avidly curious page, to find Bertrand D'Aubigny waiting, muffled in his familiar mantle, holding the reins of an elderly palfrey. Janeta saw that his own mount, the pampered Saladin, was tethered near by to a ring in the stable wall. She had been warned to dress warmly and clothes suitable for riding had been provided. She longed to run and greet Bertrand joyfully but the presence of the watchful page restrained her, and she approached shyly and ran her hand gently down the palfrey's nose.

Bertrand eyed the cheeky-faced youngster and dismissed him airily. 'Your mistress will be safe in my hands and I will conduct her to the Countess's apartments when we have concluded our lesson.'

The boy went reluctantly, several times looking back over his shoulder at the pair.

'Oh, Sir Bertrand,' Janeta breathed, 'how good it is to see you. I am quite afraid of making a fool of myself in the saddle and welcome the instructions of a friend.'

'The Countess knew that, so here I am. There is no need to fear. I've chosen the gentlest mount in the stable and I shall be close all the time.'

He lifted her into the saddle and walked the palfrey slowly round the courtyard. As the Countess had promised, Janeta soon became accustomed to being in the saddle and allowed the horse to trot. Once sure that she was confident, Bertrand mounted Saladin and they rode through the archway into the town. It was still cold but most of the slush had cleared from the walkways, though some still lay, dirty and sullied, in piles near the open kennels. The air was good and Janeta felt exhilarated. They passed the great stone church and castle and headed through the town gate into the meadows beyond. Already workmen were hammering at the stands which would house the King and Queen, their favourites and the ladies throughout the coming tournament. Janeta averted her eyes and did not refer to the event. She had no wish to alienate Bertrand this fine morning. Her gentle mount ambled happily and Janeta made no attempt to force the pace. She was content to allow herself to become accustomed to handling her. Saladin, that fierce, proud creature, kept a quiet pace at her side under his master's firm control.

Their progress was easy enough to allow talk, and he told her enthusiastically about his life at the castle. The Earl of Leicester was to stay near the King's side after he rode south to London, and Janeta wondered if Eleanor would accompany her brother or return to her own manor at Odiham. She felt a keen pang at the thought, and wished passionately that the Countess would decide to go to London.

'Do you see the Earl often?' she enquired. Simon de Montfort must have close companions, and Bertrand had only recently joined his household, so it seemed unlikely.

'Yes.' One eyebrow rose doubtfully. 'He keeps me in close attendance, which is flattering. I think he is doubtful about the loyalty of some of those around him and, since I saved his life, he appears to trust me.'

'Has his wound healed cleanly?'

'Yes, and without the services of a surgeon. He speaks of your ministrations with gratitude. He is most anxious that you should settle well into the Countess's household.'

'She treats me very well,' Janeta said thoughtfully. 'It seems that, like the Earl, she isn't quite sure about her other attendants.' She bit her lip. 'Her favour makes Lady Sandford very angry, though. She told me yesterday that I was a threat to all their hopes. What do you think she meant by that?'

He shrugged lightly. 'Jealousy is a strong emotion. I imagine she is afraid of losing her hold on the Countess.'

'But she cannot fear that *I* could take her place.'

'It seems unlikely.' He turned his mount and watched carefully as Janeta went through the same manoeuvre. 'Have you heard any word from your father yet?'

A tremor of fear passed through her. She dreaded to face her father's fury when he presented himself at Court. Even the Countess's kindliness might not protect her from his demand that she return to St Catherine's. The King was a deeply pious young man. He might well insist that her father's wishes override his sister's.

She pushed the doubts aside as they entered the town again and made for the Old Palace. She was proud of her achievement of skilfully handling her palfrey, though she knew her lack of fear was because Bertrand was there to guide her.

As they entered the courtyard she saw there were new arrivals. Grooms were about to lead their mounts into the stables. Bertrand dismounted and reached up to lift Janeta down. His attention was on his pupil, and he started as he heard his name called in an excited feminine voice.

'Bertrand? Here? Morris, do you see? Bertrand is here. What a wonderful surprise!'

Bertrand steadied Janeta and they both turned towards the two newcomers. The woman was coming towards them, almost breaking into a run in her delighted surprise. The man was hanging back, as if in doubt of his own senses. Janeta saw that he was young, stocky, not so tall as Bertrand, but, though he was darker, she saw a distinct resemblance. Was this the elder brother who had inherited the family manor?

The woman was holding out her hands in greeting. She was small and slim, wrapped against the chill wind in a mantle of green velvet. The fur-lined hood had been drawn up over her barbette but Janeta saw that she had fair hair, curling a little outside the restraints of the veil. Her flower-like face was tilted up to Bertrand for the kiss of greeting, and he bent and their lips met. Janeta wondered if his lingered there longer than was needed in the formality of greeting.

He drew back slightly, his lips parting in delight.

'Demoiselle Janeta, allow me to present my brother, Morris, and his betrothed, Demoiselle Roesia Fitzherbert. I had not expected to see you both again so soon.'

Morris D'Aubigny caught his brother's arm in a firm grasp but his grey eyes seemed to Janeta to be clouded with doubt. Had he hoped that his brother was far away from his intended bride? Certainly he was placing a restraining hand upon her arm.

'I should have known I might find you here with the tournament planned after the Holy Day,' he said in a determined attempt at heartiness. 'The King summoned me to Court for the crown-wearing and commanded that I bring my betrothed. Fortunately the weather cleared enough for us to travel in reasonable comfort.'

He glanced down at Janeta and made her a little bow. 'It seems my brother has been of service to you, demoiselle.'

'The Demoiselle Janeta Cobham is one of the ladies in the household of the Countess of Pembroke,' Bertrand explained. 'I have taken service with the Earl of Leicester and I have been requested to escort her on her ride.'

There was a distinct coldness in Morris D'Aubigny's acceptance of his brother's news. He stood, feet astride, looking from Bertrand to Roesia, and said somewhat flatly, 'Then you will not, after all, be leaving our shores for Normandy? How fortunate. You must tell me how all this came about, but now we must settle Roesia and her ladies into their lodgings.'

'You'll find me at the castle, Morris, when you have leisure to talk.'

Sir Morris D'Aubigny bowed to them both and firmly led his betrothed towards the door of the palace. Bertrand followed their progress keenly and Janeta thought she detected a wistful twist to his lips.

Janeta took her leave of Bertrand very hurriedly. He seemed unaware of the perfunctory nature of her leave-taking and she was wrapped up in her own thoughts as she hastened to the Countess's apartments to present herself for duty.

The Countess was in attendance on the Queen in the bower, and it was some hours before Janeta found herself needed. Even then her thoughts were elsewhere and she had to be sharply called to order by Martha before she understood that the Countess had requested her presence in her chamber. All through the day Janeta had craned her neck for glimpses of Roesia Fitzherbert, but there was no sign of her. Possibly she had been presented to Queen Eleanor in the Queen's bower.

The Countess nodded to her ivory comb and Janeta began to unbraid her hair. There was no sign of Lady Sandford and Eleanor dismissed Martha.

'Well, how did the lesson go?' Eleanor enquired, peering at Janeta through the polished iron mirror on her large travelling-chest.

'I think well, my lady. Sir Bertrand was very patient and provided me with a very docile mount. My early lessons came back quickly and I think I shall soon be competent enough to ride wherever——' she hesitated '——Wherever you wish to go after the Christmas festivities.'

Eleanor looked at her newest attendant shrewdly.

'Did Sir Bertrand speak of the Earl of Leicester's plans?'

'I understand the Earl's household is to ride south with the King, my lady.'

'Indeed. And the Earl—is he recovered from his wound?'

'I think entirely, my lady, since he is to ride in the jousts and the mêlée. Bertrand—is to ride with the other household knights. . .' Janeta's voice trailed off awkwardly.

'You are concerned?'

'I have never seen a tournament, my lady, but at the convent we were taught that it is displeasing to God for men to risk their lives in vain show.'

'It is dangerous,' the Countess said, biting her nether lip, 'and a way of settling old scores. The King disapproves of the practice but it is traditional at this Holy season and he has been constrained to give his permission. He will be present on this occasion and I too.' She caught Janeta's hand within her own. 'Do you wish to attend me, Janeta?'

Janeta's brow creased in doubt. 'Yes,' she breathed, 'I do, my lady. If I were not there. . .'

'You would worry even more. Good. You shall sit with me in the stand. That is enough brushing, child. Call Martha now, and go to your bed. Tomorrow is the Eve of Christ Mass. We shall all be busied, helping to fix the greenery in halls and bowers.'

Janeta was kept busy next day, running errands for the Countess and her ladies who were excited by the prospect of the Holy Day to come. Most were occupied in choosing gowns for the Crown-wearing feast and giving orders to the pages and squires occupied in decorating the ladies' bower. Again Janeta looked among the throng of brightly clad ladies for the golden-haired Roesia, without success. She had no idea whether she would be present at the symbolic feast of the Holy Day herself and, if so, what she would wear. Would Bertrand be present in attendance on the Earl of Leicester? It was more than likely, since this was the day when oaths of loyalty were renewed as a Holy rite, and Simon de Montfort must be present with the other barons.

To her delight the Countess informed her that she would take her place at the central table with the rest of Eleanor's ladies and bade Martha to provide her with a suitable gown. This one was of crimson velvet with an over-tunic of midnight-blue. Lady Sandford grumbled that the style and colours were far too sophisticated for so young a maiden but the Countess laughed at her remarks.

'Nonsense. This is a grand occasion and Janeta must play her part in it, as we all must.'

No one, thought Janeta irritably, thinks of me as more than a child. She frowned at her reflection in the scratched mirror Martha had loaned her. The years in the convent had schooled her to lower her eyes and walk demurely. These mannerisms made her appear younger than she was, she concluded.

The day had been a hectic one: morning mass celebrated at the minster, followed by exchanges of gifts by the ladies. Janeta had no money or trinkets to offer and felt somewhat out of it but, prior to descending for the feast, the Countess Eleanor presented her with a golden chain and refused to accept her tearful whisper that she did not deserve such kindness.

'Take it in gratitude for your care of my lord earl,' the Countess said briskly. 'As for the gifts of gowns, that can soon be remedied when your father arrives. I shall insist he make you an allowance so that you can be suitably dressed for all occasions.'

Janeta's heart was beating very fast when she entered the hall that evening, walking behind the Countess with the other ladies. Would Bertrand approve of her new finery? Would he even notice her, or would his whole attention be given to his brother and Roesia Fitzherbert?

She had become accustomed to the splendour and chaotic bustle of the huge feasting-hall, with its central hearth and long tables groaning under the weight of trenchers, silverware and plate, but tonight everything was overwhelmingly magnificent. This was the Holy feast of Christmas and the King would appear wearing St Edward's crown, after showing himself to the people. The place was thronged with the kingdom's nobility, from the greatest earls to the lowest barons and knights of their households. Everyone was attired in his very best and boisterously determined to drink himself under the table and miss not one of the choice delicacies from the many removes brought to the table; peacock and roasted swan, carp in rich sauces, eels, pastries and jellies. No expense would be spared to show the world that the King was indeed the lord of his people, generous and forgiving. And there was much to forgive. Already Janeta had heard from her companion ladies of the many petty jealousies and spites that marred the peace of the realm. The King was too much under the influence of the Church, they said, and those foreign nobles he favoured, the most prominent of which was the upstart Simon de Montfort, the Earl of Leicester.

This time there was no opportunity for Janeta to seek out Bertrand at a lower table. She was seated among the Countess's ladies, facing the high table with its embroidered cloth of estate suspended over the chairs for the King, his queen and his sister.

The clamour hushed momentarily as the steward

thumped his wand upon the rush-strewn floor, and then the cheers of the multitude outside in the torchlit courtyard with its high balcony collected again to witness the young King and Queen wearing their golden crowns and robes of state. As one man the company within the banqueting hall rose as the steward again rapped for attention and Henry entered the hall, leading his queen by the hand. Both were dressed tonight in scarlet and cloth of gold and the torchlight gleamed on their crowns. There was a soughing of stiffened cloth as they passed down the length of the hall to take their places at the high table, and the men bowed low, their spurs and sword-hilts ringing against the table supports, and the women sank into curtsys.

The King seated himself after acknowledging the homage of his court, and the clamour resumed as the company did likewise. Nervously Janeta reviewed the benches for sight of Bertrand D'Aubigny. The Earl of Leicester, in defiance of the hostility of many of the King's earls, was seated close to the high table, and it was some time before Janeta at last saw Bertrand and Morris D'Aubigny, much further down the length of the facing long table. Roesia Fitzherbert was seated between them and wore a gown of pink and silver, a silver fillet holding her gauzy veil in place.

Next to Janeta was Cecily Sandford and Janeta was soon conscious that that lady was as uncomfortable about the proceedings as she was. Like Janeta she ate and drank little. Her eyes were fixed unblinkingly upon the Lady Eleanor, Dowager Countess of Pembroke. Janeta followed her gaze and saw that Eleanor's eyes were equally determinedly fixed upon Simon de Montfort. He looked magnificent tonight, in a pale blue tunic with deep embroidered bands in the English fashion at shoulder and hem. His heavy velvet mantle in crimson was thrust back from his broad shoulders and his dark eyes were shining with excitement. Eleanor had never appeared so beautiful. Tonight she wore a gown of rose silk under a mantle of cloth of gold and her glorious hair fell about her shoulders loose beneath her veil of white and gold gauze. Round her brows she wore a princess's coronet. Simon's dark eyes met and held Eleanor's blue ones, and Janeta understood in a simple moment of revelation. Simon loved the King's widowed sister and there was no doubt in her mind that that love was returned. There was a magnetism between them tonight which no one could fail to recognise.

Janeta smiled happily to herself. Now she had realised the reason for Eleanor's particular kindness to her newest attendant. Janeta had been present when the attack had been made on Simon and had been of some small service to him. Moreover, she was in contact with someone in the Earl's household and could carry news of him to her mistress. Why not? Eleanor had wed once, an older man to please her king; now, surely, she was free to follow her heart's desire, and Janeta would be delighted to help her. So, Cecily Sandford was jealous that her years of influence were soon to be ended. There could be no bar to the match. Simon de Montfort was held in high esteem by his king and Henry would, perhaps, be persuaded to give his consent to the marriage.

Janeta gave a little sigh of pleasure and turned her attention to the three at the lower end of the bench.

Roesia Fitzherbert was bending so close to Bertrand D'Aubigny that their lips almost touched. Janeta experienced that feeling of murderous rage that had often threatened to engulf her totally at St Catherine's. Her fingers clenched on the table-edge so tightly that the bones showed white beneath the flesh. She felt she would choke with fury. How dared Roesia, pledged to

another man, flirt so shamelessly with his brother?
Janeta made a little inarticulate sound, just as hastily
stifled, and Cecily Sandford turned her cold eyes upon
her. Hurriedly Janeta turned away. She could not rise
and leave the King's board, though she longed to do
so. She sat on, the bright scene blurring through a mist
of tears.

CHAPTER FIVE

JANETA sat with the Countess's ladies within the wooden stand erected for them to view the Christmas tournament outside the town walls. Fortunately the snow had totally disappeared and St Stephen's day was bright and crisp, leaving the lists and already trampled grass hard beneath the feet of men and horses. The wintry sun illuminated the bright scene, glinting on the colourful fur-lined mantles in green, blue and crimson of the spectators, the gaudy tunics of the heralds and the painted devices on the shields of those taking part in the coming events. It was the second day of the proceedings, the preliminary bouts having already taken place before Christmas, and the champions were now anxious to come to grips with their respective opponents. This was the first day that the King's party had come to the stands.

Janeta looked curiously over the field. At both ends were the tents housing the knights. Over one floated the device of the King's brother, Richard, Earl of Cornwall, over the other that of Simon de Montfort, Earl of Leicester. Below her was a scene which appeared chaotic, but, she realised, was actually well-organised. Heralds moved from tent to tent, squires bustled about bearing mailed hauberks and helmets, some leading destriers. Since Bertrand had no squire as yet, she wondered who would do him service today.

The Countess appeared animated, and was clearly looking forward to the colourful show. Her brother, in his carved cushioned chair, did not appear to share her gaiety, though his queen was excitedly pointing out to

him one or two of the champions' shields. He nodded
to her half-heartedly and continued to sit slumped in
his chair.

Janeta dared not turn to see if Roesia Fitzherbert
had joined the company. She had seen nothing of that
lady nor of Bertrand since the ceremony of the crown-
wearing on Christmas night.

Firmly she tried to put behind her those violent
emotions which had shaken her. It was ridiculous. She
had no claim on Bertrand D'Aubigny. He had proved
himself a friend and benefactor and his relations with
other women were no concern of hers. Besides, she
had more than likely exaggerated in her own mind the
importance of their seeming closeness on that evening.
Was not Roesia Morris D'Aubigny's betrothed wife?
Yet there had been an eagerness to greet him that day
in the courtyard, and melting looks in his direction
throughout the banquet, which Janeta had found
impossible to dismiss.

She told herself fiercely that if Bertrand wished to
make a fool of himself and a possible enemy of his
brother it was no business of hers. The girl was stupid
to encourage his interest and Janeta could not dismiss
the thought that she did it deliberately. Was there
some perverse streak in Roesia, which needed to pit
brother against brother to the destruction of the frater-
nal affection which should bind them together in the
natural order of things?

Janeta had known only one other person possessing
such a flaw of personality. A young novice had come
to St Catherine's, Sister Anne, outwardly modest,
demure and anxious to please, yet she had managed to
set many of the nuns against one another within days
of her arrival at the convent. Fortunately the abbess
had been quick to notice the sudden unrest which had
beset her formerly peaceful establishment and Sister

Anne had left without any explanation being offered as to the reason for her abrupt departure.

Janeta frowned as she thought Roesia Fitzherbert just such an unsettling being. Had this been the reason why Bertrand had abandoned his home and set his face towards life as a mercenary? Now he was once more thrown into her company, temptation might be more than he could bear. Sighing, Janeta wondered if she was being unfair to the girl; perhaps her own strong feeling of friendship towards Bertrand prompted her to distrust the motives of the other woman. But Bertrand had found a place in Simon de Montfort's household. It would be a pity if now his peace was shattered by some unfortunate liaison which could only be termed dishonourable by his companions.

There was a sudden bustle below and squires came to collect their knights' shields. The heralds advanced and took up positions immediately before the King's stand. The crowds lining the fences which determined the limit of the lists hushed. Trumpets sounded and heralds proclaimed the names of that day's champions. The knights emerged from their pavilions and moved towards their destriers. Janeta craned her neck for sight of Bertrand. It had been decided that today and the following day's mêlée were to be mock-combat under the commands of Richard of Cornwall and the Earl of Leicester, and the knights lined up behind each of their leaders. Each of the champions would take as his opponent a knight from the opposing side. Janeta quickly recognised the device of the de Montfort lion and wondered if the man riding beside the Earl could be Bertrand, for by now all the knights were helmed. The man now moved his shield into view and she saw that it bore a bar argent on an azure-blue field. Could this be the arms of D'Aubigny?

The lesser stands on either side of the Royal one

were now hurriedly filling up, and with a sudden sense
of shock Janeta saw that Morris D'Aubigny and his
betrothed were now seated in the stand to her right.
Roesia Fitzherbert was scanning the lists as anxiously
as she was.

The King was sitting upright and took from his
chamberlain the small gilded baton which would signal
the start of the jousting.

The knights advanced their mounts and halted them
directly before the Royal stand. Each tipped his lance
in salute, then solemnly wheeled his mount and moved
round the field again. This time each knight took his
position before some lady of his choice and dipped his
lance before her to request her favour. Janeta was rigid
with fear that Bertrand might be foolish enough to
request one openly from Roesia.

She gave a little shiver of expectancy as the knight
with the blue shield and its silver bar drew in his
destrier directly before the King's party. To her surprise and virtual disappointment he tipped his lance
before the Lady Eleanor. Laughingly she tied upon it
a scrap of silvery gauze veiling. Janeta could be in no
doubt now. She recognised the caparisoned destrier as
Saladin. So Bertrand had chosen to honour his lord's
lady. That glance between Eleanor and Simon on
Christmas night had convinced Janeta that the Earl
and she were in love. It was likely, then, that Simon
had requested Bertrand to do this, since nothing would
have persuaded Bertrand to displease his lord in this
fashion and so publicly. Clearly it was still unwise for
Simon to show openly his passion for the King's sister.

Covertly Janeta half turned to see whom Simon
would choose to honour. He stopped his curvetting
mount before the Queen's chair and tipped the head
of his lance at her small feet. There was a little ripple
of applause for the gallant gesture.

Janeta was puzzled by the Queen's reaction. She sat stiffly upright and did not look towards her husband for guidance. There was an awkward pause and the lists went strangely silent. Would the young Queen deliberately insult her husband's chosen friend by refusing to grant him the traditional favour? Very slowly she unhooked a kerchief from her sleeve, where it had been placed purposefully, and tied it with trembling fingers to the shaft of the Earl's lance. Once more he saluted her and the King, then rode off in the direction of his own silken pavilion.

Janeta's companion murmured uneasily, 'That was a bad moment. It was a good thing the Queen recollected herself so quickly. It might have caused friction between herself and the King had she revealed to the world her hatred for Leicester.'

Janeta whispered, 'I don't understand. Does the Queen resent the King's friendship with the Earl of Leicester?'

The woman shrugged, her head lowered, her eyes cautiously upon the Royal party. 'The Queen cannot forgive the de Montfort family for their part in the Albigensian Crusade, which caused such destruction in her own province of Provence.'

Further evidence of intrigue and undercurrents here at Court! Janeta felt more and more uneasy. She had heard talk of the depredations that the French knights had made in Southern Europe, hunting down those heretics who dared to hold opposing beliefs to that of Mother Church. Though she was anxious for the souls of such people, she thought the terrible torturing and loss of life needlessly cruel and pitied them, particularly those poor folk, many of them women and children, who were innocent of malice towards their neighbours. She was not sure what part Simon de Montfort had played in those proceedings.

She waited now in a state of acute anxiety for the joust between Bertrand and his opponent.

When he rode into the lists and was announced by the heralds the Countess laid a restraining hand on her arm.

'Do not be afraid. Both today and tomorrow the King has decreed that this tournament is to be a *plaisance*. The lance-heads are fitted with harmless cronels. Sir Bertrand can come to no harm.'

Despite this reassurance, Janeta watched, tense with fear, as the two knights rode at each other. Their first pass missed contact and again the two rode to their respective ends of the lists. Even if the lance-heads were not deadly she feared Bertrand would be thrown heavily from the saddle and might harm his neck or back. Again the combatants approached each other and the ground seemed to shake with the thunder of the destriers' hoofs. This time lances were splintered and the two were now to dismount and fight on foot with swords, their edges rebated.

To her profound relief Bertrand won his bout and was able to claim his opponent's horse and armour. The two rode off amicably to settle the matter. The man would retain his property but Bertrand would obtain a sizeable ransom. Simon de Montfort also was triumphant and declared champion of the day on points. Gravely he presented to the Queen on his lance-tip the small gilded coronet granted to the victor. This time she took it smiling, and the King leaned down to speak with Simon, now unhelmed by his squire.

Janeta had looked for further signs of concern from Roesia for Bertrand's well-being, but that lady had remained seated sedately beside her betrothed, betraying no obvious distress. Janeta was relieved to depart with the Countess from the stand to wait upon her in her apartment in the Old Palace. Tonight there would be further feasting before the final day of the tournament.

She was not cheered during the banquet to hear further gossip concerning the rivalry between the Earl of Cornwall and the King's friend. Each time she glimpsed Simon, seated in triumph at the Queen's right hand, she thought how loyally Bertrand would fight at his side on the morrow. The Queen clearly despised Leicester and resented the favour her husband showed him. Could she have given the order for that ambush on the Winchester road that had almost resulted in his death? If so, could Janeta rely on the Countess's assurance that tomorrow's combat would be a *plaisance* and not something entirely more sinister?

Janeta helped prepare the Countess the next morning for her second visit to the tournament stand. She had mixed feelings about the Countess's declaration that she would again be one of the ladies accompanying her to the ground. While Janeta's thoughts seethed with fears for Bertrand, she was not sure that she could bear to be present to watch the mêlée. She was hesitating about what to wear. All the ladies were determined to outdo each other in the splendour of their apparel, for this was the final day of festivities, but Janeta had few garments to choose from. It was still bitterly cold so she must wear her warmest cloak. When a young page appeared and informed her haughtily that she was wanted in the Countess's private solar she was astonished, for Eleanor had only just dismissed her kindly, with instructions to change into her warmest clothes for the journey to the tournament stands. Deciding that her green woollen gown would have to do, she snatched up her cloak and followed the boy.

Eleanor's voice bade them enter as the page hesi-

tantly tapped on her door, and he stood back for
Janeta to precede him. On the threshhold she stopped
dead, staring, bemused, at the sight of the tall man
facing the Countess's chair. He swung round at
Janeta's entrance and she heard him give a hiss of
concentrated fury.

'Janeta.' The Countess welcomed her warmly, and
apparently without dismay. 'As you see, your father
has arrived, at last, and is anxious to discuss your
future with me.'

'My lady,' Sir Hugh Cobham barked hoarsely, 'I
have already said my most pressing desire is to see my
daughter returned to the nunnery of St Catherine's.
She has seen fit to disobey me but I cannot allow her
to remain a charge on your generosity and——'

Eleanor cut in, her voice honey-sweet, 'I knew you
would see matters in this light, Sir Hugh, and be
prepared to see to it that Janeta is provided with
suitable clothing and funds to uphold her position in
my household. Already she has proved herself invaluable. Did you know how superbly she sews? Several
garments I had reluctantly decided to discard, because
they were damaged, have been expertly repaired by
Janeta and she has a directness and ready obedience I
find refreshing, often missing in other ladies about my
person. You will concede my need to keep her with
me.'

Despite the pleasant tone in which her request was
couched, Sir Hugh recognised the determined will
beneath, inherited from her Plantagenet sire, and a
hint of the remembered displays of temper the late
King had revealed, which might result if that will were
to be thwarted. He looked helplessly from his trembling daughter to the lovely regal woman in the chair
and cleared his throat awkwardly.

'For reasons I feel it best not to reveal, I still consider

it best for Janeta to take her vows into the noviciate,' he said less assuredly.

Janeta's hopes plummeted, but at the Countess's beckoning gesture to advance she came further into the room and, eyes lowered, curtsied to her and then to her father.

'What do you say to your father, Janeta? Do you wish to remain in my service?'

The question was peremptory and Janeta managed a nervous nod, then strengthened it with a strangulated, 'Yes, my lady.'

'Janeta is scarcely more than a child. . .'

'I am nineteen, Father,' Janeta found the courage to remind him, and Eleanor raised her eyebrows in faint surprise at this information. Possibly she had considered Janeta younger.

'Nevertheless, she knows nothing of the world and is hardly qualified to judge what is best for her,' he blustered.

'And you consider that I am not?' Eleanor demanded frostily.

Again he cleared his throat in embarrassment. 'My lady, obviously you know the world, have had occasion to view events which my daughter——'

'And I am qualified to do my best for her welfare?'

He quailed before the flash in those arrogant blue eyes. 'My lady Countess, I would not presume to contradict you, but. . .'

The door swung abruptly open and the King stood framed against the lintel. He was frowning imperiously and was clearly annoyed.

'Eleanor, what is keeping you? We are all waiting on your presence and ready to leave for the tournament ground.' His gaze fell on Sir Hugh, who dropped on to one knee in the presence of his sovereign. 'Who is this?'

'Sir Hugh Cobham, sire, Janeta's father. You will recall I sent a message to inform him of his daughter's presence here.'

'Ah, yes. We thought he might well be concerned.'

'Sir Hugh is anxious about Janeta.'

The King waved a hand airily. 'No need, Sir Hugh, none at all. Your daughter, as you see, is in good hands. She is fortunate to be included among my sister's ladies. The Lady Eleanor has taken quite a fancy to the girl and my queen has expressed admiration for her skill with the needle and, I understand, has received the benefit of the demoiselle Janeta's expertise on some piece of torn expensive embroidery.' He beamed with pleasure. His young queen had quickly established herself in his affections, and what Queen Eleanor wanted or praised was worthy in his eyes.

Sir Hugh turned a speculative eye in Janeta's direction. She had sunk into a deep curtsy in the King's presence and her head was lowered so he could not read her expression. He was defeated and he knew it. He bowed formally, first to King Henry and then to the Countess.

'I am honoured that my daughter has distinguished herself in your notice, sire,' he said evenly. 'I shall make it my business to put funds at her disposal. She will not be embarrassed by any shortage, I assure you, my lady. Now, if Your Grace will excuse me. . .'

'Certainly, Sir Hugh. We shall look to see you often at Court to visit your daughter when she is in attendance here, and now, perhaps, you would accompany us to the day's entertainment, since you are here. You will wish to see more of Janeta, I'm sure, but we cannot wait longer to leave the palace.'

Nothing was less calculated to entertain Sir Hugh at that moment than the prospect of paying respects to his sovereign throughout the prolonged ceremonies of the tournament. Rather, he needed privacy to nurse his fury, but he swallowed his inner rage and bowed again.

'Your Grace does me great honour. . . .'

'Yes, well, let us go. I have little stomach for these occasions and desire to have this business over as soon as possible. The Queen's champion rides in the mêlée and we cannot be absent. That would be discourteous.'

One of the Countess's ladies came instantly to her side with her fur-lined mantle and the King held out his hand to lead his sister out of the room. The Countess's ladies hastily followed and Janeta was left to walk, silent and unrepentant, beside her father in the wake of the Royal brother and sister.

If the field had appeared chaotic to Janeta the previous day it was yet more so now. As she entered the Royal viewing stand the Countess called to her.

'Come, sit beside your father here, near me.'

Sir Hugh, who had moved towards the back of the stand with the lesser barons, started, but came obediently forward to take his place beside the Lady Eleanor. Self-consciously, for she was aware of the jealousy of the other attendant ladies, Janeta took her place by his side.

Below her were the heralds and squires of the opposing forces, hastening into their respective tents with stands of armour, helmets and freshly painted shields. Even from this distance Janeta could hear the hum of frenzied activity, the shouting of men and the blowing and whinnying of the destriers behind the tents. Soon this flat, open space would resemble a battlefield. She shivered in anticipation and turned to see if the Countess was similarly disturbed. Eleanor did not appear to be so. She was talking animatedly to Sir Hugh, as if there had been no contest of wills between them less than an hour ago. Feeling suddenly cold, as if someone had physically stabbed her in the back, Janeta turned suddenly to see Roesia Fitzherbert seated behind her with Sir Morris D'Aubigny. Bertrand's brother acknowledged her with a courteous nod of his head and Janeta smiled at him a trifle nervously.

There was a flourish of trumpets and the knights emerged from their tents and the squires led up their coursers. Janeta leaned forward for a glimpse of the silver and blue shield which would identify Bertrand for her now he was fully armed and helmeted. She gave a little sigh as she saw him riding by the Earl of Leicester's side.

Her father said sharply at her elbow, 'I understand you were escorted into Winchester by the Earl of Leicester and one of his household knights.'

'Yes, Father.' Janeta indicated the two men with a little gesture of her hand. 'Sir Bertrand D'Aubigny has been giving me instruction in riding at—at the request of the Countess.'

He nodded and she saw his mouth tighten. 'I imagine the fellow is penniless?'

'I fear that is so,' she replied very softly, 'but Sir Bertrand is high in the Earl's favour and will, no doubt, find a suitable niche for himself in that household.'

'Hmm.' Sir Hugh looked over the field, shielding his eyes from the cold beam of the wintry sun. 'Let us hope he distinguishes himself in this business.' He gave a sudden sharp exclamation.

Janeta followed his gaze to where a knight, sitting proudly on his prancing charger, rode unhelmed beside the herald to rein in before the King's chair. She saw that he carried a small baton similar to the one by which the King signalled the beginning of the day's events. Her father was staring at the man intently, his eyes narrowed. Obviously he knew the man, who was unknown to Janeta, but surely he knew many other barons present; she had seen him acknowledged by several on the short walk from the palace, yet this man in particular engaged his total interest.

Janeta turned to her nearest neighbour, one of the Countess's ladies who had not too openly shown her resentment of Eleanor's marks of favour towards Janeta.

'Do you know the knight riding beside the herald?'

'Fulke L'Estrange. He has only recently returned to Court from his own manor. He is acting as president of today's tourney. It will be his responsibility to see to it that all combatants abide by the rules of chivalry.'

The two had kept their voices low and Janeta's father did not turn, so he had probably not heard what was said. He was still intent on his scrutiny of the newcomer to Court. Were they neighbours? Did Sir Fulke hold land close to the Cobham manor? Janeta had the strangest feeling that her father and this man were enemies, yet she had never heard talk of dissension between the Cobhams and any of their neighbours. Her father, to her knowledge, had never sought favours from his sovereign, keeping himself well from Court, so there could not be jealousy between them. She gave a little shrug and turned her full attention to the proceedings below.

The president of the tourney and another man, who dismounted now and walked beside him, were moving among the assembled knights drawn up in two lines at either end of the lists, inspecting weapons.

Janeta's previous informant now leaned towards her again. 'That other man is the Chevalier d'Honneur. See the *couvre-chef de merci* tied upon his lance? Like the president, it is his task to see to it that no man bears dangerous weapons, and he will ensure that any knight down and threatened with serious hurt will be touched by his lance and allowed to depart with honour from the field.'

'Ah.' Janeta gave a little sigh of relieved satisfaction. It would appear that her fears for both Sir Simon and Bertrand were groundless. This tournament was simply a vehicle to allow these knights to display their skill in arms, a colourful show which would end in mutual goodwill and allow the victorious and vanquished to enjoy themselves at this evening's revelries.

Despite these reassurances, and the fact that the watery sun was touching the field with gleams of gold, she was deeply uncomfortable during the preliminary courtesies. She was aware that her father's disapproving eyes were on her, the eyes of a stranger. The Countess had won this first battle for her future but Janeta was sure that her father had not given up the game. She frowned in bewilderment as the knights lined up before the Royal box and then began to disperse to the spaces before their own tents. Why was he so determined she should take the veil? Of course it was as true as ever it had been that she was physically marred and unlikely to become a bride. A sharp pang went through her at the thought. Roesia Fitzherbert possessed two rival champions. But Bertrand would eventually marry. The Earl of Leicester would find for him a suitable minor heiress. She, Janeta, might well spend her life as a dependant upon the Countess of Pembroke's charity. Perhaps her father was right, after all. Had she remained in the contemplative world of the nunnery, she might have become a prioress or abbess.

The lady beside her touched her arm as the heralds put their trumpets to their lips and the combat began.

At first Janeta could distinguish nothing. There was

a confusion of horses and men, a flurry of hooves and blown spume, mud-tufts thrown up by the destriers, and shouts, and the deafening clangs of weapons upon wooden shields. She leaned forward now on the bench for sight of Bertrand, but it was impossible to recognise anyone in the mêlée. Her father was breathing fast now at her side and she realised he was remembering other times when he had taken part in such martial exercise, and sometimes actual combat itself. What side did he favour? He had shown no preference. Janeta's eyes went to the King's chair. Like the other spectators in the stand, he was gripped with the excitement of the moment, leaning forward, intent. His brother was leading one side, but his friend, Simon de Montfort, the Queen's champion of the tournament, the other. Queen Eleanor had been reluctant to offer the Earl her gage but she was clutching tightly to a kerchief now, her embroidered veil blowing in the wind as she cheered her champion. Beside her sat the Countess, tense and watchful. She cheered no man, but sat rigid in her seat, her fingers tightly clenched on the arms of her gilded chair, her eyes seeking a sight of de Montfort in the field.

The ranks parted momentarily. Several knights had fallen and squires ran with litters to draw them clear of the conflict. Janeta's heart thudded painfully as she saw that both the Earl of Leicester and Bertrand were still in the saddle. The tournament president signalled a renewal of the battle and the two sides closed again. Janeta could hear the shouts 'A moi, Cornwall' and the answering 'De Montfort, Leicester for champion'. Her teeth were biting down so hard on her nether lip that she tasted salt-blood.

Again the combatants were hidden by flying mud and mist-like spume, but the clangs and thuds seemed to be following each other more slowly now and Janeta realised that the knights were tiring. She had watched some of the squires practising in the courtyard and noted how heavy the two-handed swords and axes were, and the weight of the hauberks must be considerable. Even on this winter day the men must be sweating heavily.

To her eyes this tournament seemed a futile, deadly game. Even with the safeguards men could be badly injured, as she had witnessed as the litters had been borne past the stand. Bertrand might well have been one of them, or Simon. If de Montfort were to be killed, Bertrand's hopes would be vanquished, and, besides, she liked the tall, dark Frenchman who was the apple of the Countess's eye. Eleanor would be devastated if de Montfort were to fall.

Janeta watched as the Chevalier d'Honneur rode about the milling knights, occasionally touching one man or another who was sore beset, and seeing him safely to the side of the lists. She began to hope that Bertrand would be one of their number. She knew he would begrudge such an interference but at least she would not have to suffer these fears for his safety.

Now there were few knights left in the fray. Cheers went up as both de Montfort and the Earl of Cornwall were seen to be of their number and Janeta saw a quiver pass through the Lady Eleanor's body. Soon, now, it must be over. The King was becoming tired of the business and would soon call a halt; yet it should proceed until one side or the other was declared victorious. Honour demanded it.

Another knight rode from the field and Janeta saw that he was half fainting in the saddle; his squire ran up, his face a mask of fear.

Cornwall rode clear of the field, his sword broken. He urged his destrier towards the wooden fence near his tent, where the extra weapons were kept. There was a sudden stir among the watchers and Janeta's attention returned to the fray. She almost felt in her own body the terrible jarring blows as the frenzied conflict continued. One man was surrounded, beset by Cornwall's knights, and, dry-mouthed, Janeta realised that it was Simon de Montfort. As if in answer to her conscious fear, she saw Bertrand D'Aubigny ride to his assistance. The blue of his sorely dented shield flashed in the pale sunlight. There was little left of the brave paintwork, so chipped and crushed was it. She could not see Cornwall now, so concentrated was she on the slowly revolving destriers as the knights moved in close, struck and withdrew, and then came in close again.

She gave a sudden cry as one man went down and it seemed the circling knights swept in for the kill. Her instinctive terror told her that Bertrand had fallen and de Montfort was dismounting and standing over him. Still the blows continued, men leaning low in the saddle to deliver them, and Janeta, horror-stricken, waited for the tardy Chevalier d'Honneur to act. The man seemed struck dumb, his destrier stilled, his helmeted face turned towards the Earl of Cornwall as if for instructions. The King had risen to his feet, his baton held high. There were shrill cries of alarm from the spectators. The day's enjoyable spectacle had suddenly become ugly and sinister. Janeta found herself struggling to leave the stand, but was held back by an iron hand she later realised had been her father's. Her lips moved in silent prayer. Sweet Virgin, go to Bertrand's aid. Do not let him die in this ridiculous display, and the Earl. . .

Before her terrified eyes Fulke L'Estrange rode his destrier into the mêlée, his baton high. She could hear his muffled bellows of rage even from this distance. The warring knights parted before him, as if he were some avenging angel, and in Janet's eyes he was indeed. It was now possible to see clearly the fallen man and the tall figure, his mail dented and blood-smirched, standing astride his twisted body. Janeta gave a terrible cry and fought the blackness which threatened to engulf her senses. Why was there blood on the Earl of Leicester's mail? If all men bore the regulation cronels upon their sword-points, how was it that these two men had come close to death?

The King was issuing orders. Janeta had never seen him so agitated and so plainly angered. Squires ran to de Montfort with a litter and Bertrand D'Aubigny was carried tenderly from the mud-churned lists into de Montfort's silken tent.

Janeta turned, white-faced, to her father. 'The injured knight is the one who was so kind to me. I must go and find out how badly hurt he is.'

He kept a tight hold on her arm. 'Janeta, you are to do nothing which would excite gossip.'

Janeta's heart was pounding, her legs about to give way. She felt the familiar threatening rage beginning to build up within her. Bertrand might even now be dying inside that tent, and her father was refusing leave for her to go to his side. She mastered her rising temper with an effort and was about to plead again when the Countess unexpectedly came to her aid.

She had risen and moved towards the entrance to the stand. Imperiously she waved to Janeta to accompany her.

'Come with me. I go to enquire about the Earl of Leicester and his injured knight.' She turned one burning glance behind her, upon her brother the King. 'You should initiate enquiries, sire. Something is very wrong. Why did not the Chevalier d'Honneur go immediately to the aid of the stricken knights? No one should have been gravely hurt in these bouts.'

The King leaned down to summon L'Estrange to his side. 'Certainly, there are questions to be asked. L'Estrange, you are president of this field of honour. It is for you to discover how this came about.' He gestured testily as the president began to offer apologies. 'There is no fault in you. Once you saw the need you went quickly to the rescue, but someone was to blame. Weapons could not have been inspected well enough. Ask my brother, Cornwall, to come to me. It seems his knights are implicated. . .'

Janeta, hastening after the Countess, heard the King's words fade into the distance as both ladies raised their hampering skirts and began to run towards the tent. An agitated knot of squires and servants, gathered round its entrance, gave way respectfully as the Countess approached.

Simon de Montfort greeted the two women just inside. His eyes went to Janeta's stricken countenance.

'There is no real cause for alarm. Sir Bertrand is not close to death but he has sustained a severe shoulder wound and has lost a great deal of blood. My field surgeon is attending him now. He lost consciousness for a few moments but has regained his wits now. His back is not hurt.'

The Lady Eleanor looked anxiously into Simon's face. 'And you? Are *you* hurt again?'

He gave that distinctive French shrug. 'Nothing to concern you, my lady. Minor hurts, scratches and bruises only.' His gaze turned on the litter where the gaberdine-clad doctor was examining his patient. A servant came awkwardly towards them, carrying a bowl of blood-stained water. The man was clearly anxious not to alarm the ladies. Eleanor drew aside for the fellow to pass outside to empty the bowl and Janeta bit down savagely upon her bottom lip, watching for the doctor to turn again and confirm his first assurance that

Bertrand was in no danger of dying. Yet the wound could prove grave enough. If a shoulder or upper arm muscle had been lacerated Bertrand might never again use his sword-arm. How, then, would he make his way in the world?

As if to reassure her, the Earl said quietly, 'Do not be concerned, demoiselle. Bertrand will have the best of care and I will see to it that his future welfare is assured.'

Janeta nodded, swallowing hard. The doctor straightened and withdrew from the litter. He crossed to the entrance flap to report to the Earl.

'The patient can be removed to the castle soon, my lord. The main danger is over. We must watch for wound infection, of course. Will you allow me now to attend you?' He glanced apologetically at the Countess. He was a grizzled veteran of many campaigns and had seen too much blood-letting to allow this happening to alarm him; neither did he stand in awe of his master, the Earl.

De Montfort frowned in irritation. 'I am well enough, man. I'll send for you later, back at the castle. Go and arrange for the removal of your patient.'

The man bowed and withdrew. Janeta waited for no permission but went instantly to Bertrand's side.

They had given him an improvised pillow made from folded cloaks and he was lying back, eyes closed. He looked waxen-pale, but sudden movement near the litter alerted him to Janeta's presence and he stirred, then, recognising her, struggled to lift his head, his lips curving into a smile.

'Demoiselle Janeta. How good of you to come.' He moved awkwardly and she realised his wound pained him more than he would confess. 'You look very frightened. There's no need. The bleeding has stopped. I shall soon be up and about again.'

She stooped to touch his good hand briefly.

'The Countess was concerned for—for both of you,' she said in a sudden rush. 'You should not have taken part in the mêlée, not after. . .' Her voice trailed off uncertainly, then she added, 'It seems the Earl has many more enemies than we thought.'

His brows drew together and he winced in sudden pain.

'He appeared to be the target for the onslaught but——' he also gave that irritating shrug '—there may be nothing suspicious in what happened. Weapons do sometimes suddenly lose their protective foils——' He broke off, staring at her distraught expression. 'There are so many rivalries at Court, petty jealousies. . . Cornwall is known to disapprove of the King's affection for de Montfort.' He grinned perkily. 'It seems I chose a master who will continue to have a real need for my services.'

Janeta bit back the words which might alarm him, about the severity of his sword-arm injury. She forced a smile. 'I expect your brother will be soon at the castle to see you and—and the demoiselle Roesia.'

If she had expected a strong reaction to the name she was disappointed. He nodded weakly and she realised he was more exhausted by talking than he wished her to guess. Again she touched his hand. 'I should go now. I'm tiring you, and the surgeon said they would soon be moving you to your quarters in the castle.'

His smile was reassuring and she hastened back towards the Countess and Simon de Montfort. Eleanor was leaning very close to him, her expression both determined and pleading.

'Simon, this cannot be allowed to continue. We both know that business in the mêlée was no chance accident. You were meant to die out there. Henry must be convinced and those men concerned named and punished.'

The Earl's answer was equally determined. 'If I were to go to the King and ask for your hand openly. . .'

'No, no.' Eleanor's voice conveyed real anguish. 'You swore to me you would not do that, not until I have obtained——' She broke off, her eyes gazing huntedly around the tent for eavesdroppers.

'I love you, Eleanor. I shall not be content until you are my bride. Ambition for power is nothing to me beside that need. We could retire from Court. If we wait, Henry could choose another husband for you. . .'

'No,' she said softly, 'you know he will not do that. From that fate, at least, I am safe. Do nothing yet, my love,' she implored. 'We are young. We can afford to wait. But do not allow yourself to be goaded into any more martial feats and—and do not ride out unescorted. It would break my heart if——' She turned hastily at the sound of the soft pad of feet near her but relaxed visibly at sight of Janeta.

'How is young Bertrand?'

'Recovering, my lady, but still weak. I did not stay for fear of further tiring him.'

'Of course.' The Countess forced a smile. 'We should leave. Our presence here inhibits the surgeon's preparations for evacuating both his patients to their own quarters, where they can be more properly tended. The King will be anxious for a report of their condition.'

She offered her hand in farewell and Janeta noted that Simon caught at it and held it, reluctant for her to leave his sight, but she gently extricated herself and withdrew, with Janeta in attendance.

CHAPTER SIX

JANETA was summoned to the Countess's chamber late that night, after all her attendant ladies were sleeping. Eleanor was sitting up against the pillows, her face flushed, clearly unready for slumber. She patted the bedside near her and ordered Janeta to sit close.

'Is the chamber door latched securely?'

'Yes, my lady.'

'You saw no one but Martha near by in the corridor?'

Janeta seated herself nervously, her expression somewhat startled.

'No one, my lady. I am quite sure.'

'Good.'

The Countess sat silent for a moment, pleating the cambric sheet abstractedly, then she turned her startingly blue eyes on Janeta in a direct stare.

'You heard what we said, didn't you, this afternoon, in the Earl of Leicester's tent?'

It was Janeta's turn to flush darkly. She lowered her head to avoid that almost accusatory stare, then she murmured very softly, 'I am sorry, my lady, I could not help——'

'No matter,' Eleanor cut in urgently. 'I know I can trust you.'

The blue eyes held Janeta's smoke-grey ones steadily, and Janeta gave a little nod.

'Good.' The single word was whispered. 'Then you will be prepared to help us?'

Janeta gave another startled little jump. 'But how, my lady?'

'You will wish to visit the castle over the next few days to enquire about the health of a certain injured knight.' Eleanor chuckled as she saw the flush on Janeta's cheek spread to her throat. 'You will have seen how things are at Court. My brother's Poitevin advisers are detested and Simon is considered with them, a hated foreigner who has no right to be in the King's councils. Even the Earl of Cornwall, as the King's brother, feels he has a much greater right to be trusted and listened to, and his jealousy of Simon is well-known. You saw that rivalry show itself clearly in the lists today.'

Janeta said in a shocked tone, 'My lady, you cannot mean that my lord Richard was behind that dastardly attack upon the Earl?'

Eleanor frowned. 'I don't know. I have no proof, but the Queen takes little pains to hide her detestation of the Earl of Leicester. There are many who wish him dead, and his attendant knights with him.'

Janeta went pale as the full force of the fear which had been rising in her assailed her with the Countess's words.

Eleanor continued, her eyes narrowed in thought. 'Henry will have enquiries made. The Chevalier d'Honneur would seem to be at fault, but there must be someone more important who gave him his orders. It was fortunate that Fulke L'Estrange stopped the engagement in time.' She turned to Janeta, her lips curving wryly. 'It is not a good time for Simon to approach the King on the subject of a possible marriage between us. We must be circumspect. I must stay from his side for a while. Gossip is rife at Court but——' she paused significantly '—I can send frequent messages, with your help. I will have that?'

Janeta drew a long breath. 'Of course, my lady. You know there is nothing I would not do for you. You have taken me in, protected me from my father's fury. . .'

'Yes.' Eleanor tapped her white teeth reflectively with her fingers. 'How strange is your father's determination to consign you to the nunnery! One would have thought he would welcome a chance for advancement by keeping you in my household. He is not an ambitious man, your father?'

'I confess I know little, my lady. I was but ten years old when sent to St Catherine's for my education. Even before that he paid me scant attention.'

Eleanor sighed. 'I was even younger when my mother abandoned me to the care of governesses and went about her own concerns.'

Janeta had been told how, after King John's death, his widow, the beautiful Isabel of Angoulême, had returned to her former love, Hugh de Lusignan, and married him, even when Hugh had been negotiating a marriage with her own daughter. Eleanor, her youngest child, like Janeta, must have felt very lonely and vulnerable as a child.

Eleanor was looking at her again, very intently, her blue eyes shining with excitement in the candle-flame.

'I have to warn you that if you were discovered in such clandestine business it could mean your disgrace and dishonourable discharge from my service. You would be returned to your father and he could well treat you very harshly.'

Janeta hesitated. She knew that well enough, and it had to be considered and faced squarely. Her newfound freedom would vanish like mist on a summer midday if that were to happen. She shrugged. 'I understand that and am ready to take the risk.'

'Then I can rely on you to deliver my letter in person—and no one the wiser? Not even Lady Sandford must know.'

Janeta inclined her head. Her heart was pounding so loudly in her own ears that she thought Eleanor must be aware of it. She was being offered opportunity to visit the Earl of Leicester's household and she would see Bertrand—often. Even the dread possibility of her father's fury could not be counted against the thrill of that.

Accompanied by a young page as escort, Janeta set out early next morning for Winchester Castle, where Simon de Montfort had his lodgings. A morsel of parchment crackled against her breast where she had hidden the Lady Eleanor's letter. On recognising the device of the Countess of Pembroke upon the boy's surcoat, they were admitted into the bailey. Janeta haughtily informed the sergeant-at-arms that she had her mistress's permission to enquire, in person, after the health of the Earl of Leicester and the knight who had been so sorely injured at yesterday's tournament. She was escorted into the great hall while her request was conveyed to the Earl. The place echoed with the noise and confusion of a large martial establishment. Men-at-arms sprawled at their ease, some playing dice, others attending to the sharpening of daggers and swords or the careful examination of the fletching of arrows. Two clerics argued at a table at the far end over piles of unrolled vellum, presumably the castle accounts. Dogs rolled and snarled in fights to determine leadership of the pack. A falcon screamed shrilly from its perch. Janeta, still unused to this state of chaotic management of a huge and martial household, moved nervously closer to her youthful escort. The boy, on the other hand, let his eyes rove excitedly over the high-raftered hall, missing nothing. Janeta thought wryly that he would be instantly willing to relinquish his safe and comfortable existence in the Countess's service for this more adventurous and seemingly less restricted life.

The sergeant returned very quickly. He offered apologies from the Earl.

'My lord would come himself to greet you, demoiselle, but at this moment he is being attended in his chamber by his surgeon. If you would be pleased to follow me I will take you there.'

Janeta and her page were hard put to it to keep up with the man's long strides as he led them through the hall and a corridor to the Earl's apartments.

'I hope,' Janeta said breathlessly, 'that the Earl's injuries were not more grave than was first thought.'

'Nay, nay, demoiselle.' The grizzled veteran turned to give her a grin, a flash of yellowed teeth in the dark-bearded countenance. 'His lordship suffered only grazes but they needed dressing. He will not keep you waiting long.'

'And the young knight?' she asked hastily. 'He is not worse?'

The sergeant blinked less confidently now. 'I hear there is no fever,' he said cautiously, 'but it will go hard with him if he loses the use of his sword-arm. Sir Bertrand proved himself a doughty warrior. We all pray for his full recovery.'

He knocked upon the heavy wooden doorway and the doctor Janeta had seen in the Earl's tent the previous afternoon emerged, his surgical satchel slung over one shoulder. He turned to give one last word of warning to his master.

'Take heed, sir, and rest the right arm. That long scratch could turn nasty if you over-use the limb and the edges of the wound open again.'

He scuttled hastily away at sight of Janeta, his eyes sliding from the sergeant's obviously concerned gaze.

Despite the surgeon's admonition, Simon de Montfort's hand-clasp was reassuringly strong.

'You have come from the Lady Eleanor? You are very welcome, demoiselle.'

Janeta curtsied and looked hurriedly to the sergeant and page, hovering within earshot in the doorway. She hoped Simon de Montfort would read her need for privacy in her expression. It seemed he did so, for he gave a quick nod of his head and dismissed the two, ordering them to close the door and wait outside until he should call.

Wasting no time, in case they were interrupted, Janeta quickly handed him the Countess's letter. He murmured an excuse for his discourtesy in taking his attention from her even for moments and strode to the unshuttered arrow-slit to read Eleanor's words to him.

When he turned back to her again she thought she detected a glitter about his eyes which had not been there before. Was that the faint sheen of tears, and from one of the realm's most famed warriors?

'You will perhaps wish to see Bertrand D'Aubigny, Demoiselle Janeta?'

She resisted the urge to appear too eager and nodded, her lips a little tremulous with longing.

De Montfort smiled. 'I will send my sergeant with you. He knows the virtue of discretion. I'll keep the boy with me. Pages gossip, as I know to my cost. When you are ready to leave I will have an answer for you to convey to the Countess.'

Her previous escort came immediately at the Earl's summons and grunted at the order to take her to Sir Bertrand's chamber. He stood back for her to precede him through the door and then took the lead through the maze of passages which led from the Earl's apartments to a small room in the west tower.

'We put Sir Bertrand here on his own,' he explained,

as Janeta eyed him questioningly, knowing privacy was a rare commodity within the households of the great. 'The surgeon said he needed lots of rest and he's been with us on campaign long enough to know that you don't need to bleed a warrior who's already been blooded in combat. Sir Bertrand's in good hands. You don't need to fret yourself about that.' He cast her a quick, discerning glance from beneath bushy brows and Janeta found herself beginning to feel the warmth of blood staining her throat and cheeks.

There was little enough room within the tiny chamber, scarcely more than a hollowed-out space within the thickness of the castle wall, off the spiral stair which led to the leads and battlements above the tower. A truckle-bed covered with a straw palliasse and rough blankets had been pushed against the wall and a faldstool laid against it, on which had been placed a jug and earthern cup. Bertrand's mail hauberk stood on a wooden stand at the bed-foot and his good mantle was covering the bed for extra warmth. Janeta was glad to see that the one brazier stood near the leather-curtained opening to the room. Bertrand was propped up against straw-stuffed pillows and managed a game smile as she entered. There was a hectic flush on his cheeks she did not like, and his hand was clammily unhealthy as he grasped hers. She paused uncertainly, but he waved her to sit on the side of the cot while the sergeant waited stolidly by the entrance, the curtain pushed well back to allow air inside.

'Bertrand,' she whispered anxiously, 'are you still in pain? You look to have a fever.'

'It was bad in the night but the surgeon says it's broken now. I'm certainly sweating. The pain's not bad unless I try to move my arm,' he muttered fretfully. 'Don't be afraid for me. I'll mend.'

She forced a smile. 'I'm sure you will. The Earl

assures me his surgeon is to be relied on. Even the
sergeant appears to think well of him.'

Bertrand gave a brief splutter of laughter. 'That's
praise indeed. Most soldiers fear the battle surgeons
and avoid their ministrations as they would the plague.'

'The Countess sent me to enquire. She was very
concerned about you.'

His eyes mocked her and he gave a harsh, barking
laugh. 'Then you did not come out of a personal fear
for my welfare?'

'Hush,' she said sharply. 'Of course I did. You know
I shall always hold the warmest of friendly feelings for
you. Although,' she added tartly, 'you know well
enough I was against your taking part in this ungodly
tournament from the very beginning. It is against the
tenets of the church and——'

'You will not pray for me that my soul will be
forgiven and not go to its maker unshriven?'

'Do not talk such nonsense,' she said fiercely. 'I
should think you had the good sense to confess your
sins before embarking on this foolishness, and of
course I pray for you—continually—both for the good
of your soul and for your complete recovery.'

He laughed, his eyes still bright with fever. 'God
could not fail to be moved by the prayers of my little
novice.'

'I am no novice and you know that well enough.'

The smile left his lips for a moment and he tried to
lean forward, as if to question her, but his injured
shoulder pained him and he sank back, holding in a
soldier's curse beneath his breath.

'I am blessed indeed,' he said softly. 'Thank the
Countess for her goodwill.'

She frowned and leaned close after glancing back to
see that the sergeant was now looking the other way.
'She is alarmed, as I am, about what happened, and

believes both the Earl and you were purposely attacked
so savagely. You must take constant care.'

His eyes widened momentarily and he was about to
reassure her when voices were heard below and mailed
feet began to ascend the stair, followed by the quick
patter of lighter shoes, as if the visitor was accompanied by page or woman. Bertrand frowned and
gestured Janeta to silence.

The sergeant's voice was heard remonstrating with
someone outside, then a deep male voice spoke commandingly and the veteran's head appeared in the
curtained opening.

'I'm sorry, demoiselle, and Sir Bertrand, to inter-
rupt, but this knight declares himself to be your
brother, sir.'

'Morris?' Bertrand did not appear to be as pleased
by the news as Janeta would have supposed. 'Thank
you, Sergeant, admit him. That's if he can get in.'

Janeta moved to leave but he threw out his good
hand and detained her.

Morris D'Aubigny ducked his head beneath the
entrance archway and, seeing Janeta, froze near the
door.

'Ah, I see you have company. The Earl's men did
not appear to wish me to see you. I had to exert my
authority, believing you must be worse than I had first
feared, but you look fit enough to receive visitors.'

Bertrand grinned. 'The Countess of Pembroke was
gracious enough to send her messenger to enquire as
to my welfare. I am somewhat better, Morris, but the
sawbones says it will be some time before I can use my
sword-arm. I can only pray he is not holding back bad
news about my future capabilities.' He grimaced. 'My
sword-arm is my livelihood.'

A sweet voice broke in before Morris could enter
and Roesia Fitzherbert squeezed herself into the small

space left in the chamber. 'You will always be welcome at the manor, you know that, fit or well, Bertrand. Isn't that so, Morris?'

The elder D'Aubigny swallowed and nodded. 'Of course. Birtwood is your home, will always be so. If the worst comes to the worst, we'll find you suitable employment.'

Bertrand's lips twisted wryly and Janeta inwardly cursed his brother's lack of tact. The one thing Bertrand did *not* wish to consider at the moment was the possibility of becoming an encumbrance on his brother's charity.

Roesia was staring at Janeta pointedly and there was no mistaking the hostility in those limpid blue eyes. She turned again to Morris D'Aubigny. 'We should have him conveyed out of here to your lodging in the town, Morris. He should be with members of his own family. I—we can give him more close attention than he can receive here in this great fortress.'

Morris D'Aubigny opened his lips as if to argue, but she swept on. 'Morris, you know he will be much quieter and more comfortable there.'

Bertrand said weakly, 'There is no need for that. I am getting adequate care and shall soon be on my feet again now the fever's beginning to abate.'

An authoritative voice settled the question. Simon de Montfort could be heard clearly from the stairway. 'Moving Sir Bertrand at this juncture would be fool-hardy. The bleeding could begin again. My surgeon has experience in dealing with this type of injury and it is essential that he should exercise under the guidance of an expert in such matters if he is fully to regain his skills.'

Morris D'Aubigny bowed and withdrew to just out-side the chamber, drawing Roesia with him. Janeta also, embarrassed by her presence here, struggled to extricate herself. Bertrand relinquished his hold on her and she curtsied and moved towards the Earl, who had entered the room.

De Montfort looked smilingly down at the younger man. 'You wish to stay here with your companions, sir knight?'

Bertrand's gratitude was obvious. Janeta could see that he had no wish whatever to be carted off to his brother's lodgings.

'If it is your wish, sir,' he said quietly.

'It is my command. You are one of my household and I am responsible for your welfare.' The Earl turned and smiled benignly at the discomfited Roesia. 'I can understand your concern, demoiselle, but really, Sir Bertrand is best to bide where he is.'

She swallowed and curtsied, averting her face. Janeta was sure that the woman was furious with the Earl for thwarting her plans. For herself, Janeta was delighted. The less those three associated, the better the relationship between the brothers.

Outside, the Earl put a hand under her arm and drew her gently down the stair.

'The message is ready for you, Demoiselle Janeta.' his eyes twinkled. 'I'm sure you will agree that Bertrand is best kept away from dangerous distractions at this stage in his illness.'

Janeta's blue-grey eyes looked troubled and he exerted more gentle pressure on her arm. 'It will be best when Demoiselle Roesia is finally given in marriage to Sir Morris. I notice she is given to travelling, often unchaperoned by her maid. Such behaviour could pose problems for our hero, don't you think?'

Janeta could manage only a faint shrug and the Earl's expression sobered. 'I know you have strong feelings of gratitude towards the man who so gallantly came to your rescue. I have seen you look intently at

Demoiselle Roesia, as if you wished she had not appeared on the scene just now.'

Hastily Janeta choked out her explanation. 'My lord earl, my feelings towards Sir Bertrand are kindly only, and I would not wish you to think——'

He interrupted her smoothly, 'You have Sir Bertrand's welfare at heart. I assure you, demoiselle, I understand that. I would be foolish indeed if I did not realise that that vain young woman's desire to set brother against brother with her stupid posturing could be dangerous in the extreme.' He handed her a sealed missive. 'It is fortunate that both the Countess and I were tutored in writing skills. It would be hazardous for this to be seen by any eyes other than hers. You take my meaning?'

'Yes, my lord.' Janeta took the folded vellum and secreted it within the tight cuff of her sleeve. 'You can trust me to be discreet at all times, sir.'

He gave her that dignified half-bow she was beginning to know well and, since they had reached the great hall, beckoned to the Countess's page, who was lounging against one wall watching four archers dicing. The boy hastened over at once and Janeta took her leave.

During the short journey to the Old Palace her thoughts were filled with her fears for Bertrand. Would he truly recover his health? He appeared now to be out of immediate danger but there was still the matter of the shoulder wound to concern her. She gave a brief sigh of relief. At least the Earl had removed from her the more pressing fear that Bertrand would once more come within the influence of the beautiful Roesia Fitzherbert. His sickness might well have made him more vulnerable. Despite Morris's apparent displeasure, would the woman continue to visit Bertrand?

Janeta sincerely hoped that Bertrand's brother would discourage her from so doing.

Janeta found herself being used as messenger several times over the next few days. The Earl came often to feast with the King, but carefully kept his distance from the King's sister. From her place further down the board Janeta noted that the Queen's hostility towards her husband's friend was still clearly apparent to all who could read the signs. Should the Earl make his desires known to the King he would find opposition to the match from the Queen. That was certain.

Each time Janeta arrived at the castle she was relieved to discover that Bertrand was growing steadily better. She did not see him every time, but often the Earl himself made it easy for her to do so, jovially announcing that she must be anxious about her riding instructor. On the fourth occasion Bertrand himself came to the hall to greet her. He still carried his right arm in a silken sling Janeta thought must have come from Roesia, but he was clearly now much stronger and out of pain other than when some unwary movement reminded him of his disabililty.

She was delighted when he used both hands to grip hers in greeting and draw her to a cushioned window-seat.

'It is good to see you again.'

'And you. You are using your arm more freely. Does the surgeon offer more hope now of complete recovery?'

He beamed at her. 'Yes, he does not think it will be long before I can resume practising again in the tilt-yard.'

She gave a little sigh of relief. 'So you will not be returning to your brother's house to convalesce?'

He gave a faint grimace. 'No, praise the Virgin.

Morris will be going home soon. The marriage ceremony will take place next week at Roesia's manor and they will then be leaving for Birtwood.' His golden eyes looked clouded and Janeta's heart turned over.

'You will miss them coming to visit you here. I suppose your brother will not come very often to Court.'

'Very unlikely. Morris is not an ambitious man. Court life would not appeal to him even were he wealthy enough to live there in style, but Roesia will miss it, I think. This short visit has given her a taste for high living.'

Janeta said softly, 'She is very lovely. She must have had many admirers here.'

His lips parted in a rueful smile. 'Indeed, she has never stopped boasting about her many conquests.'

Another stab of pain coursed through Janeta. Bertrand must have suffered pangs of jealousy laid up here away from the Old Palace while Roesia enjoyed herself at the feasting. Janeta knew now that she herself had deep feelings for Bertrand. Of course she could not love him. She had heard her companion ladies giggling in corners, discussing the amorous adventures of others at Court, many of the stories embellished with salacious titbits of gossip which had brought burning flushes to Janeta's cheeks. The sisters at St Catherine's would have been horrified, scandalised. Janeta, used to their strictures, had not allowed herself even to think of Bertrand in such outrageous terms. She loved him as a true friend who had used her with kindness and consideration. Had it not been for him, she could never have reached Winchester. To her he was imbued with every knightly virtue — except that she feared he entertained unworthy thoughts about Roesia. That lady had made it very clear, sometimes nakedly, even in the presence of her betrothed, that she had strong feelings for Bertrand.

Suddenly she said sharply, 'It must give you great pain to think of her so soon to be wed to your brother.'

Unguarded came his answer. 'Indeed it does.'

She said through stiffened lips, 'I can see why you were forced to leave your manor.'

His golden-brown eyes were regarding her steadily. 'It is so evident?'

She nodded, averting her eyes to stare through the horn window at the misty image of squires practising at the quintain in the tilt-yard outside. She whispered softly, 'I can understand how deeply you love Roesia and consider you gallant and brave to leave her vicinity so that you will not be constantly tempted.'

There was a short silence and, turned away as she was, she could not read his expression, then he said in an amused tone, 'Then you read the signs quite wrongly, Janeta. I certainly have no amorous feelings for Roesia whatever.'

She jerked her head back to face him, her lips parting in wonder. 'You really don't love Roesia?'

'That vain little creature? Of course I do not. I cannot see how Morris could become so besotted. He is usually a very sensible soul.'

'But she is so lovely.'

'Pretty, yes, desirable, I suppose, to many, but you are beautiful. A man would have to be blind not to compare the two of you to her disadvantage. I wonder that you, too, have not been besieged by admirers. I suppose you have, but have had the good sense not to recount your victories.'

She was totally bemused. How could he consider her beautiful, she being a dark, ordinary creature compared with the glorious golden tresses of the Lady

Eleanor and the daintily fair pink and white freshness
of Roesia Fitzherbert?

'But I was sure. . . Why did you leave Birtwood
then, when you love it so, and why are you so reluctant
to go back?'

'I left because Roesia's attentions were becoming a
veritable embarrassment. I was afraid Morris would
notice finally and that it would place a constriction
between us, even bring about virtual enmity. Morris
and I have always been close. He tutored me in the
skills of war, took me on campaign. Were it not for
him and the chances he gave me I would never have
won my spurs. Birtwood can never be mine. I told you
when we first met that I have no fortune, must make
my own way. It was time enough, and I decided
to make the final break with my home ties. I love
Birtwood but the manor is small and can barely keep
Morris and his bride in comfort, certainly not in the
style of living to which Roesia is accustomed to preen
herself. That is the reason why I said I regretted the
nearness of the ceremony. I wish Morris free of her,
but he is ensnared. He will have to make the best of
life with a woman who will never fully appreciate his
qualities.'

She was silent, her thoughts seeking to digest this
startling information.

As if to push home the truth of his assertion he said
sharply, 'I confided my predicament to my lord Simon.
It was for this reason he was so adamant in declaring
that I was unfit to be moved to Morris's lodging.'

He stood up abruptly and took her hand, drawing
her to her feet.

'Do you trust me—to walk with me alone in the
herb-plot?'

She nodded dumbly and he drew her swiftly out of
the hall. It was less cold today than it had been before

the Holy season had begun and it was exhilaratingly fresh outside. Janeta hungrily drew in the fresh, bracing air. Both had been wearing cloaks, since the hall and corridors of the castle were always chill, even in summer, and it was pleasant to fall into step together and pace through the tilt-yard, ringing with the sounds of practice blows, iron on iron, and the challenging shouts of the participants in the training programme. Someone called to Bertrand and he returned a cheery answer then led her through an archway past the stables and armourers' hut and through another archway leading into a small sheltered garden. The ground was empty of foliage now, except for a few withering cabbages, and iron-hard still. The herbs had died down but Janeta could note and approve the small divided plots which would provide the castle with the flavouring and medicinal herbs it required in the spring once more. The place was surrounded by a high wall and the two were alone together. The noise from the stables and tilt-yard came to them only faintly. Janeta was without chaperon, her escort page left to idle in the hall, but she was not afraid. A tingle of excitement swept through her body and she dared not look at Bertrand and reveal the naked longing in her eyes.

She could hardly believe it even now. He did *not* love Roesia Fitzherbert. His concern was only for his brother, that Morris was making an unworthy match, and—and this made her tremble so that she could hardly press her weakened limbs to obey her—he had said she was beautiful!

He stopped suddenly, and, taking both her hands within his own, he turned her to face him.

'Little Janeta, you are so very lovely I can hardly trust myself——' He broke off harshly. 'But there, you knew you were safe with me and safe you shall be.'

'And what if I do not wish to be safe?' she whispered, peering up into his unsmiling countenance. 'Oh, Bertrand, all this time I have been torturing myself, believing that you loved Roesia and fearing you would be ruined by it, and now—now you tell me you think I am beautiful. But that cannot be. No one has said. . .'

He released his grip on one of her hands to touch her cheek. His lips curved into an amused smile. 'I had forgotten how strictly you were reared, no vainness allowed in the convent. Perhaps you never saw yourself clearly. But surely, now, you have looked at your image in one of the Countess's mirrors or seen admiration reflected in the eyes of the younger knights at Court?'

She shook her head fiercely. 'I—I never sought to look, and the men, they speak pretty speeches but they do that to all of us. I thought it was required behaviour at Court, meaning nothing.'

'And they would not dare to touch the Countess's protégée. So you have failed to realise how lovely you are. Your eyes are so difficult to define, sometimes grey, sometimes blue like the Countess's, and in fact there are times when——' He broke off, staring at her intently again, tracing the line of her mouth and nose with a questing finger. 'I think de Montfort has noticed it too.'

She moved nervously at the touch of his finger. His gentle caresses were sending strange sensations through her body again and she was hard put to it to stay quiescent in his arms.

He shook his head in bewilderment, as if something was troubling him but he could not truly place it in his mind. 'No matter, you are lovely in your own right. I thought so that night I found you, could not believe your family would be so negligent as to allow you out without protection. . .'

She was wearing a tight wimple swathing her throat,

and her head veil was held in place by a simple silver fillet. He lifted his hand to push back the concealing cloth and glimpse the hidden glory of her astonishing dark hair but she resisted his movement fiercely.

'No, no you must never do that. Do not touch my throat. . .'

A terrible constriction welled up so that she found herself choked with tears. He had said she was beautiful but he did not know—must never know—her secret, the ugly wine-coloured stain her father had called the mark of the devil.

He released her immediately, so that she almost stumbled. 'I'm sorry, Janeta. I had not the right. I am a poor man with nothing to offer. Your father would never consider me fit to approach you.'

'No,' she whispered hoarsely, 'you don't understand. Please, Bertrand, it is not what you think. . .believe me. . .'

He cupped her face in his two hands again, then wiped dry her welling tears with one thumb.

'Don't cry, my lovely Janeta. I *do* understand. You came with me, trusted me, and I took outrageous liberties. Forgive me. I must take you back to the hall.'

She wanted to tell him, beg him to be patient, but the words would not come, and how could she bear the horror in his eyes, which her father had sworn would come when any man gazed upon her? Let him think what he would. Better to leave him free to love some other woman more worthy than Roesia Fitzherbert, who could only have brought him unhappiness and deep disgrace. He deserved better, her Bertrand.

He took her hand and began to escort her back but just before they reached the archway he stopped again and drew her closer to him. She could hear the harsh rhythm of his fast-beating heart and her own began to race in response.

He said hoarsely, 'When I first realised your predicament, how you desperately wished to leave the convent, I thought, in time, perhaps I would make sufficient gold to find you again and wed you. Now—now I know you are beyond my reach but I want you to know that I truly love you, Janeta Cobham. I shall never want another woman as I ache for you.'

She could not believe he was saying these words to her. If he really loved her so deeply as he said, perhaps—and she hardly dared hope for such happiness—perhaps he would be willing to overlook that disturbing blot on her beauty. She must pray to the Virgin that it could be so.

Her eyes were swimming with tears. 'I—don't know what to say to you. Dear Bertrand, I have trusted you and longed to see you near me each day. . . I think—I think I love you too. . .if you were to approach my father. . .'

'When the Earl requested that you enter the Countess's household, and I realised at the time that it was the best thing possible to assure your future, I knew then that you were lost to me. She will want to arrange a suitable match for you and your father will agree to it. He must. To do otherwise would offend His Grace the King.'

'My father does not wish me to wed.' She shook her head vehemently as his dark eyes grew troubled again. 'I cannot explain now. I think—I was never meant to marry. . . Yet, Bertrand, if I were free to give myself as I choose, I would want to give myself to you. Cannot the Earl do something for us? He knows what it is to love beyond his station.'

His lips curved into a faint smile. 'So you know of his deep and constant love for the Lady Eleanor?'

'She trusts me. I carry her messages to the Earl. If she knew—how deeply I felt for you. . .'

He bent and kissed her gently upon the lips. 'Then we must be patient, my love. If the Earl and Countess achieve their hearts' desires, they could possibly be brought to look favourably upon *our* needs, but the Virgin knows I wish I could offer you a home. If we wed, it will mean that we must always serve in the household of someone else.'

'And would that be so hard?' she breathed softly. 'We love and admire them both. It would be a privilege to serve them. Bertrand, the King must grant them permission to wed. I think her heart will break else.'

'He is high in the King's favour. I think pressure could be brought to bear so that he will approve the match and, with that, renewed hope for the fulfilment of our own happiness.'

His kiss had been gentle, undemanding, and left her vaguely unsatisfied. She had displeased him by her hasty withdrawal earlier. She thrust aside her doubts about his eventual discovery of her secret. He loved her—it would make no difference to him—yet she had seen, when a child, the responses of others to the sight of that offending wine-dark stain.

He took her hand and kissed the palm, then led her hastily back the way they'd come. There was no privacy when they were once more back within the crowded hall for him to do more than bow politely as the page, eyes wide in curiosity, came to her side, and she curtsied in answer and left.

She silenced the boy's chatter as she hurried him through the streets, her thoughts dwelling hungrily on the words of love Bertrand had spoken. He wanted her, would have asked for her now if he dared. She would speak to the Countess, make her understand.

Eleanor loved as she, Janeta, loved. She would make it possible. . .

Janeta was walking so swiftly on her high pattens that she almost outran her puffing youthful escort. It was as if her heart winged towards her mistress, desperate to reveal the secret of its love.

She was thankful that the boy was too far behind to observe her flushed cheeks. She had wanted Bertrand to push back the wimple, caress her throat and breast, finger her hair. . . Dear God, she was wanton! Of what use had been all the dire warnings of the nuns concerning sins of the flesh? She was in love with Bertrand D'Aubigny and gloried in the knowledge.

CHAPTER SEVEN

JANETA'S happy mood was abruptly broken as she entered the Old Palace and made for the Countess's apartments. To her amazement she found the palace in a state of utter chaos. Servants were frantically rushing about, laden with heavy travelling-chests and saddle-bags, getting into each other's way and tripping over their own feet in their desperate attempts to obey the bawled instructions of the red-faced chamberlain.

She was confronted in the entrance to the Countess's apartments by a furiously angry Lady Cecily Sandford.

'And just where have you been hiding yourself, my proud young madam? There are so many tasks to be finished by nightfall and you nowhere to be found.'

Janeta stared at her open-mouthed. 'I'm sorry, Lady Sandford, I don't understand. I—I went on an errand for. . .' Her voice trailed off miserably. She was not sure if she should divulge to Lady Sandford that she had indeed been out on the Countess's business. She stared around her, bewildered. 'What is happening? It looks as if the household is preparing for departure.'

'Just so.' Lady Sandford looked triumphant. 'If you had been where you ought to have been, performing your duty, you would have known and been at hand to help with the work. All the Countess's personal property, except that which will be needed for tonight, needs to be packed. The Royal household leaves Winchester tomorrow at first light for Westminster and the Countess is to be in the company. Hurry, demoiselle. Don't stand about gaping. First of all ready your own belongings for the journey and then report to

Martha in the Countess's chamber. I have enough to do without having to dispatch pages all over the palace to find absent attendants.'

She disappeared round a bend in the corridor with a flurry of her black draperies and Janeta turned to the page, who was grinning from ear to ear, amused by her discomfiture.

'You, boy,' she snapped, irritated by his insolence, 'you heard what Lady Sandford said. You'd best get to the master of pages and report for duty.'

He hurried off, stung by the sharpness of her tone, and she turned, pausing before entering the apartment, almost colliding with one of her companion ladies, carrying one of the Countess's jewel-chests.

'Oh, there you are, Janeta Cobham. My lady has been asking for you, said you were to go to her chamber the moment you returned to the palace.'

Janeta nodded. Her heart was thudding uncomfortably. This could not be happening, not now. She could not be torn away from Winchester just at the moment when she and Bertrand had been able to confess their love. If she had been able to continue to visit him at the castle or he come to her here at the palace, to continue her riding instruction, there would have been opportunity to wait until matters resolved themselves between the Lady Eleanor and the Earl, and it would have been possible to speak with one or other of them on the delicate matter of Janeta's marriage. Knowing her father, Janeta understood only too well that it was imperative she have the Countess's support for a match with Bertrand D'Aubigny for the idea to have any chance of success.

What had occurred for the Countess to make such a sudden decision to join her Royal brother in Westminster? Surely she too would have preferred to remain within sight of Simon de Montfort? Had their correspondence been noted and the King angered, so commanding his sister to leave the vicinity of the Earl of Leicester? If so, that would be a calamity for both of them; neither Eleanor nor Janeta could hope to achieve happiness.

She thought, fiercely, of Bertrand's recent nearness, the male smell of him when he had drawn her close, the arousing scents of leather and the armour-oil used to clean his weapons, the innate strength of his muscles, the dear, familiar sight of him. She could not be parted from him with the dread likelihood of that separation becoming permanent! She loved him; she knew that now; their meeting had been predestined. He was the one man, she thought, who would accept her. The fear that had haunted her from the moment she had been able to understand the significance of that stain upon her breast was laid in abeyance whenever she was with him. Only once, this afternoon, had the fear returned, at the second he had sought to free her hair and throat from the concealing wimple. That dread had threatened to destroy her faith in him, but later that trust had been restored. Now she would not have that hope withdrawn, even if she was forced to leave the Countess's household.

Eleanor was in her chamber, gathering up a selection of soft leather belts to hand to Martha, who looked up questioningly at the sight of Janeta, still cloaked and rosy-cheeked from hurrying through the cold Winchester streets. Eleanor caught Janeta's eye and smiled, picking out a blue belt studded with chased gold and gesturing for her serving-woman to leave her.

'This will do for tonight's feasting. The rest can go with the remainder of my jewels in the smallest chest. See to the final arrangements, Martha, will you? And come back in an hour to prepare me for supper. Take some time to see to your own packing. You have been on your feet all afternoon. You will be up all night at this rate. I'll see you have a place reserved in one of the carriages. I know how you hate to ride pillion.'

The older woman made a face and grinned in answer. 'Aye, my old bones feel the harshness of the saddle-leather these days. Thank you, my lady. You should try to rest for an hour before supper. The journey could be hard tomorrow.'

She went off, grumbling softly beneath her breath and obviously ticking off in her mind the final tasks left to her. The door closed and Eleanor gestured Janeta to come close.

'You saw the Earl? He received my note?'

'Yes, my lady, but. . .' Janeta handed over the small vellum scroll which had been Simon's reply and waited with scarce-concealed impatience while the Countess read its contents. At last Eleanor looked up, her eyes shining.

'You do not know what you have done for me over these last few days, child.'

'All is well, my lady?' Janeta's question was tremulous.

'Very well.'

'But. . .'

'What is it, Janeta? You look positively downcast. Did someone offer you an insult? Surely not Sir Bertrand?'

'No, no, my lady, quite the contrary; in fact he — we. . .' Janeta paused, tears welling in her eyes, her fingers gripping tightly to the arm of the Countess's chair. 'Oh, my lady, must I come with you? I thought you would not wish to leave—I cannot leave Bertrand now. I might never see him again. Please. . .'

'Foolish child,' the Countess reproved, smiling. 'Whatever makes you think you and Bertrand are to be parted? Of course the Earl of Leicester will escort

His Grace the King to Westminster. His Grace has commanded him to be present at the Twelfth Night festivities and I have no doubts Sir Bertrand D'Aubigny will be in the Earl's train.'

Relief flooded Janeta's taut body, so that she was forced to grip the chair-arm yet more tightly as the tension relaxed and left her limbs weak.

'Oh, my lady, my lady,' was all she could say.

'Your father has been persuaded to travel with us part of the way at least.' The Countess made a little wry grimace. 'So you will not have the opportunity to bid him goodbye for the present. Do not be tempted to speak to him of—of what we must hold secret yet awhile. Trust me, Janeta. You have done me great service. I will not forget, and when the time comes these favours will be returned.'

The palace household was up before first light, breakfast taken very early, and they were ready to set off before the wintry sun was up. Janeta had tossed and turned throughout the night, her thoughts seething. The Countess had assured her of her support but after Janeta's first feelings of elation she had been left in the small hours with many doubts. The Countess's mention of her father had reminded her of the first hurdle. She had had few conversations with him over the few days he had remained at Court and she still felt she hardly knew him. He had made no more objections to her leaving St Catherine's, but she was aware that his submission had been forced upon him by Royal command. Bertrand's lack of fortune would still be an outstanding obstacle and her own father's refusal to provide a dower for her would not ease matters. There was still a great deal to be overcome.

She was delighted to find, when she emerged from the palace with the other attendant ladies, that the

Earl of Leicester's company had already attached itself
to the royal household and Bertrand came looking for
her, a gentle palfrey held by the leading rein.

'Do you feel confident to ride, demoiselle?' he
asked, smiling, and, at her quick nod of acquiescence,
lifted her into the saddle then brought up Saladin and
mounted himself. Janeta felt herself crimsoning as her
companions regarded her curiously, some giggling,
some openly contemptuous. Any fears she might have
had concerning her competence to make the long
journey mounted were dispelled when she found her
palfrey docile and Bertrand detailed by the Earl to stay
by her side.

'I was so afraid,' she whispered, 'when I heard of
the King's intention to ride north. I was afraid I might
not see you again for months, possibly never. Have
you any idea of the reason? The decision appeared to
be made so suddenly. The Countess appears to be
happy, though, now that the Earl is to accompany the
party.'

He nodded thoughtfully. 'The whole of the Earl's
household was taken by surprise. He was expected to
return to his Midlands holdings for the rest of winter,
but he suddenly announced the change of plan in the
castle hall at supper.'

'I feared it was a plan to part the Countess from
him.'

He shook his head. 'The King likes to have my lord
Simon near him. It seems likely he has no notion of his
sister's correspondence with Simon. If he had——' he
shrugged '—I hardly think the Earl's attentions would
be welcomed, not to the extent of looking so high as to
wed with the King's sister. He would probably be
dismissed from Court.'

'I understand from the gossip of the other ladies that
there is little love lost between the Queen and the

Lady Eleanor, so it is even more surprising that she is travelling to Westminster, rather than returning to her own manor at Odiham where she generally prefers to reside.'

Bertrand's eyebrows rose slightly, and again he shrugged.

'Curious indeed, but fortunate for us.' Despite the nearness of others in the company, his affection for her was revealed all too clearly in his expression.

'My father is travelling with us,' she informed him hastily. 'Do not reveal your desires too openly. I spoke to him only in passing at breakfast. We ladies were too occupied with the Countess's business to be held in talk. I do not know if he will go to Westminster or leave for his own manor soon. I hope he does,' she said nervously. 'I know him only slightly—we have been apart too long—but the way he looks at me so broodingly fills me with apprehension. He has given way under pressure for me to remain in the Countess's household but I know he wants me safely shut away in the convent.'

'But why, if the Countess's favours to you can bring him into notice at Court? I don't understand this determination of his.'

'Nor I,' she said with a slight shudder. She averted her face from Bertrand's gaze, aware that she was not being completely honest with him.

An hour later Bertrand was summoned to the Earl's side by a man-at-arms and his place taken by Fulke L'Estrange, who rode in close, murmuring that he understood Janeta to be a novice in the art of riding and that he was willing to place himself at her disposal as mentor until her instructor was able to rejoin her.

She thanked him civilly, glancing obliquely at his handsome countenance. He had made himself pleasant to her several times over the last few days, but she had

been always conscious of her father's black fury whenever he had come across the two of them chatting.
Always she had parted from L'Estrange quickly on
these occasions, unable to speak to him of what had
been most closely on her mind. Now her father was
riding ahead in talk with one of Simon de Montfort's
knights and she was free to express herself frankly.

'I have not thanked you properly, sire, for coming
to the rescue of the beleaguered knights that awful day
at the tournament. Without your prompt intervention,
I fear lives would have been lost.'

'And one of those dear to you, demoiselle. Is it not
so?'

Her face flamed with embarrassed colour. 'Sir
Bertrand D'Aubigny has been kind to me on many
occasions, sire, and naturally I feared for him.'

'Just so.' The mobile lips, framed by a golden beard
and moustache, twitched into a ready smile. 'I am sure
he is deeply grateful for your concern, Demoiselle
Janeta. He is a fortunate fellow.'

Again she flushed and he laughed.

'Do not be alarmed, demoiselle. I would not dream
of gossiping about your concerns. I am only anxious to
serve you. I understand you are new to Court and
would profit by the advice of one who knows it well,
with all its imperfections and hidden dangers. Please
come to me if you have need. I knew your mother.
Sometimes I catch her expression, fleetingly, in yours.
She was very beautiful.'

Her lips parted in wonder. 'You knew her, truly?
But how, sire?'

'I came to your manor on two occasions with the late
King. I served him then as personal squire. Your
mother was a charming and gracious hostess.'

'King John—came to our manor?' She was astonished. 'My father never spoke of it, nor can I remember

anyone else doing so. How strange that so great an honour was not mentioned.'

'The visits were of a purely private nature. The King came to hunt and your father, in those days, was more frequently at Court. He supported his sovereign during the difficult days of the barons' opposition, was present with the King at Runnymede when the Great Charter was signed. Later——' L'Estrange sighed '—problems intervened, and he was not with the King when he died at Newark.'

'And you were?'

He nodded gravely. 'I was privileged to ride with the marshall to the young King and be present at his hasty crowning.' Again he gave a gusty sigh. 'Times were hard then for all of us, the country in disarray and needing William the Marshall's firm hand.'

She was staring at him, her eyes shining. 'I cannot really remember my mother. She died a few months after I was born. My wet-nurse said she never really recovered from the birth. I suppose my father was not able to forgive me for that and for the other. . .'

His light blue eyes were regarding her intently and she gave a little nervous laugh. 'He sent me to St Catherine's convent for my education when my nurse died. I was just ten years old then. He wished me to take my vows.'

'And you had no vocation?'

She shook her head.

He gave a little barked laugh. 'I should think not. What a waste that would be. I'm sure Sir Bertrand D'Aubigny would be the first to agree with me.'

Her lips curved into a warm smile and he thought how truly lovely she was, despite that tendency to wrap herself so tightly in that unbecoming wimple.

'You say my mother was beautiful—and charming, that she was a pleasing hostess to the King?'

His eyes flashed as if with pale blue fire. 'Indeed she was. I can go so far as to say he was quite entranced by her.'

Janeta laughed merrily. 'And yet they say he was so very wicked, and godless. I could never quite believe that. My nurse said he loved England far more than his brother, King Richard, who cared nothing for our island and would have sold it if he could for more gold to fight his crusading wars. You knew John. Did you fear him greatly, Sir Fulke? The nuns said he would fall suddenly into the most dreadful rages.'

Fulke L'Estrange's bearded mouth parted in a grin of pure delight. 'Aye, demoiselle, he could do that. All the Plantagenet princes were prone to them. His father, King Henry, would fall to the ground and gnaw the rushes, it's said, if his wishes were thwarted. I cannot help thinking that was done mainly for effect. For all I hear King Henry was a canny ruler. For all that John could exert great charm. We who were close to him learned to love him well, despite all his failings. Women loved him to distraction, you know. But there, I should not talk of such things with so innocent a lady, brought up so strictly by the nuns.'

Her lovely blue-grey eyes were watching him thoughtfully. 'You are teasing me now, Sir Fulke. I'm sorry; you must think me a foolishly curious creature. It was only that everything I heard of King John at the convent made me consider him almost an agent of the devil. He avoided mass whenever he could, they said, and the land lay under interdict while he refused to accept Stephen Langton as his archbishop. Was he really pagan?'

Fulke looked away from her and there was a little silence. She felt she had gone too far in her impertinent questioning, then he turned back to her again and was smiling once more.

'No, John had his weaknesses and God knows they were many, and he could be cruel, but where he loved he loved greatly, and I revered him as my sovereign lord. As to his beliefs. . .' Fulke shrugged. 'I cannot say. They attempted to force him into the church as a child oblate, you know. There, probably, were sown the seeds of rebellion against the papacy and clergy which he displayed later.' He chuckled. 'The saints know his father, King Henry, had his own troubles with the clergy too.'

Janeta gave a little gasp, remembering the martyrdom of St Thomas at Canterbury for opposing the King's will, and how the nuns had taught that pilgrims, visiting the place of his murder in the cathedral and later his grave, had been cured of their ills. It was all beyond her understanding. Kings who strove to be strong and rule were said to be wicked, yet she knew, without words having been spoken, that the Countess considered her brother, young King Henry, weak-willed and too easily led by his wife and his advisers, despite her genuine love for him. Henry was deeply pious. Perhaps that tendency could spell danger for his people. So many of his favoured clergy were foreign and avaricious, like Peter de Roches. Even the nuns had been overheard to comment on the fact that too many of the parishes were given to absent foreign priests and their flocks left to languish without true pastors.

L'Estrange turned as sounds of an approaching horseman checked their talk.

'Whoever it is is in a very great hurry.'

The sergeant-at-arms stopped the newcomer to question him and Janeta, craning her neck, saw that the horseman was young, probably a page. Had someone ridden from Winchester with urgent news for the King?

Her curiosity was soon satisfied, for the new arrival,

allowed to proceed by the sergeant, pulled up his lathered mount as he approached her.

'Demoiselle Janeta Cobham?' The boy leaned forward over his horse's shoulders, his youthful, high-pitched voice eager.

'Yes?' Janeta's reply was guarded. She glanced nervously back to where she knew her father was riding with lesser barons in the household. Had he, even now, found some means of parting her from the Countess?

The boy urged his mount nearer, while careful not to agitate hers. 'I'm right glad to have caught you in time, demoiselle. My mistress was so anxious you should get her message and gift before you left Winchester, but when I got there I discovered the royal household had started out much earlier than expected. I had to ride hard to catch up.' Smilingly he bowed his head and, reaching inside his tunic, handed her a small parcel wrapped in silk.

'With the compliments of Lady D'Aubigny, demoiselle. She wishes you to accept this as a mark of her gratitude for your care of her husband's brother after his recent injury in the Winchester tournament.' He saluted her, one hand raised to his forehead.

Janeta was somewhat bewildered, her heart thudding wildly at the sound of the donor's name. She had a view of the broad, youthful features, and the shock of curly hair falling over his eyes, then he had excused himself and was turning his mount. She stared after him as he rode cautiously, picking his way back through the cavalcade, then she turned as he was lost to view to find Fulke L'Estrange regarding her quizzically. She took a quick breath, then she recalled that only a day or so ago Roesia Fitzherbert had become Lady D'Aubigny by her marriage with Morris, Bertrand's brother. She managed a wry smile and tucked the package away inside the tight cuff of her gown. Why on earth had Roesia Fitzherbert thought to send her greetings, let alone a gift? She was astounded. Why should Roesia even remember her? Surely her thoughts now should be only on her new husband?

If Fulke L'Estrange noticed her heightened colour, he passed no comment as they rode on.

Janeta had hoped Bertrand would soon return to her side, but obviously the Earl had found need for him to remain near him and she was a little piqued that she was left in the company of Fulke L'Estrange when the party halted at a village for noon refreshment. The King, Queen and the King's sister, as well as the Earl of Leicester, were accommodated within the house of the local lord of the manor, together with important members of their households, but L'Estrange escorted Janeta and several of the Countess's lesser ladies to the local inn, where he swept aside the innkeeper's protests and ordered out all other customers, to give some measure of privacy for his charges. Janeta was amused by L'Estrange's lordly manner, but though the place was poor enough she was glad of its protection from the chill wind outside and respite from the growing discomfort of her saddle.

Other ladies kept L'Estrange's attention and it was after they had all dined on cold bacon, rye bread and ale, which was all the innkeeper could provide for such unheralded company, that Janeta found herself a little withdrawn from the rest and drew out the package she had received so unexpectedly. Her fingers fumbled with the silken ribbon which tied it and managed to extract a small, soft leather pouch.

She tipped out the contents and found a beautifully crafted brooch pin, in gold and enamel. The design was of a rose, clear red in colour, and supported by

leafed branches and stem. The leaves and petals were
finely veined and Janeta exclaimed at the beauty of the
thing, holding it tightly to examine it more closely, and
so not realising that the stem was also embellished in
life-like manner with a very sharp thorn. She gave a
little startled gasp and looked down angrily at the
bright red bead of blood upon her finger.

'Oh, dear.' She looked up to find Fulke L'Estrange
once more at her side.

'Despite their undoubted beauty, roses do bear
harsh thorns. Whatever have you done to the lady,
Demoiselle Janeta, that she finds it necessary to remind
you so forcibly?'

Janeta's lip trembled as she met his searching gaze
and she gave a little tight smile. 'Nothing whatever
that comes to mind, sir knight. The brooch pin is so
pretty and realistic that I'm sure the giver completely
overlooked the thorn.'

'You think so?' His eyes were mocking her, and she
flushed darkly and turned away.

Despite her reassuring words Janeta knew well
enough that the gift was an open challenge. Such a
design was not to be easily found among a goldsmith's
stock. So fashioned it must have been deliberately
commissioned, and well paid for too, to be completed
so hurriedly. Though she had wed his older brother,
Roesia was informing her that she still retained an
interest in Bertrand D'Aubigny and meant to pursue it
at the first available opportunity. With a jealous
woman's intuition, she had noted Janeta's growing
affection and singled her out for malicious intent.
Janeta gave an uncontrollable shiver and replaced the
deadly little pin within its leather pouch.

As they resumed their journey Janeta was relieved
to see Bertrand riding towards her, and faintly embar-
assed by the presence of Fulke L'Estrange still in close

attendance. She was further irritated when her father suddenly arrived by her side and pointedly edged L'Estrange away from her.

'I shall be leaving the company a few miles further on. I would welcome the opportunity to speak privately with my daughter, sire.'

L'Estrange bowed in the saddle and moved his mount aside, smilingly accosting Bertrand, who was anxious to return to his pupil. Janeta glanced at Bertrand helplessly as her father masterfully took hold of her lead-rein and led her somewhat apart from her companions.

'I see Fulke L'Estrange is paying you close attention,' he snapped, frowning, glancing over his shoulder to where the elegantly attired knight was laughing and chatting with Bertrand, who was showing distinct signs of frustration at even now being parted from Janeta.

Janeta looked up at her father's grim countenance and back at the two men.

'He was instrumental in saving the Earl of Leicester's life,' she reminded her father, 'and, with him, Sir Bertrand D'Aubigny. I owe both men a great deal. I had no wish to appear discourteous.'

'Hmm.'

Janeta was not sure what the grunt was meant to convey. She said thoughtfully, 'Sir Fulke spoke to me of my mother. It appears he knew her.'

She turned to find naked fury sparking from her father's eyes. It was so obvious, she was shocked by it. There was more than dislike here—there was antipathy, arrant hatred.

'You have had reason to distrust Sir Fulke?' she questioned softly.

His mouth tightened, as did his grip on the reins. 'The man is blatantly ambitious, a time-server. He thinks only of preferment at Court. Keep from him, daughter, as you would a poisonous snake. The slime he exudes could coat you too.'

She gave a little nervous smile. 'He could gain little by paying me attentions. I think he is anxious only to help someone new to Court ways. He will soon find more noble company once we reach Westminster.'

'Aye, possibly.' He glanced ahead and then back at her again. 'Remember you will always be——' he hesitated '—different from other women, daughter. Obey the Countess, perform your duties well and look to your soul's welfare. You know I would have preferred you to remain at St Catherine's but I have been gainsaid. I exhort you not to disgrace me. I expect to hear nothing but word of discreet and dutiful behaviour of you.'

'Yes, Father,' she replied mechanically, hoping, at this moment of parting, that he would make some show of affection. As usual there was none. He nodded, grim-lipped.

'Farewell, child. The Countess will send me word if there is need.'

He was off, shouldering aside other riders, before she could even reply and she impatiently dashed away the sudden tears as Bertrand took his place by her side.

'You are crying. What did he say to upset you?'

'Nothing.' She blinked back further tears. 'Perhaps that is the trouble. He exhorted me to be a faithful servant and not to disgrace him.'

Bertrand swore softly beneath his breath. 'I'm sorry I had to leave you on the journey, but the Earl had special business for me.' He hesitated. 'I cannot say more just yet, but I assure you I did not neglect you without urgent good cause. L'Estrange assures me you are a credit to my teaching and ride well.'

She laughed. 'He is very kind. My mount is very

accommodating, otherwise I think I might have encountered trouble. How much longer must I endure this aching of my buttocks?'

He grinned. 'We stay the night near Guildford. The King's houshold will occupy the guest-house at the monastery there. The Earl's men will take what lodgings they can find in the town, but tomorrow I'll find you in the cavalcade very promptly, I promise.'

She wondered if Fulke L'Estrange had mentioned the present Roesia had sent to her. She hoped not. She had no wish to trouble Bertrand with the knowledge of his sister-in-law's malice. Common sense told her she should rid herself of the gift as soon as possible, yet she hesitated to do that. If Morris should one day comment on it, she would feel considerable discomfort at having to explain away her reason for no longer possessing it. The trinket was expensive and, outwardly, a mark of gratitude. For the present, she would not show it to Bertrand.

She occupied cramped quarters in the monastery guest-house. The Countess slept with Lady Sandford in attendance and Janeta's services were not needed. She lay wakeful, listening to the snores of other ladies close by, reflecting both on Roesia's resentment and the reasons for her father's hatred of Fulke L'Estrange. He had passed no comment when she had mentioned that the man had known her mother and she had pressed him no further, recognising it was that knowledge—that L'Estrange had been present during the late King's visit to their manor—that had prompted that expression of downright loathing which had distorted his features. Had Fulke L'Estrange made amorous overtures to her mother? No, that could not have been. L'Estrange had been scarcely more than a boy on those occasions yet. . . .

Janeta turned over wearily on her straw-filled pallet and tried to summon up sleep. Her whole being ached. She grimaced at thought of resuming her seat in the saddle for the last miles of their journey to Westminster and hoped, fervently, that she would have Bertrand constantly by her side. That would make the whole business endurable.

The weather proved fine next morning and there was no delay on the next leg of their journey. Bertrand presented himself early at her side, much, she thought, to the envy of her companions, and entertained her much of the way with stories of Simon de Montfort's household. At an inn near Windsor they shared a table, and though Fulke L'Estrange bowed to her from a distance he made no attempt to pay her undue attention, for which fact she was grateful.

Janeta was not surprised by the sprawl of huts and domestic buildings which made up the palace of Westminster, having already had experience of such a royal building at Winchester, but she *was* impressed by the superior appointments of this palace. There was a profusion of wall-tapestries to keep out the winter chill and, in the private apartments, even fur rugs and carpets upon the floors, brought from Outremer during the Crusades. The Countess of Pembroke's quarters were some distance from those of the King and Queen and Janeta thought she detected an expression of relief on Eleanor's features, as if she was glad there was no longer need to keep her dislike of the young Queen concealed.

Janeta was kept busy that evening unpacking the Countess's immediate needs, and the next day helping with settling in further. Eleanor appeared withdrawn, wrapped up in her own thoughts yet not unhappy, so Janeta guessed there had been no expression of disapproval from the King which had prompted him to insist that his sister accompany him back to Westminster.

The Twelfth Night festivities were kept up in the great hall, and once more Henry appeared before his barons wearing his crown. Janeta was seated at the foot of the high table and so separated from Bertrand, but Simon de Montfort was once more seated near the King, to the evident spleen of Queen Eleanor.

It was after the boards had been cleared and dancing and more boisterous games begun that Bertrand appeared at Janeta's side and led her out of the hall into one of the wind-swept corridors. Janeta protested, glancing up at the wavering flames of the torches, and pulled her mantle more closely round her shoulders.

'It is so cold and draughty out here. Why could we not have stayed nearer one of the braziers?'

'Because I want to reveal to you the reason which kept me from your side during the first part of the journey. I couldn't do it before because people might have overheard, and they might easily have done so now were we to remain in hall.'

'Oh! It is so important, then?'

He nodded and drew her close. She longed to surrender, but his nearness was playing havoc with her heart and her limbs again. She struggled and protested, though only half-heartedly.

'Someone will see us and report this to Lady Sandford. Already she dislikes me because of the Countess's favour.'

'There are so many other amorous couples taking advantage of nooks and crannies in the palace on this festive night, I doubt *we* shall attract notice. Do you not love me, then, wench?'

'Bertrand,' she murmured, 'you know that I do, but. . .'

He released one hand from her shoulder and placed

it gently over her lips. 'Then listen to what I have to say. It concerns us. The King has given his consent to the Earl's marriage with his sister.'

She gave a great gasp and drew away slightly, her eyes widening in wonder.

He resumed his pressure upon her mouth. 'It is to be secret and take place tomorrow night in the private chapel. I was summoned by the Earl and given instructions for preparing the escort for them to leave for his Midlands holdings very soon afterwards. I sent couriers on ahead to prepare their chambers. The King has given the Earl the castle of Kenilworth as a wedding-gift.'

'Then we shall be together for some time?' Her eyes were shining.

'Better than that, my love. I have spoken with the Earl and he has promised we shall be married very shortly. It will be for him to beg the Countess for her consent and to wait on word from your father.'

'He will never give it.' Her words were anguished.

'He will. The King's wish is law, and the Countess's virtually the same. Soon, my love, we shall be wed, far quicker than I had dared to hope.' He laughed triumphantly. 'And then there will be no reason for you to freeze in my arms. No one will dare to say us nay, and there'll be no cause for us to be stealing moments like this in draughty corridors. Kiss me, Janeta, and say you will marry me as soon as possible.'

She gave a great sigh of content. 'Sweet Virgin, Bertrand, I can hardly believe it. They wed tomorrow, you say?'

'Aye, love, but in strictest secrecy. You must not breathe a word of it to anyone.'

'I would not. My lord Simon trusts you?'

'He does.' Bertrand chuckled. 'I think he knows how I understand his need.'

'Twice you helped to save his life.'

'And he is grateful. Our marriage is the finest gift he can grant me and he has promised me preferment in the household, so your father will have no cause for complaint at my lack of standing.'

'St Catherine, the patron of all virgin maids, has answered my prayers,' she whispered. 'Oh, Bertrand, I shall pray so hard that my mistress will be as happy in this match as I shall be with my chosen mate.'

'Amen,' he whispered fervently as he bent to kiss her again.

CHAPTER EIGHT

JANETA hugged her secret to herself after Bertrand had escorted her back to the hall, where the feasting had become indecorous and the King and Queen signalled their desire to retire to their own apartments. Lady Sandford, whose expression clearly showed her distaste for the whole rowdy proceedings, beckoned to Janeta, who took hasty leave of Bertrand and presented herself at Eleanor's side.

She looked anxiously at her mistress for any sign that the momentous tidings she had received from Bertrand could be true, but Eleanor was outwardly unmoved. She curtsied as the King and Queen departed and as Simon de Montfort moved to follow she smiled her farewell, then she too gathered her ladies round her and left the hall. Janeta wondered if she would be required to sleep within Eleanor's chamber that night, but no such summons came, and she retired to the crowded chamber she shared with the other ladies somewhat disappointed. She, aparently, was not to be the recipient of Eleanor's confidence, as she had expected, since she had carried the messages between the parties now preparing to take such an important step in their respective fortunes.

She lay wakeful for some hours, as she often did these days, despite her weariness after the work of the day and the evening's festivities. Bertrand was so hopeful that they would soon be wed. It was a prospect she had never really dared to contemplate. Oh, she had dreamed of it, but it had not been a reality. Always, in the back of her mind, she had thought some obstacle would rear itself to prevent her true happiness. When she had unpacked her few gowns and belongings she had pricked her finger unwarily again on Roesia's gift, and a stab of fear had gone through her as if, even from a distance, Roesia could harm her. Was there some deadly witchcraft bound up within the hateful thing, born of Roesia's relentless malice? Yet Janeta was unwilling, still, to dispose of it.

The next day the Countess appeared as usual, considerate and kindly, unaffected as many were by the over-drinking and unruliness which had occurred during the previous night's carousal. Lady Sandford watched with a keen eye for signs of reaction to over-indulgence from her charges. Guiltily, Janeta thought the woman was watching very closely indeed, as if she knew what had been revealed in that short meeting in the corridor. Did Lady Sandford know? Would she be in attendance at the ceremony? Surely she would be chosen, since she had been the Countess's governess and her close friend over many years? Janeta sighed as she watched Eleanor covertly. What tremendous excitement must be being concealed beneath that attitude of calm solicitude for the sufferers among her attendants!

Eleanor finally sent for Janeta towards the close of the afternoon. Her servant and old nurse, Martha, closed the door on Janeta and barred it, standing with her back against it to prevent any unwanted visitor. The Countess was seated on her bed and she beckoned Janeta to approach.

'Can I trust you utterly, child?'

'Of course, my lady.'

'I am to be wed tonight to the Earl of Leicester within the private chapel. Since you are already aware of my feelings towards my lord, I think it only right that you should be a witness to the ceremony along with Martha here.'

Janeta swallowed the hard lump which had formed in her throat and blinked back tears of joy not unmixed with a rising feeling of apprehension. Since this ceremony was to be kept a close secret, was she risking her future in the royal household by taking part in it? If the King and Queen were to discover her part in the proceedings she could be permanently disgraced.

Eleanor reassured her. 'As you surmise, the news of my marriage is to be kept from the Court for some time.' She paused. 'The Earl is still a newcomer to court, or considered so by many of the principal barons, and therefore there will be some resentment of his rise to power by so important a match; but the King, my brother, has given his consent. You will be in no danger of his anger by being present. I wish to have someone by me who understands my love.' She gave a little nervous laugh. 'For I think you above all women do, Janeta. You will sleep in my chamber tonight and, after all have retired, you will help prepare me with Martha and then we shall go down to the chapel. The Earl will send someone he trusts——' a smile dimpled the corner of her mouth '—as escort. I am sure we shall have no reason to doubt the probity of that someone, Janeta. I do not have to remind you how important it is that you give no sign to anyone during the rest of this day that anything is untoward. No one is to know.'

'Lady Sandford?' Janeta framed the question almost silently.

Eleanor's expression hardened. 'No one.'

'Oh, my lady, I am so very glad for you both. I shall pray for your future happiness.' She rose from the kneeling position near the bed which she had assumed to hear Eleanor's softly uttered instructions, curtsied, and moved back to the door which Martha was guarding so jealously.

Though Cecily Sandford glanced at Janeta sharply when she took her place with the other ladies in the bower and took up her embroidery again, she passed no comment. Janeta was thankful that she was not questioned as to the reason why the Countess had required her services. She lowered her head to the intricate work, parrying enquiries by intimating that it needed all her concentration.

She waited in trepidation for the summons to the Countess's sleeping-chamber, though she was wildly excited too. A page came at last, and she and the other ladies prepared Eleanor for bed, after which the Countess dismissed them all except for Janeta and Martha. Cecily Sandford's expression conveyed her disappointment at being excluded, but she curtsied with the others and withdrew.

Eleanor drew a deep breath of relief, then, eyes shining with anticipation, she gestured the two conspirators to sit by her.

'We must wait for at least an hour before I begin to dress. The ceremony will take place at midnight. We must find some occupation for our minds until that time.' She laughed. 'Oh, Janeta, are you not longing for your time? I promise it will not be long delayed.'

Janeta nodded, flushing with her own delight.

'A nuptial chamber has been prepared for us near the King's own apartment. You two will keep guard in the ante-chamber there—afterwards. Simon has been accommodated in apartments there since his arrival at Westminster.' She glanced at the darkened window, where the light from the flaring sconces did not reach. 'How the minutes drag! I do not think I can bear the suspense.'

Martha grunted. 'The hours before your first marriage you spent in dread. Not this time, my hinny, eh?'

'Not this time. Martha, I love Simon so. Tell me I am doing no wrong.'

'You follow your heart, hinny. How can that ever be wrong?'

'Yet I am afraid. . .' The anguished little words died away as Eleanor thrust a hand across her mouth, as if to stifle some further doubt.

Martha rose determinedly. 'Come, I think it is more than time we began to get you ready.'

It was a joyous task, undertaken by the two of them alone. Usually Eleanor was surrounded by a score or more of giggling ladies; she now stood docilely while Janeta and Martha attired her for her wedding. She had already bathed in scented water and washed and dried her lovely hair, which Martha lovingly undid from its braids to lie in curling tendrils upon her shoulders. It would be cold in the chapel and Eleanor had chosen to wear a full-skirted gown in the newly imported velvet cloth of the darkest midnight-blue. Janeta was gratified to note that the mantle, in softest wool of a lighter blue shade, was embellished with bands of cloth of gold embroidery she had herself only recently completed. The gilded leather belt which confined Eleanor's slender waist was studded with gold and sapphires. Its ends fell almost to the hem of her gown. She wore little jewellery, only a golden cross, again studded with sapphires, on a heavy gold chain. Since she was no longer a virgin bride, she did not wear her red-gold hair loose, but confined in a golden crespinette, and round her brows she wore a golden coronet proclaiming her royal rank.

When she rose from her kneeling position, where she had been engaged in adjusting the hem of the gown, Janeta caught Martha's eye and smiled her gratification for work well done. The Earl would have good cause to be proud of his bride.

Eleanor impulsively hugged her old nurse, her bright eyes sparkling with tears, and bent to cup her hands round Janeta's chin.

'Thank you, both of you. My lord and I will remember you in our prayers for your work this night.'

Again Janeta felt that familiar lump in her throat. It had never been her lot to help prepare a beloved sister for this wonderful moment. Now she felt that the Lady Eleanor stood in this role. With all her heart she wished her well and longed for the time when the marriage could be proclaimed to the world and the Earl take his place proudly by his wife's side.

When the knock sounded on the door Martha nodded for her to answer. Instinctively Janeta knew she would find Bertrand outside. His brown hair was shining under the light of the sconce on the opposite wall. He carried a torch to light them down the gloomier passages of the palace. His eyes lit up at the sight of Janeta, dressed in her best gown of saffron wool, the Countess's gift.

'The Countess is ready,' Janeta breathed.

He nodded and stood aside, bowing, as Eleanor came to the door, Martha, behind her, adjusting the folds of her mantle.

The altar appeared out of the grey gloom of the small chapel like a veritable jewel, the golden pattern, pyx and crucifix lit by the glow from the candles which haloed Eleanor's coronet and golden crespinette. Simon de Montfort turned at their approach and gave a little sigh of wonder. His dark eyes took fire as he moved to take Eleanor's hands, indicating by the graciousness of his smile that he was grateful to her attendants. The King's chaplain appeared and signalled for the pair to approach the altar.

Almost at the same moment the chapel door was flung open and the King stepped into the candlelight and came forward to stand beside his sister. Janeta was astonished to see that he was attended by Fulke L'Estrange, whose garments were fully as gorgeous as his master's. The Earl, though dressed finely in his habitual scarlet, which complemented his darkly handsome features, had chosen not to over-embellish his apparel. Janeta saw no sheen of gold on his person and she smiled to herself in the half-darkness. How sensible he was, indeed, not to seek to outshine his bride, or her royal brother. Bertrand was dressed neatly but discreetly in a dark green tunic and brown homespun mantle.

She stood well back from the bridal pair, her hand tightly clasped within Bertrand's; Martha was behind them, her back pressed to the door, as if, once again, she was on guard to keep out intruders.

The King glanced back briefly once and Janeta wondered if he had deliberately kept the secret of this marriage from his own queen. If so, he judged there would be complaints to hear, possibly hard words later, for Queen Eleanor had no love for the bridegroom. L'Estrange turned almost at the same second and his blue eyes twinkled at the sight of Janeta's hand in that of Bertrand. His level brows drew together and he put up a hand, as he was wont to do, to stroke his golden beard.

The King and Eleanor made a handsome Plantagenet pair, yet Simon too, standing straight and tall as he quietly made his responses, was not to be outdone in noble dignity. The couple knelt for the blessing, dark head and golden bent close together. Janeta had not been near enough to them to hear clearly the whispered words or to see the exchange of rings but she rejoiced when the King's chaplain covered their clasped hands with his stole, pronouncing them man and wife together, and gave them the final blessing which made Eleanor, Dowager Countess of Pembroke, Princess of England, now Countess of Leicester, Simon de Montfort's wife.

Bertrand's fingers tightened on Janeta's and she turned to him with a ready smile. It was done. No one could gainsay it, no matter how this match displeased the King's brother, Richard of Cornwall, and the majority of the barons. Simon de Montfort was now the King's true brother-in-law and one could see by the look of adoration in his eyes as he turned to his bride that she alone was the object of his worship. Ambitious Simon de Montfort might be, and many would speak of this match as a deliberate stepping-stone to further heights of the King's favour, but Janeta would declare stoutly for the rest of her days that that was certainly not the man's reason for requesting Eleanor's hand of the King. All who had eyes to see had the proof before them of how deeply the two loved each other. Radiance shone about Eleanor as she lifted her face for her brother's kiss and Janeta saw him give a slightly uncertain smile as he grasped the hand of his new-made brother-in-law.

They were escorted by the King himself, Bertrand and Fulke L'Estrange to the apartments reserved for the use of the Earl of Leicester. It seemed the other servants had been dismissed to their beds, for it was Bertrand who lighted his new Countess and her two attendants into the Earl's sleeping-chamber, the King and Fulke L'Estrange remaining outside for a while with the bridegroom.

Quickly Martha and Janeta undressed their mistress, attired her in a fur-trimmed bedgown, and Martha, with the privilege of the old nurse, combed out Eleanor's beautiful hair again and led her to the bed.

There was the sweet and sharp smell of freshly strewn herbs both around the bed and beneath the pillows. The torchlight lingered on Eleanor's features; her eyes were shining again. There seemed no nervousness in her manner. Eagerly she waited for Simon's arrival.

Finally Martha kissed her and Janeta drew close at Eleanor's invitation to receive a like kiss upon her cheek. There were huskily spoken words of gratitude for their hard work and loyalty and then the door opened as Martha informed her new lord that all was ready and he could now join his lady. The King stood back to allow the entrance of his chaplain to bless the marriage-bed, then Janeta was curtsying and withdrawing into the ante-room with Martha. There was none of the bawdy badinage she had heard was common on these occasions. The King was a deeply pious young man and would have considered such behaviour unseemly, and there was none of Simon's fellow barons to take part. L'Estrange prepared to light the King to his own apartment and Janeta was relieved to see that Bertrand was preparing to sleep across the entrance of the ante-room. All would be secure.

She slept dreamlessly and soundly, and it seemed only moments before Martha was shaking her up from her truckle-bed.

'See to it that the Countess has warmed water and towels. I shall attend to all in the chamber. We must hurry. My lady wishes to return to her own apartments before the household is awake. Both she and the Earl will leave the palace before the news breaks. It will be better that way.'

Janeta rubbed her eyes and nodded. There was no sign of Bertrand outside in the corridor so he must have been sent on some errand. She hastened in search of a serving-wench who would procure the things she needed.

As she was about to enter the Countess's apartments, her way to the sleeping-chamber was barred by Lady Cecily Sandford. The former governess was fully dressed and did not appear to have slept throughout the night. In the pallid grey light of dawn her face looked drawn and set.

'Where is she?' Her voice was sharp and without the respectful tone Janeta would have expected in her reference to her lady.

Janeta paused uncertainly, her eyes looking warily to the chamber where many of the ladies slept.

'The Countess—where is she? No, do not bother to lie. She is with him, the De Montfort creature, isn't that so? And you and that foolish wench, Martha, arranged it for her.' The words were flat, hollow-sounding and weary. Janeta was shocked to the core of her being.

She hesitated. Could she allow Lady Sandford to think badly of her mistress? Surely the former governess should now be informed that there was no sin in Eleanor's lying with her wedded lord?

Before she could make some evasion, she saw Lady Sandford's deeply set dark eyes widen as if in sudden shock.

'She has not wed him?'

Janeta whispered, 'The King was present but the marriage is not to be made known yet. You must keep silent, Lady Sandford——'

Her words were cut off as the irate woman seized her by her shoulders and began to shake her as if she were a rat within the jaws of a hunting-dog.

'*You* were at the bottom of this. You carried messages between them. I feared as much. The moment I set eyes on you I knew you would cause trouble, a runaway from a convent. Have you no conscience? Don't you know what you've done?'

Exhausted by her overnight vigil, she gave up her frenzied attack and Janeta was thrown back violently against the wall of the corridor, bruising her elbows as she braced herself to remain upright. She was totally taken aback by this unjust charge.

'Th—the Lady Eleanor loves the Earl,' she stammered. 'Lady Sandford, can you not be happy for her? The King will announce the match in due time. There can be no impropriety. The Countess is a widow and——'

'No impropriety?' Despite their need for caution against waking the attendant ladies, Cecily Sandford's question was shrill with outrage. 'You talk of sacrilege as "no impropriety"? As if we spoke of the lovesick surrender of some ignorant dairy-maid! Eleanor knew well what she was doing. She *cannot* marry, you foolish girl; she is already sworn as a bride of Christ. Have you not noticed she wears his ring as I wear mine?'

Janeta was unsure, at first, if the strange numbness of her thinking process was due to some blow to her head when her body had struck the wall, yet she soon knew that that was not so. She stepped forward, facing the distraught Cecily Sandford, trying desperately to assess the meaning of the words she had just heard. Her chest felt suddenly tight and hard, as if she was unable to breathe properly. She took a gulp of air, put out her hands as if to ward off the awful truth, yet knew instinctively that Cecily Sandford's distress was genuine, and not the outpouring of some jealous friend whose closeness had been usurped by another, less worthy.

Janeta said stupidly, 'I saw the ring—I thought—believed it was her wedding-ring, given by my lord of Pembroke. . .'

'When Pembroke died, Eleanor mourned him truly. He was an old man but he had treated her well and she had been deeply fond of him, although naturally she had not loved him as a maid loves a man. . . She feared her brother would force her into some new politically useful state marriage. She was also a pious daughter of the Church, as I was.' The formerly harsh voice had broken and fallen to a whisper. 'I knew how she felt. I too had only recently lost my husband. We took counsel from the Archbishop of Canterbury, the sainted Edmund, and, after much consideration and prayer, we decided together to take vows of eternal chastity. Though it was not the wish of either of us to enter a convent, we were as much bound as any nun. Eleanor swore then that if she was ever tempted to break that solemn vow she would, indeed, ride to some nearby convent and take the veil. Why do you think I wear this habit? I have often wished that I had become a true bride of Christ, but I felt I must stay by Eleanor, strengthen her in her resolve——' She gave a great sob. 'Then *he* came—this foreigner, Simon de Montfort—and I feared—I feared. . .'

Janeta said with deadly calm, 'And you are telling me that this is well-known, that the King himself was aware of it——?'

'Everyone was aware of it. She made her solemn vow in the cathedral on her knees, dressed as a true bride of Christ, before Archbishop Edmund, and he placed the ring upon her finger, as the bridal ring a novice takes at her final vows proclaims her nun in truth.' Cecily gave a little impatient movement of her hand and then said slowly, 'But *you* were not aware of it. I see now why you, and you alone, were chosen to be her go-between.'

Janeta felt a cold, sick feeling at the pit of her stomach. Of course she had been chosen. The woman she had admired above all other had deliberately used her. Her thoughts flew to the moment when she had

helped Martha prepare Eleanor for Simon de
Montfort's bed. They had both known they were
committing one of the gravest sins and she, Janeta,
had helped them. It was useless to tell herself that she
had not known. Again there seemed proof that she
had been destined from birth to do harm to others.
She was marked for it, as her father had constantly
told her. For this reason he had placed her within the
nunnery, but she, in her sin of pride, had thought she
knew better, and now she had caused another to break
her sacred vow.

Had Bertrand known? The thought struck her as a
deadly blow. He had needed the Earl's patronage. He
had encouraged her to enter the Countess's household
and her very reason for visiting Simon de Montfort's
lodgings in Winchester Castle had been, ostensibly, to
visit Bertrand, to enquire after his health. The Earl
and the Countess had conspired together to make
Bertrand her riding instructor, so that the two of them
would be able to move freely between the two households without particular notice.

She shivered violently. She had depended upon this
royal marriage to make it possible for her own match
with Bertrand. A bribe? Oh, Eleanor would not have
seen it like that, but as a reward for two loyal servants
who had served her so well. That last letter she had
taken to Winchester Castle had most likely been
Eleanor's final message to Simon that the King was
prepared to give his consent to the match, and they
had left almost immediately for Westminster!

Cecily Sandford was watching her intently. She said
awkwardly, 'I misjudged you. I thought that, having
decided against the convent life yourself, you had allied
yourself with the Countess—agreed to help her—but it
was not like that, was it?'

'No,' Janeta said through stiffened lips. 'I did not know.'

Cecily Sandford's lips twisted in a wry smile. 'How could you? You were immured in your convent when the vow was taken and no one in the household would gossip about what they must have known was going on.'

'What will happen? Is the marriage valid? But the King was present. He must have known.'

Again Cecily Sandford's lips tightened. 'Oh, he knew all right. Possibly Simon de Montfort did not know of the situation until it was too late.' She looked away hastily. 'I know she loves him,' she said softly, almost tenderly. 'It is always possible he loves her, though ambition plays an important part in men's affairs, and this marriage is certainly advantageous to Simon. The King gave his consent because—because he feels he needs the man at his side. De Montfort is a capable councillor, I give him that. I don't know what will happen. There will be a terrible scandal. The bishops will object, as will the principal barons, who only need a good excuse to oust Leicester from Court.' She sighed heavily. 'None of this weighs so heavily with me as my fear for the well-being of Eleanor's soul.'

Janeta crossed herself, her lip trembling. 'Could the bishops declare the marriage invalid?'

'I believe they could, but the harm is done. You say they bedded?'

Janeta nodded, her colour heightening.

'Child, it is not your responsibility—nor mine now, thank the Virgin.' Lady Sandford turned briskly away. 'I still have duties. I must set about them and afterwards ask permission to withdraw from the Countess's household.'

The words were ominous, like a knell sounding on

Janeta's hopes. Lady Sandford had made her decision according to her conscience. It was now up to Janeta to make hers.

The palace was already stirring. Soon her companion ladies would be up. She must not be seen in such distress. And the Countess still required the needs to fulfil her toilet. A spasm crossed her face as she thought that Martha would, even now, be removing the evidence of the night of passion the lovers had shared.

Like Lady Sandford, she must complete her business before requesting permission to leave the household that she now knew to be tainted. She found a yawning serving-wench and dispatched her to the kitchens for a ewer of hot water, and went herself in search of towels, a dish of soap and perfumed oil from the travelling-chest in Eleanor's sleeping-chamber.

She was on her way back to the Earl's apartments when Bertrand hastened to her.

'Where have you been? I've been looking for you. Here——' he stopped a passing page '—deliver these to the Earl of Leicester's chamber. Hurry.'

The boy took Janeta's burden from her, sniffed curiously at the small pot of oil scented with attar of roses, set on the tray beside the ewer and the beautifully embroidered towel. He was used to amorous intrigue. Whatever went on within the chambers of the great was not his business. He had learned from painful experience that his ears would burn, and possibly his back if he allowed himself to gossip. He smiled slyly at Bertrand and hastened off on the errand.

Bertrand hurried Janeta along until they entered the ante-chamber where she had spent the previous night with Martha. She saw that he was already dressed for riding.

'Martha wondered why you were taking so long. The

Countess will need clothing from her own apartments. I was about to set off but did not wish to leave without bidding you farewell. I'm to ride ahead and smooth arrangements for Simon to leave for the Midland shires.' He stopped abruptly, staring at her white, set face. 'What is it, Janeta? You are not ill?' He moved to take her into his arms and furiously she dashed away his hands.

'Do not place your hands on me.'

He backed off uncertainly. 'What is it? I don't understand. Has someone been speaking ill of me?'

She was experiencing that approach of uncontrollable rage which had always frightened her, both as a child and, later, at St Catherine's. Her body was trembling, she was deadly cold and sick, and the dear, familiar form of Bertrand was obscured by a reddish mist which developed before her eyes.

'They are still together?' She spat out the question.

'Who? You mean the Earl and the Countess?'

'I mean the Earl and his whore.'

'What are you saying?' His tone sounded bewildered, but equally angry. 'You witnessed their marriage in the presence of the King and solemnised by the royal chaplain.'

'But you knew, as the King knew—yes, and as all at Court knew—that she was not free to take husband. Everyone knew but Janeta Cobham, the poor dupe who was taken in charity into the household and who could prove so useful as a tool.'

He flinched back from her, hardly believing he could hear such words from her, and spoken with such venom.

'Oh, you mean that vow she took some years ago, when she was hardly more than a child, full of grief for a husband who had always petted her like a doll? She was under the influence of Cecily Sandford, who had been like a mother to her. I imagine the Countess has regretted it ever since.'

'She took an oath in the cathedral before the altar. The Archbishop of Canterbury himself placed the sacred ring which bound her to Christ upon her finger. She is not free to take another husband.'

He shook his head impatiently. 'That can be overset. Simon will obtain a dispensation. Since the King gave his consent to the match, himself witnessed the ceremony, the Pope will hardly dare to refuse him. It will need a considerable sum of money to convince the clergy. I am sent to Leicester to see about raising the necessary funds. She did not take the veil, entered no noviciate. This vow will not be held as binding. There were extenuating circumstances.'

'Did you know?'

He sighed heavily. 'I heard of it, certainly. When the oath was taken it was the subject of considerable talk throughout the land. A suitable foreign marriage for the King's youngest sister would have been a bargaining counter. Most people were surprised that he allowed her to take such a step but Henry was ever pious in the extreme.'

'And now he is less pious, it seems, or he values the Earl of Leicester so highly that he is prepared to let his sister be foresworn.'

Bertrand's face was mottling with angry colour. 'Those are strong words, Janeta, and. . .'

'And none the less truthful for that?'

He looked anxiously around him, as if fearful of eavesdroppers. 'You must be careful. Your words could be interpreted as treasonable.'

'And that would cause you concern? At the very least it might lose you the favour of the Earl.'

'Yes,' he said soberly. 'I want you to think very

carefully. Such open disapproval of the Earl and his lady could lose both of us favour.'

'And you think that will count with me?'

He frowned, clearly bewildered by her attitude. 'What the Earl and the Countess have done is no business of ours. The affairs of the great are not to be commented on by simple folk. You have lived at Court long enough to understand that, surely? Do you think Lady Sandford will openly criticise her mistress, whatever she may think in private?'

'Lady Sandford was not involved in the arrangements for the marriage, did not prepare the bride for her lover's bed. I was—unknowingly. Bertrand, I have committed a mortal sin.'

'Nonsense, how can you be implicated? Whatever the clergy decide, you cannot be blamed. You and Martha were simply obeying the instructions of your mistress. The sin does not lie on your soul.'

'But I helped her—the Countess. I carried the letters between her and the Earl. Bertrand, I have brought disaster on them both.'

He drew a hard breath. 'These are the foolish fears of a girl too strictly brought up. You yourself decided you could not live the convent life. You ran away. Can you not sympathise with the Countess, caught in such a trap?'

She nodded vehemently. 'Of course I can. I suffer for her—deeply—but I took no vows. Though I could see little future for me outside the convent walls I left before committing myself to the noviciate. The Countess must have had good men to advise her—the Archbishop of Canterbury, for one. Are you telling me he did not warn her of the irrevocable nature of the vow she was taking? This marriage is doomed, Bertrand, cursed by God. The two of them could be excommunicated and I—in innocence certainly—was instrumental in the final moves. I cannot speak out. Who am I to condemn her? But I have to leave her household. To stay within it would compound my sin.'

He came close to her then and took her by the shoulders, his face working. 'Are you mad? Do you realise what you will be doing? Our own marriage hopes will be totally destroyed if you take this step.' He was shaking her, and she felt the fury rise up in her again. She lifted one hand and struck him hard across the face.

'I have told you not to touch me. You are tempting me to commit further sin. You placed me in that household, allowed me to act as their go-between, unknowing. . .'

'I neither knew nor cared whether you knew. I tell you again, it is not our business. Our business is to serve our respective master and mistress. As to our meeting on the Winchester road, you speak as if it was planned.'

'It was preordained.'

'I'm beginning to think this convent education of yours has sent you half mad. How could it have been ordained? We came upon the Earl beset on the road and I went to help him. Do you tell me I was sinning in going to the help of a man outnumbered and completely at the mercy of his enemies?'

Tears were stinging her eyes. 'I don't know, I don't know. My father said—he said—he placed me in the convent so I could not harm others, that I was. . .'

'Your father wanted to be rid of you.' His reply was brutal. 'He merely wanted to put you out of sight and mind so that he would not be forced to pay out a sizeable dowry. You've said that yourself, many times.'

She had freed herself now and her hands covered her face. He watched helplessly as tears dripped through her fingers.

'I love you, Janeta,' he said desperately. 'What shall I do if I lose you?'

'I love you,' she sobbed, 'more than life itself, cannot you see that? I do not blame you for what has occurred, those were foolish words, but I blame myself. I knew the association was secret. I should have realised. . .'

'How could you?'

'I wanted to meet with you. Ever since I met you on the Winchester road I felt—I knew—I had never experienced such strong feelings. I felt they must be wrong. And there was Roesia—I thought you loved her and I was jealous—I wanted to be near you constantly in case she—she. . .'

'I have told you I had no love for Roesia Fitzherbert. If there is love, it is on her side only. Janeta, be sensible. What hope have we of obtaining consent for our marriage without the help of the Earl and Countess of Leicester? If you insist on leaving her service, I shall lose you.'

She lifted a tear-stained face to his. 'I know,' she moaned softly, 'but cannot you understand? I must do what is right.'

'Cannot you understand that they love one another, as we love, that he needs her? Simon de Montfort is destined for high office. The people of England need him. The King needs him. She will help to make him great.'

Janeta nodded, her eyes averted. 'I understand all that too but——' she shivered violently '—nothing can change the fact that this marriage is accursed. It is against the will of God. I fear for them both, and the children they bear.'

He said briskly, 'This is more superstitious nonsense. I believed you would put our love higher in your priorities than this.'

Suddenly he had swept her into his arms again and

she felt the hardness of his body against her, bruising
her flesh beneath the folds of her gown. He rained
kisses down on her face, pushing aside the wimple and
pressing his lips on the white skin of her throat. 'I will
make you love me,' he murmured thickly, 'make you
come to your senses. Now tell me you will throw our
love away for some stupid whim. . .'

She was melting against him, her treacherous body
prepared to surrender. If he took her now she would
not care yet—just as suddenly—she thrust him from
her, exerting all the strength of her two extended arms.

'No,' she moaned, 'I cannot do it. I cannot damn my
soul. Not even for you, Bertrand D'Aubigny.'

'Then you will give up all that we hold precious
because of this religious belief of yours?'

'I must.'

He gave a hopeless little shrug. 'What will you do?
Where will you go?'

'I don't know. Perhaps my father. . .'

'I doubt if you will find your father ready to take you
in if you anger the King and his sister.' His tone was
dry.

'Then—then perhaps the nuns of St Catherine's will
take pity on me. There——' she gave a little sob
'—there I can atone for my sin.'

'I cannot pretend to understand you, Janeta. I am
prepared to accept the decision of the clergy on this
matter. The Earl has been good to me. I wish to go on
serving him.'

She nodded. 'I know that you do. I cannot expect
you to see this grave matter as I do. You have your
future to consider.'

'Promise me you will give yourself time. Nothing
can be decided until the Curia makes its wishes plain.
If a dispensation is then granted, surely you will not go
against the decision of the Pope?'

'I feel partly responsible,' she said wearily. 'The Countess will decide for herself what is right for her. As I see it, she has already done so. I only know that I feel guilty and must atone.'

'At the cost of our love?'

'You think I do it lightly?'

'I think, perhaps, your love for me is not as great as the Lady Eleanor's is for my lord Simon,' he said very deliberately.

She turned from him. Her legs were trembling violently again, and if she stayed near him now she would surrender to his stronger will. He must not see her face now, guess at the agony which was tearing her in two, or he would exert greater pressure, and she feared she could not withstand that temptation.

'I'm sorry,' she said tonelessly. 'I must go now and find Martha.'

'Then it is goodbye? You will leave Westminster?'

'You must go about the Earl's business. Try to forget me—in time—and try to forgive me, Bertrand.'

She gathered her skirts then and ran from him. Tears blinded her and she stumbled into the path of a bewildered page, who had to put out his hand to steady her lest she fall. She could not tell if Bertrand had called after her or if he had attempted to follow her. She could not bear it if he had. Her one wish now was to hide herself like a wounded animal who sought out a secret place to die. Something deep within her had died and she had no hope of a resurrection.

Martha, it seemed, was closeted with her mistress and the Earl, and Janeta could not have borne to face them even if she had been granted entrance to their chamber. She turned away from the Earl's private apartments and made for the open air. The palace corridors were already becoming busy with servants and officials scurrying to report for their morning duties. She found herself pushed and pressed against the stone walls and longed to be free of the place, if only for moments, while she forced herself to face facts and prepare for the steps she must take.

The rear of the palace faced the river and Janeta, without a cloak, shivered in the chill air. The walk facing her led to the palace steps, where ferry boats plied their trade to the city downriver. The mighty Thames flowed sluggishly and seemed shrouded in a damp mist. The prospect was cheerless, in keeping with Janeta's anguish of mind. She walked down to a low wall which separated the river path from the palace gardens, brown and apparently bare now in this season of winter. She ignored the one or two people who passed her on their way to and from the palace landing-steps and stared oddly at the girl so ill-clad against the fog-bound cold air. She was rapt in her own despair.

One man paused in his way to the palace door, checked, and then walked decisively towards her where she stood, arms folded on the wall in front of her, staring out, unseeing, over the brown expanse of the river. Fulke L'Estrange stripped off his fur-lined mantle and, turning her towards him, wrapped her securely within its folds.

'Demoiselle Janeta, are you trying to catch your death? What are you doing out here without your warm cloak?'

She stared at him uncomprehendingly then, despite her apparent lack of care for the inclemency of the morning, snuggled into the comforting warmth of the coney-fur lining.

He spoke again, gently but commandingly. 'Something is very wrong, Demoiselle Janeta. I was your mother's friend, remember? For her sake, will you not give me your confidence?'

Again she stared at him blankly, and then began to

weep. He put a firm hand beneath her arm and led her
back towards the palace.

She went with him obediently and found herself in a
window embrasure of the great hall. It was still far
from the central hearth and from the inadequate
braziers, placed at safe and strategic places near the
unshuttered windows in a vain effort to combat the
deadly chill and draughts of the place, but they were
out of the damp river mist now and he pulled her taut
form down on to the window-seat, tucking his cloak
more closely round her.

'Have you displeased the Countess? Did she berate
you or even strike you? She has the Plantagenet
temper, you know, and gives rein to it at times. It
means little. She has much on her mind. She will soon
get over it and regret she upset you. She is fond of you
and has much to thank you for.'

Janeta shook her head, her eyes filling with tears.

'Has she decided to leave you behind when she
departs for the Midlands? I thought she found your
services invaluable, but she must go in haste now and
will probably send for you within the next few days.'
He smiled broadly. 'You will not be parted long from
your Bertrand, I'm sure.'

She found her voice then, and told him what had
ruined her new-found happiness. They were apart from
the servants, busied laying the boards for breakfast,
and her whispers were hoarse with pain.

He sat silent for a moment. 'It occurred to me that,
perhaps, you were not aware. . . It will all come right,
you know. The King approved the match. He will not
wish to part with Simon. Though there will be scandal
and railing in Council Henry will have his way in the
end, and the marriage will, in due time, receive the
consent of the Curia.'

'I know that,' she said stiffly, 'but I will not be able

to forgive myself for *my* part in it, and I cannot continue to live within the favour of the Earl and Countess and profit from it.'

'And what says young Bertrand?'

'He is honoured by the Earl's patronage. His future is assured within the de Montfort household. He will stay with the Earl.'

L'Estrange was standing slightly in front of her, shielding her from the gaze of others within the hall. He tapped his thigh with one gauntlet thoughtfully.

'Your father will not be best pleased by this new decision of yours.'

'No.' Tremulously she said, 'I must return to the convent.'

'Don't you think that is a very precipitate decision? You are upset. You are not thinking clearly.'

'Bertrand has said as much and—besides——' she swallowed hard '—I do not know how I can get there without escort or help. . .' Her voice died away uncertainly and tears threatened again. She dashed them aside impatiently. How foolishly weak she must seem to this man. When she had stubbornly determined to leave St Catherine's she had not been so fearful. This would not do. She still had her mother's reliquary and—if the worst came to the worst—Roesia's brooch pin. They would provide the means for her to travel and she could ride now tolerably well—thanks to Bertrand's instruction. The thought of him threatened to wreck again her determination to be sensible.

'I would be perfectly willing to escort you,' L'Estrange said quietly, 'but first you must obtain the Countess's permission to absent yourself from her service. No——' he put up a hand to silence her as she made to protest '—leave that to me. You would not find it easy to find a convincing excuse in your present state, but I still think you are hastening to immure

yourself within convent walls too quickly. You need a
breathing-space and I believe I have the answer to that
as well. I have a cousin who has lodgings at present in
Thames Street, near to the bridge in the city. I could
take you there today. She would be delighted to
receive you. You would be company for her. She has
recently become a widow and is often lonely.'

'Sire, I could not put you to this trouble. You are
not responsible for me and, besides, if it is discovered
that you helped me run away from service it could
bring you into disfavour with the King. . .'

He laughed. 'My back is broad enough, Demoiselle
Janeta. For your sweet mother's sake I would be
honoured to be of service to you. Will you put yourself
in my hands?'

Her grey eyes sought his, troubled, then she gave a
little sigh and placed one icy cold hand in his. 'Yes,
sire, I will, and be ever grateful,' she said gravely.

'Good, then go to your chamber and collect your
belongings. I will make your excuses to the Earl and
his lady. They will both be too much occupied with
each other this morning to be over-concerned about
your behaviour. Meet me here soon after noon and I
will hire a ferry boat to take us downriver.'

She slipped, thankfully, from the shelter of his
mantle, stood up and curtsied. He bowed, his light
eyes twinkling encouragingly. She turned and looked
about her, as if saying farewell to this experience of
life among the great, turned back to him again with a
little rueful smile and hurried from the hall.

CHAPTER NINE

THE house where Fulke L'Estrange took Janeta proved to be amazingly small. Used as she was to palaces and the nunnery, she found it almost squalid.

He had been waiting for her as he had promised in the great hall when she returned to it at noon, clutching a canvas bag which contained her pitifully small collection of possessions. She had taken only a change of shift and one extra gown besides the one she was now wearing, that one in which she had left St Catherine's. The gifts given to her by the Countess, with the exception of the simplest and least valuable, which she carried with her, she had left in the small chest by her bed. She had decided to leave no message for Martha. The elderly nurse could not have read one anyway and would have been forced to find some clerk to decipher it for her and Janeta could have offered no explanation which could have been read by other eyes than theirs. Sir Fulke had sworn he would deal with her excuses and she trusted he would do that service for her faithfully. Fortunately she had encountered no one while she had packed hastily, and she had waited in a secluded corner of the hall until Sir Fulke had arrived to collect her.

It had been icy cold and damp in the ferry boat which carried them downriver and Janeta had had no heart to look about her or take in the sights. She had found the experience of passing through the fast current beneath the bridge-arch frightening, but L'Estrange, flashing her his bright blue smile, had assured her that the ferry-boat owners were experts in

190

dealing with the river hazards, tackling them every day of their lives as they did.

She had been startled by the gigantic size of the famous bridge and had stared wonderingly at the seemingly tumbledown hovels and shops which lined its thoroughfare. They had landed at the steps in Thames Street and Sir Fulke had taken her burden from her and led her immediately to his cousin's house. Like all the properties in the vicinity it was made of plaster and lath and was crowded in between a tavern on one side and another, slightly larger and more prosperous-looking building on the other.

A young maid had admitted them, wiping a dew-drop from her reddened nose. Janeta had thought the girl appeared slatternly, but she had been polite and even welcoming at the sight of Sir Fulke.

The small solar they were now taken to was dark, and at first Janeta could see little of her hostess, although it was still early in the winter afternoon. There was a small fire in the hearth which gave little real warmth but the voice of her hostess was pleasant enough and when she called for the candle to be lit Janeta saw Mistress Spooner, as Fulke L'Estrange announced his cousin, to be much younger than she had expected.

The room was sparsely furnished but there was arras on one wall to help keep out the draughts near the door; what furniture there was looked well-polished and the rushes upon the floor smelled reasonably fresh.

Sir Fulke hastened to his cousin's side and kissed her soundly upon the cheek while Janeta hung back uncertainly, feeling the curious gaze of the slatternly maid almost piercing her back.

'Avice, my dear, I have a favour to ask, and could send no word ahead of me.' He turned and indicated that Janeta should come near to the room's one chair, from which Mistress Spooner had risen. 'This is Demoiselle Janeta Cobham. She has been in service on the Dowager Countess of Pembroke but now finds herself in difficulties and, for reasons I would rather not mention, finds herself no longer able to remain in that household. I think I once told you I knew her mother and I would be eternally grateful if you would receive her into your house for the next few days. Then I will come again and we can reconsider her future. She has no other protector at this time.'

Avice Spooner was a tall, well-made woman of perhaps twenty-three or -four years of age, obviously considerably younger than her cousin. She was dressed in a fine woollen gown of brown wool with embroidery at neck and hem, and Janeta saw that she wore a gold chain round her neck. The gilded leather belt she wore was also studded with gold. Since she wore no mourning Janeta considered that her husband's passing had been at least a year ago. She had ample curves and her face was plump but pretty, her eyes light brown and a trifle protuberant. Her mouth was full and, when she smiled in welcome, Janeta saw that her teeth were rather large but still good and white. It was possible to see wisps of curling brown hair from beneath her veil, and the dimpled chin which rested upon the snowy crispness of her wimple would soon reveal a double line. Her plumpness would turn to fat in a few more years, but at present she was still remarkably handsome.

'Fulke, of course I am always willing to do you service, you know that. Come close to the fire, my dear. It is hard to keep out the chill on raw days like this. Gytha——' this to the serving-wench '—bring bread and meat and mulled ale.' She indicated a stool near her chair. 'Please sit, demoiselle. Fulke, must you return to Westminster today? At least stay and take supper with us.'

'I'll be glad to do that but I must return to Westminster again before morning.' He hesitated, looking meaningfully at the maid until she had sidled out. 'There is some general disquiet at Court and I should be near to His Grace in case he should have need of me.'

Avice Spooner's pencilled brows rose in interrogation. 'There has been no attack on the King?'

'No, no, nothing of a dangerous nature, but much gossip and back-biting.' He made a disclaiming gesture. 'As usual there is friction between one or two of the barons in Council.' His eyes met those of Janeta fleetingly, a glance which was not lost on Avice Spooner, whose brows rose again, but she forbore to comment. Fulke L'Estrange smiled at his cousin engagingly. 'It does me no harm to be found to be staunch for the King at these difficult times. In a couple of days the matter in dispute will be forgotten and the furore will blow over. I shall be back then and we can discuss what is best to be done for Demoiselle Janeta.'

His remarks to Mistress Spooner, Janeta felt sure, had been made with the intention of reassuring her that all would be well but when, after a hasty meal, he left, she felt completely bereft.

Her hostess yawned and rose. 'You must be very tired. As I'm sure you've noticed, this is but a small house and I'm afraid it will be necessary for you to share my bed. Gytha, my one serving-maid, sleeps on a truckle near by, so I cannot offer you a private space but I'm sure you will find the accommodation comfortable enough—though,' she added rather slyly, 'I suppose, living within the vicinity of the great ones of the land, you are used to better things.'

'I—I—thank you,' Janeta stammered. 'I hope I do

not put you out—I have frequently been asked to share
my chamber with others. Palaces are very bleak and
crowded. . .'

The light brown eyes flashed a little and Janeta
wondered uneasily if the woman was envious of her,
but dismissed the thought instantly as Mistress
Spooner's manner again became pleasant and she
assured Janeta she would cause her no undue trouble.

Janeta followed her hostess up the stair and thought
ruefully that she had indeed often shared a chamber,
but never before a bed. If Mistress Spooner was to see
her disfiguring mark would she still be willing to offer
shelter to her cousin's protégée?

It seemed, however, that Mistress Spooner was
economical with candles and prickets, for there was
only one small taper alight on the chest by the bed and
Janeta was thankful to undress hurriedly by its dim
light and scramble into the bed before Avice Spooner
had an opportunity to see her form clearly.

As she took her place beside her visitor, Avice
Spooner gave her a shrewd glance, which made
Janeta's cheeks burn. Fulke L'Estrange had murmured
something to his kinswoman at the door before leaving.
Just what reason had he given for Janeta's need to
leave the royal household? Could it be possible the
woman believed she was with child, so often the reason
for some unprotected woman to be abandoned by her
mistress? Janeta trembled in the darkness as she considered that. If Mistress Spooner entertained such
thoughts of her, did the woman think Sir Fulke
L'Estrange held himself responsible for Janeta's
welfare?

Gytha, the serving-wench, could be heard moving
about the house extinguishing lights and ensuring that
bolts were drawn across the doors.

Not for the first time Janeta found it almost impossible to sleep. Gytha snored noisily on the truckle pulled out from beneath their bed and established next to Janeta's side, so close that she could reach out and touch the girl. Avice Spooner's even breathing soon told Janeta that she slept soundly.

The street outside was uncommonly rowdy. She could hear footsteps constantly passing by on the cobbles, laughter and raised voices. The tavern next door appeared to accommodate its customers throughout the night. After falling finally into an uneasy doze Janeta was wakened early by the clanking of the iron wheel-rims of carts on their way to the nearby Chepe, or to the river wharves, and later the throaty cries of apprentice lads from the shops lining London Bridge, and the calls of the ferrymen already plying their crafts through the dangerous currents of the bridge-arches.

It was all so unfamiliar and daunting. As she lay waiting for Mistress Spooner to rouse Janeta began to question her presence here. Though the woman had given no real sign, Janeta was convinced that Avice Spooner resented her presence in this house and would only have consented to receive her under pressure from Fulke L'Estrange. Janeta pondered on the thought. Had Fulke L'Estrange some hold over the woman? Perhaps he contributed to her keep. Certainly, though the house was small and economies were made—and Janeta was soon to observe those measures—Avice Spooner gave no sign of being in straitened circumstances. Had her deceased husband been of the knightly class? If so she would surely have been addressed as Lady Spooner? Yet, if not, was it likely she would be a kinswoman of Sir Fulke, whom Janeta understood to be reasonably wealthy? His clothes proclaimed him so and he would have needed considerable gold to establish himself comfortably at Court.

For the first time, while she lay watching the pale,

wintry sun move across the horn window opposite, she began to assess what little she knew about her protector. He had told her he had been squire to the late King and she judged him to be near forty years of age, though she thought he looked much younger. There was no trace of silver about his temples and he bore himself like a young man in the full flush of youth. None had dared to withstand him on the tournament field when giving judgement, so she concluded his prowess in the lists was well-known. Had he been married? There had been no talk of a wife and she realised she had been over-hasty in not establishing that fact for herself before entrusting her person to him. He had been kind and amusing, also gallant, but uneasily she recalled how her father had obviously detested him and had warned her against him. Had she been too trusting? She knew nothing of the woman in whose charge he had left her. Suppose Avice Spooner defied his wishes and threw her out into those crowded, stinking streets outside?

Betrand D'Aubigny made haste about his errand in Leicester and set off back to Odiham the moment it was concluded. Fortunately the weather favoured good progress, it being cold but dry, and the snow had not fallen again. Saladin did not founder on the hard mud of the road and Bertrand was thankful to ride into the courtyard of the Lady Eleanor's manor-house on the evening of the fourth day following her wedding to Simon de Montfort. He had finished the task set for him and now he was eager to ask permission to withdraw from the Earl's service so that he could rejoin Janeta and persuade her to forgive his seeming indifference to her distress. The Earl had been untold good to him; it had been necessary to do him this final service.

The Countess's steward informed him that the Earl and his lady were even now finishing supper in the great hall and his sniff of disapproval told Bertrand that he had little chance of being admitted to the Earl's presence until he had at least set to rights his appearance.

'My lord did instruct me,' he said icily, 'that you were expected and that I was to inform him as soon as possible of your arrival. A chamber has been put at your disposal. I will find a manservant to conduct you there immediately and I will see to it that food is provided very quickly. You must be both weary and hungry after the journey. I will give strict instructions about the care of your horse. The Earl explained how valuable the animal is. . .'

'I've seen to that myself,' Bertrand replied imperturbably, 'and reinforced the order with a flea to the groom's ear. He wasn't sufficiently anxious to please or respectful enough. I think he has understood my meaning now, but I think if orders are received from you that should see to it that my wishes are not ignored. I have little time now to go there and discover for myself if Saladin is comfortable and rested.'

The steward bowed and signalled for a young serving-lad to come forward. He whispered in the boy's ear and the lad shot round to face Bertrand, his eyes very round with wonder. He was a tow-headed, sturdy youngster but, unlike the surly groom, he seemed more than ready to please.

He led Bertrand to a small chamber set into the thickness of the wall of the north tower, sketched a hasty bow and retreated, promising to return very quickly with food and wine.

This manor had been given to the Countess by the King and she had chosen to spend a great deal of her time here following her first husband's death. Bertrand had had little opportunity to see much of it but the place looked comfortably appointed and snug enough. He wondered if Eleanor would regret leaving its welcoming familiarity for the more northern castle of Kenilworth, Henry's wedding-gift to the couple.

The boy came, as promised, and Bertrand, after a hasty wash, changed into fresh garments so that the Countess's royal nose would not be offended by the stink of horseflesh and the dust and gathered grime of the journey.

He was sent for almost immediately he had concluded his meal of broth, roast meats and manchet bread, swilled down with good, refreshing ale. Thankfully he descended the stairs again in the boy's wake and at a run. The sooner he delivered his report, the sooner he could receive news of Janeta and be off again to find her.

He was conducted to the small solar behind the great hall. Eleanor was seated in a cushioned chair by the blazing fire with Simon standing behind her, his arm laid across the carved chair-back.

'Welcome, Bertrand. We had not expected to see you quite so soon.'

Bertrand advanced and dropped to one knee before the new Countess of Leicester. Graciously smiling, she extended a hand for him to kiss.

'I hope you have not killed your fine stallion, Sir Bertrand, glad as we are to have you returned to us so quickly.'

'No, my lady. Saladin has stamina and I take good care of him. It makes for more speed in the long run.'

She nodded and half turned her head to look at her lord.

'You delivered my command? It will be executed with dispatch?' said the Earl urgently.

'I made it very clear how necessary speed was, my

lord. The steward assured me that the sum you require
will be provided within the week and that he will issue
instructions for trees to be cut down in the woodland
to the south of Leicester town. The cost of the felled
timber will provide you with yet more gold to add to
that immediately available.'

Simon smiled bleakly. 'I expect you were received
less than cordially. I'm sorry that I must call so soon
on my newly acquired earldom and manor lands but,
since you left, my need for funds has become even
more urgent.' He moved to seat himself on a chair
opposite his countess and waved Bertrand to a faldstool near by. 'Sit man, sit; you must be near
exhausted.'

Bertrand did as he was bid. He had learned not to
stand on ceremony in the Earl's presence when it was
not required. He frowned slightly in enquiry at the
Earl's final statement.

'You will dispatch messengers for Rome so quickly,
my lord?'

Simon grimaced, his dark brows drawing together in
a frown.

'I feel it necessary to go myself. It is imperative I
plead my cause in person. I regret I must leave my
countess so soon but it cannot be helped. I shall
establish her at Kenilworth within the next few days
and then make arrangements to travel.'

Bertrand was surprised. The roads would not be
easy to travel before spring, especially through the
mountainous Alps from France into Italy. He had
thought there would be months yet before his master
would need to set out. Eleanor sighed deeply and
Bertrand sympathised with a bride left so abruptly.

Simon's expression was very grim. 'You are aware,
of course, that I have enemies at Court, and I have
always feared they would turn the King against me.

The Queen is hostile towards my family. I can understand that, but it seems someone has been pouring
more poison into her ears. She informed the King that
one of the ladies newly come to Court—and I think
here, Bertrand, you will be astonished—the Lady
D'Aubigny, told her that she was sure I had seduced
my lady Eleanor before marriage. It is a foul lie. My
lady would never have allowed anything so dishonourable, especially in the circumstances of her vow, but
mud sticks, and the King is furious. He has dismissed
me from Court and told me, roundly, that he is no
longer willing to support my pleas to the Pope. I had
intended to remove Eleanor from Court but I did not
expect such condemnation from the King. It will make
our cause far more difficult. I shall need all the gold I
can muster and, as I've said, it necessitates my leaving
for Rome in person.'

Bertrand looked from one to the other of them in
mystification.

'You say my brother's wife, Roesia, has accused you
both of misconduct?'

'So I am informed.'

'Why should she do such a thing, and what evidence
could she possibly put forward for such an accusation?'

The Earl shrugged. 'As to why she should do it, I
cannot imagine. Unless it was to curry favour with the
Queen. Evidence?' He pursed his lips. 'Apparently she
talked of messages sent to Winchester Castle by
Eleanor through Demoiselle Cobham, which is true,
unfortunately. However, they were merely letters of a
purely private nature, speaking of our feelings for each
other and our longings to be joined in wedlock. The
final message from Eleanor informed me that she had,
at last, obtained Henry's acceptance of our need and
that he would make arrangements for a private
ceremony at the chapel in Westminster palace. There

was never any suggestion that there had been intimacy between us and I swear there was not until the night we were joined by the King's chaplain and you yourself helped to prepare me for my wedding-night.'

'I cannot think why Roesia should maliciously go to the Queen with such a tale.' Bertrand checked and his lips tightened. 'Unless. . .?'

'Unless. . .?'

'The day you prevented her from carrying me off to Morris's lodging. . . She must have been choked with fury.'

'She has deep feelings for you, my friend?'

Bertrand nodded slowly. 'There was never any chance that her father would consent to a match between us. He knew that I had no fortune. His choice had to fall upon Morris.' He averted his face and said through his teeth, 'In all events I never gave her encouragement. I could never have loved her.'

'Did you make that plain?' The Earl's question was posed in a somewhat harsh tone.

'I thought I had—though I had no wish to hurt her. The problem was growing daily and, for that reason, I left the manor precipitately.'

'But she had hopes you would remain and serve your brother?'

'Possibly.' Bertrand's tone was uneasy. 'Roesia is self-willed and—vain. Morris is besotted with her.' He broke off and chewed at a ragged thumbnail. 'To be honest, I see little happiness for him ahead, but I was powerless to prevent the marriage and I could not tell him why. . .'

'Just so.' The Earl gave a little snort of agreement.

'So you think she wished to make mischief for Janeta too?' the Countess asked.

Bertrand sighed. 'It is certainly likely. They met once or twice at the castle, when Morris brought her to enquire after my condition following the tournament. Roesia is a jealous creature and wished to strike back at those whom she saw as thwarting her wishes. You did, my lord, in your determination to keep me at the castle, and she probably divined, correctly, my love for Janeta.'

The Earl stretched his long legs to the hearth blaze. 'And a woman thwarted in love can be dangerous indeed. Well, we can do little about it now.'

Bertrand frowned. 'I cannot understand how Morris came to present her to the Queen. It is true he came to Winchester for the crown-wearing, as did many of the barons, but he is not in favour and. . .'

'He was encouraged in his ambitions, it seems, by Fulke L'Estrange, who unaccountably befriended your brother and, if you remember, brought him to the tournament and provided him with a seat in the royal stand.'

Bertrand bit his lip uncertainly. 'He saved our lives on that fatal day, my lord.'

'Did he, indeed?' The Earl enquired blandly, and met Bertrand's surprised glance with a little cynical smile. 'Oh, yes, my friend, I have come to believe that L'Estrange may very well have engineered that attack on us—on me, actually, but he knew you would come to my assistance, so that business was also meant to place you in mortal danger.'

'You believe him to be your enemy, my lord?'

'No, Bertrand, I believe him to be yours. He did come to the rescue finally, it is true, but only after you had been badly wounded and after the King demanded action. The Chevalier d'Honneur was astonishingly tardy, indeed downright negligent. Does it not occur to you that he was instructed to be so?'

Bertrand's amazement was growing by the moment. 'I do not understand, my lord. How can so wealthy and important a baron such as Fulke L'Estrange wish to injure one so insignificant as myself?'

'Perhaps you have one treasure he covets?' Simon's smile was broad and Eleanor leaned forward to look intently at him.

Bertrand blinked uncertainly, then his brown eyes glistened with a warm golden light. 'Janeta?'

'Just so. Janeta. Haven't you noticed how closely he watches her?'

'But the man is old. . .'

'Ho, ho,' Simon laughed. 'How quickly the young come to make such an unfair judgement. L' Estrange is by no means old—hardly forty yet, and still in the prime of life. He was recently widowed. Janeta is very beautiful, innocently fresh and youthful.'

'But she has no significant dowry.' Betrand's tone was anguished.

'Be easy, my friend. I have it on good authority that Sir Hugh Cobham detests L'Estrange. He treated him very coldly whenever they met; I doubt if he would consider giving his daughter to Fulke, despite costly inducements. And, while we are talking of the lady, I assume you can tell us where she is?'

The Countess's bright blue eyes were fixed on him and Bertrand began to feel sweat trickle uncomfortably down his back. 'Yes, I am very worried about her, Sir Bertrand. No one appears to have seen her since my wedding-night. Martha has been searching for her but she appears to have disappeared from the palace of Westminster. In the end we were forced to depart without her.' She hesitated and looked searchingly at Bertrand. 'I wondered if she could have gone with you—but that seemed unlikely. It would have been an immodest action and Janeta, convent-bred as she is. . .'

Bertrand blinked, trying to think rapidly of what explanation he should give.

'Didn't she request permission to leave your service, my lady?'

Eleanor's deep blue eyes widened. 'She spoke of doing so, to you?'

Bertrand's discomfort grew. He looked towards the Earl, as if for guidance in his dilemma. At last he said slowly, 'Yes, my lady. We spoke together briefly—after—after the marriage ceremony——'

'You quarrelled?' The Earl's question was sharp.

'Yes, my lord.'

'About what?'

'She—she wished me to leave your service and—and—I could see no reason why I should do that.'

'Why should Janeta wish to take such a step? I thought she was happy to serve me?' Eleanor's tone was high with surprise and indignation.

Bertrand swallowed and avoided her intense blue stare.

'She discovered——Lady Sandford told her of—of the vow you both made—and she—she—was distressed. She felt she was partly responsible for helping you to break—— She blamed herself, and. . .'

'Ah.' The single syllable was whispered, and expressed all the sadness of the situation. 'I see. I was not sure—if—if she knew. I suppose I took advantage of her innocence and I have to take into account her sense of outrage, coming so lately from St Catherine's as she had.'

'She left St Catherine's because she could not take such binding vows herself, my lady. I could not see why she should be so condemnatory and told her so. I refused to remove her from Court. . .'

'And have felt guilty about that ever since,' the Earl said quietly.

'Yes, my lord. I made haste about the errand, and was about to request permission to withdraw from your service. I find that I cannot imagine life without Janeta and, sorry though I shall be to leave you, I. . .'

'Yes, I understand. I should. I love just as deeply as you do.'

There was a brief silence, then Eleanor said worriedly, 'Then if she is not with you, where is she?'

Bertrand blurted out, 'I cannot believe she would leave you, my lady, so discourteously. I know how she loved you and, even if she feared to face you, I'm sure she would have left a message. I cannot think what happened. Could she have gone south to her father's manor?' He blanched at the thought. 'How could she have travelled unescorted and penniless. Anything could have happened to her on the road.'

All three exchanged anxious glances.

The Earl said thoughtfully, 'Since the matter concerned her religious principles, could she have returned to the convent?'

'It would seem likely.' Eleanor's eyes narrowed as she considered. 'Though she was so very determined not to enter the noviciate.'

'Would Cecily Sandford know?' The Earl's voice was cold.

'I do not think so. We had a frank talk. Cecily wishes me well but cannot approve my decision. She has retired to her own dower-house. She said nothing to me of Janeta. If she had determined to take her with her, or knew anything of her whereabouts, I'm sure she would have told me.'

Bertrand said eagerly, 'Have I your leave to go to St Catherine's, my lord?'

'Certainly. I suggest you leave at first light. I was about to request you stay with my lady Eleanor at Kenilworth, but I shall settle her there. Your first priority is to find Janeta. In spite of her objections to our marriage, we have much to thank her for. Find her, Bertrand, and assure her that we will make some arrangements for your future together and she will not have to live within our household if her religious scruples forbid it.'

'Thank you, my lord.'

'Tell her I understand,' Eleanor said softly, 'and beg her to try and forgive me for involving her in what she considers sinful behaviour.'

'I am sure she does realise now why you did what you did, my lady. It is just that——' Bertrand gave a bleak little smile. 'Bless you both for understanding our need.'

'Could we do less when we have such need for understanding ourselves?' Simon said, smiling.

'Go soon, Bertrand, and send us news as quickly as you can. I shall continue to worry about Janeta.' Eleanor held out her hand for him to kiss in dismissal.

He bowed low, kissed the small white hand, saluted his lord, left the solar and went instantly back to his own small chamber.

Janeta chafed continually against boredom and gnawing anxiety while she waited for Fulke L'Estrange's return to the house in Thames Street. She soon found she had nothing whatever in common with Mistress Spooner and avoided her company whenever possible, though that was difficult in the extreme as the house was so small.

Constantly she thought of Bertrand and, on the rare occasions when she was alone, the tears flowed unrestrained down her cheeks. How could she face life without him? Had she been unfair to expect him to leave service where his future was assured simply to accommodate her narrow views? Where was Bertrand now? He had been about to set off on an errand for the Earl of Leicester. Had he returned by now, and did he miss her unbearably as she did him?

No news from Court filtered down to her and she had no way of knowing if the scandal of the Lady Eleanor's marriage had brought her into disrepute with the common people or if Simon de Montfort had been forced to leave Court with his new bride. She knew it would be months, possibly even years before a dispensation could be obtained, but she also knew, with a new-found shrewdness gained by living at Court, that the Pope, eventually, would grant it. The damage had been done, the couple bedded. Simon would pay a suitable bribe and the two would resume their lives in public view without criticism. Soberly Janeta faced the facts. Doubtless Bertrand had been right; the marriage of the Countess of Leicester and her deliberate breaking of sacred vows was no concern of commoners. The fact that she, Janeta, felt blameworthy could not be put aside so easily. Penance was necessary and could only be made within the confines of St Catherine's.

Avice Spooner appeared to be totally incurious about the reason for Janeta's presence in her household. She had little conversation, went out frequently on errands into the town, where Janeta was not invited to accompany her, and gossiped with her maid more than she did with Janeta. More and more Janeta became convinced that the woman was no gentlewoman. Her clothes were gaudy and her manners coarse. Janeta was often glad to have the woman gone from the house and be spared Avice Spooner's amused scrutiny. It was almost as if she was aware of some secret unknown to Janeta, and a distinct feeling of unease began to grow in the latter's consciousness.

Janeta was profoundly relieved, then, ten days later, when Fulke L'Estrange presented himself once more in Thames Street. He was jovial as always, greeted Avice Spooner warmly, kissing her soundly on both cheeks, then lifted Janeta's hand to kiss the palm respectfully.

'I regret I was forced to absent myself for longer than I intended but, as you can guess, affairs have been somewhat chaotic at Court, and the King was loath to lose my attendance.'

Janeta withdrew her hand, her eyes on Avice Spooner. 'I did not expect you to put yourself out for me, sir, let alone bring yourself into disfavour. I have no claims on you. I am grateful for your kindness. Mistress Spooner has been put to no little discomfort by having me here and I hope you bring me news of some arrangement by which I might leave for St Catherine's very soon.'

He laughed. 'Now, demoiselle, you sound as if you are anxious to leave us.'

'No, no, sir, you mistake my meaning.' She was confused by his teasing manner. 'Mistress Spooner has been a kind hostess but—but I am sure she will be glad to be relieved of an uninvited guest.'

'You are *my* guest, demoiselle.' There was an edge to his voice she found vaguely discomfiting though his eyes continued to smile. 'However, as you say, you are anxious to leave London. I can understand that. I have been busy on your behalf. You will be glad to learn that we shall journey south tomorrow. There——' He tilted up her chin. 'That brings a light back to your eyes.'

'We?' Janeta turned, puzzled, to face Avice Spooner. 'Does Mistress Spooner travel with us?'

'Yes, you will need a female companion. Avice is perfectly prepared to accompany you. I have asked her to do so.' Again there was that faint note of steel in his tone.

'But the weather is bad—I'm sure Mistress Spooner would prefer to remain near her own hearth; I could not put her to so much trouble. . .'

'Would you arrive at St Catherine's without a woman companion? Would your nuns be pleased to receive you so compromised?'

She was not sure if he was still teasing her. She flushed darkly. 'No, I suppose not. My father would— would be displeased. I had not thought. . .' Her words trailed off lamely. He was right, of course, yet she would have been more happy to see the back of Avice Spooner and that slatternly maid of hers.

She was up at first light and impatient to leave. Fulke L'Estrange chided her gently for refusing to break her fast.

'So eager to be rid of us? Come, sit down and eat. The journey is long and the cold will bite further into your bones if you don't take the opportunity to eat while you can.'

Because she saw it would be impossible to hasten him she obeyed him, and forced down bread, meat and ale, though she feared they would choke her.

L'Estrange had provided her with a gentle palfrey and a more skittish riding-horse for Avice Spooner. Obviously the woman rode well and had accompanied him on several journeys. Janeta was relieved to find that the maid, Gytha, was to be left behind to keep the Thames Street house. That wench's barely concealed insolent arrogance had almost unnerved Janeta.

L'Estrange's tantalising manner was laid aside as they prepared to depart. Once more he seemed the kindly, considerate friend she had learned to trust at Westminster. As she came down the stair with her bundle of clothing he held out a fur-lined and hooded brown travelling-mantle of softest wool.

She shook her head, unwilling to be in debt to him any further.

'Truly, sir, you have been too good to me already. I am warmly clad and I would not wish to reach St Catherine's too richly attired. They would frown on such extravagance.'

'Nonsense. I refuse to travel worrying about you every step of the way. Your father would wish me to see to it that you are properly equipped. If it is the thought of debt which concerns you, I'm sure he will fully reimburse me. You can don your nunnish weeds once we get to your convent. In my charge you will do as I say. Please?' The final word, couched as a humble request, took from the order any sting, and reluctantly she stripped off her simple homespun cloak and donned the one he offered. Mistress Spooner, she noticed, was warmly and stylishly clad in a hooded cloak of scarlet wool. L' Estrange, as usual, was dressed flamboyantly, also in scarlet trimmed with gold braid.

A sizeable escort of ten men-at-arms was drawn up outside the house when they emerged, and Janeta was somewhat startled by the sight. Though she had known Fulke L'Estrange at Court, and had noted the magnificence of his apparel, she had not thought of him as a powerful baron, yet he had held the position of president of the tourney and was clearly in the young King's favour.

Fulke lifted both women on to their mounts and Janeta was grateful for Bertrand's loving instruction as she rode confidently, with L'Estrange on her left and Avice Spooner on her right. Six of the men-at-arms rode ahead and four fell in behind.

As they journeyed Fulke L'Estrange pointed out to Janeta several notable buildings and sights. Avice Spooner was not addressed and appeared to have little to say. Janeta wondered if the woman was angered by being forced into service as companion for this protégée of her cousin. If so, she showed no sign of it. Indeed, at all times she seemed perfectly willing to fall in with Fulke L'Estrange's plans. He had said, 'You are *my* guest,' in the London house. Did he own it? Janeta's curiosity concerning Avice Spooner's position in L'Estrange's household was growing daily. Once they arrived at St Catherine's would Fulke's cousin tamely accompany him back to London again? Was she content to remain in the background rather than press for her cousin to present her at Court?

When they turned west towards Windsor Janeta began to remember the journey from Winchester to Westminster. How high all their hopes had been then, and Bertrand had been riding beside her. In a few days now she would find the convent walls close round her, and Bertrand would be finally lost to her.

She was surprised when the party struck off the main road and turned south near Guildford. They had not passed through the town on their way from Winchester, but possibly Sir Fulke had made plans to rest for the night somewhere he knew well. He had fallen silent over the last hour, believing her wearied. She moved awkwardly in the saddle. She certainly would be glad of a break; she was becoming very stiff and her bones ached. She stole a glance at Mistress Spooner to see if she was showing any signs of fatigue. As if she was aware of the scrutiny, she turned her gaze full on Janeta, and the cold intensity of it made Janeta suddenly shiver.

'The wind has changed again. You will be glad to get indoors,' Sir Fulke said. 'It will not be long now before we can rest and enjoy a good meal. At least I hope one is waiting for us. I sent ahead with strict instructions to expect us.'

'Then you know the innkeeper?' Janeta smiled at him to reassure him that she was capable of riding for some hours yet if needful.

Sir Fulke grinned broadly at Avice Spooner. 'Oh, yes, we both know the proprietor well.'

Mistress Spooner joined in with that tinkling, unnatural laugh Janeta found irritating and somewhat frightening, though she could not have said why.

'Oh, yes, Demoiselle Janeta.' Avice Spooner addressed her for the first time since they had embarked on the journey. 'The proprietor is well-known to us.'

One of the men-at-arms turned, as if he too enjoyed the joke.

Janeta was mystified and looked enquiringly at Sir Fulke. His lips were twitching as he brought his mount closer to hers. 'We go to my manor near Guildford, Demoiselle Janeta,' he explained. 'You will have every comfort there.'

'And be totally secure from the perils of the road,' Avice Spooner added.

'I did not know you owned a manor so close to Windsor,' Janeta said. 'You did not mention it when we journeyed in to Westminster.'

'No.' He was looking ahead and she could not gauge his expression. 'I think my mind was on other matters—and, of course, I was travelling in such bewitching company that it engaged all my attention.'

Janeta always felt uncomfortable when he paid her such fulsome compliments. If she had not been convinced that he was merely teasing her, she would have felt it necessary to remonstrate with him.

Another important question rushed into her mind.

'Sir Fulke?' she began hesitantly, uncertain how to put the question. 'I—have never discovered—I mean—

I do not know if——Will your wife be there to greet us?' she finished in an embarrassed rush.

'No wife,' he said, smiling. 'Mistress Spooner will be glad to play hostess. Alas, my wife died early last year.'

'I—I am truly sorry to hear that, sir.'

He gave a gusty sigh. 'She was never very strong. We lost child after child and the last attempt killed her.' Before she could ask he added, 'The child was stillborn, and she died three days after the birth.'

Janeta gave a little gasp of pity. So many women, she knew, died in childbirth or due to complications following the ordeal. She recalled Alice Smallthorpe at the nunnery and her confessed fear of such a fate. She had dreaded her coming marriage for that very reason and would have preferred to live out her life in the nunnery, had her father agreed, rather than suffer the fate of her own mother. Janeta smothered the thought that she was denying herself the possibility of bearing children by this determination to find sanctuary at St Catherine's.

Soon they were crossing the River Thames at Guildford, and Janeta shivered involuntarily as she recalled the tale one of the nuns had told of a terrible massacre perpetrated here by Godwin the Earl of Essex, when the followers of the Aetherling, Alfred, the brother of King Edward the Confessor, had been slain. The waters ran with blood, the nun said, as many were mown down in a deliberate act of treachery. Alfred had been taken and blinded and later died of his injuries. Edward had never forgiven the Godwins, not even when he had been persuaded, for political reasons, to marry Edith, the daughter of Earl Godwin. Janeta thought how terrible it must be to be pressed to marry for reasons of state. To avoid that Eleanor Plantagenet had taken a vow of perpetual chastity and broken it when it had suited her to do so.

She was lost in her own gloomy thoughts when Fulke
leaned across suddenly and took her bridle-rein.

'Ahead of you now, Demoiselle Janeta, the gatehouse of my home. Welcome to Grimsdell.'

She looked up eagerly and her fingers tightened
involuntarily on the rein so that she jerked it suddenly
and her mount sidled, unnerved by the abrupt movement. Sir Fulke steadied her hand and brought the
animal quickly under control again.

The house was much larger than she had supposed,
a moated manor of grey stone dominating the landscape. It stood on an artificially constructed small hill
and a huddle of small cots clustered near by. As they
rode up to the drawbridge chickens squawked and
scuttled out of the way of the horses' hoofs, dogs
barked and ran after the party, but no man or woman
came out of the squalid dwellings to view their lord
and his company. Soon they were clattering over the
rude wooden drawbridge and through the gatehouse
arch into the bailey. Janeta looked back at the dark,
still waters of the moat and shuddered. It seemed to
cut off the manor completely from the vill and field
strips outside and she felt more imprisoned than she
had within the walls of St Catherine's nunnery.

Grooms ran up to hold the horses. The men-at-arms
dismounted and their booted feet and iron spurs rang
on the hard-rutted dirt of the bailey. The place was a
miniature castle. A tower stood to one side, obviously
the only surviving part of an earlier building, a hall and
undercroft had been added later, of lath and plaster,
and stone steps led up to the hall entrance. Fulke lifted
Janeta down from her horse, refusing the assistance of
one of the grooms, and led her towards them, Avice
Spooner falling in dutifully behind.

A steward, an old man, clearly much in awe of Sir
Fulke, waited to greet them at the head of the steps.

He bowed his frail back and murmured almost incomprehensible excuses as Sir Fulke shouldered him impatiently aside and brought Janeta into the hall itself.

It was growing dark already and she peered uncertainly ahead into the gloom. Two sconces burned sootily near the fireplace set in the far wall, but she thought this was a very recent innovation for the roof was blackened by smoke from an earlier central hearth.

Sir Fulke's hand was beneath her arm and he drew her to the fire, which appeared to give little heat despite the fact that the logs were burning well. She thought perhaps the hall was little used when Sir Fulke was absent from Grimsdell.

Sir Fulke shouted impatiently to his steward to provide them with wine and pushed Janeta gently into the one chair near the hearth, leaving Avice Spooner standing.

'You must stay here for a while, take wine and warm yourself, then you would probably prefer to retire to the chamber prepared for you. I will order supper to be served to you there.'

Janeta thanked him and sipped gratefully at the mulled wine the steward brought for them all.

Sir Fulke bestrode the hearth, peering down into the flickering flames. 'Mistress Spooner will show you to your chamber. She knows it well.' He cast a smiling glance in her direction and her lips arranged themselves into an answering smile, though it did not reach her eyes, and Janeta again wondered if the woman resented being used as if she were a paid attendant to the visitor.

She was aching with exhaustion and glad when, at last, Sir Fulke signalled for Avice Spooner to lead the way to the guest-chamber.

A servant went ahead with a lighted sconce, leading

them up a spiral stair with a roped support into a
tower-room three floors above the hall level. He
entered the chamber and lighted the candle placed
ready on a chest near the bed. Janeta advanced and
looked about her. The walls were of stone, unlimed,
and two of them, were covered in arras, the subjects
of which she could not see since it was too dark in the
greater part of the chamber. The bed looked comfortable and she noted a truckle pulled out next to it.
There was a brazier near the unglazed high window
and, opposite, a tapestry-covered prie-dieu. The
accommodation was very good and Janeta would be
glad of that before the arduous journey the following
day. She removed her fur-lined mantle and laid it upon
the bed.

Avice Spooner was dismissing the servant, after first
ordering him to return with warmed water and towels.
She examined the chamber's appointments critically,
almost as if she was used to acting as mistress here.

'Well,' she said, with her somewhat hard smile, 'you
will have nothing to complain about during your stay
here. Everything of the best has been provided, as
instructed.' Her gaze went deliberately to the curtain-
hung bed. 'The lady of the house spent much of her
time here——' she paused, her eyes glinting maliciously
'—on the occasions when she did not share Sir Fulke's
bed, of course.'

'I suppose he was often absent, on the King's
business.'

'Yes, Fulke was often in London or Westminster.'

'His wife must have been very lonely at times.'

Avice Spooner's arched brows rose above her high-
ridged nose. 'I think she was, and sometimes I think
she was thankful to be.'

Janeta shot her an alarmed, enquiring look but the

woman shrugged and, laughing, began to remove her own mantle.

'Do not be afraid, my dear. I shall share your chamber tonight.'

Janeta turned away to hide her grimace. She would much rather have spent the night alone, even though there was something about this fortress-like manor-house which disturbed her. She dismissed the thought. It was rarely inhabited now by the master. Fulke, more than likely, preferred to stay well away from the house where he had lost his wife and babies. She must take care she did not speak again of his loss. After his period of mourning was completed, and it must be soon now, he would seek a new wife from one of the fashionable Court ladies and, in time, he would be more fortunate, and have the heir he doubtless longed for. She would pray for him at St Catherine's.

CHAPTER TEN

THE gate portress at St Catherine's nunnery peered at
Bertrand through the opening in the wicket and he
could tell by her expression that she was very perturbed
indeed. He was not surprised. He doubted if she was
ever again likely to be faced by a visitor so grim-faced
and clad in mail. She shook her head doubtfully.

'I will send your request to Reverend Mother, but
she may not be willing to see you. It is almost time for
Vespers.'

'I will keep her only for moments.' Bertrand pressed
his face close to the opening and the portress withdrew
a little, visibly even more alarmed.

He drew back instantly and she said, a trifle breathlessly, 'I will go and find a nun to send your message.
Wait there.'

The little window opening was slammed shut and
Bertrand was left outside the gate, slapping his thigh
impatiently with his riding-gloves. He had made good
speed, the weather being in his favour. If Janeta had
arrived here before him it could only be by a matter of
a day or possibly two. Despite the chill of the winter
day his upper lip was marked with a trail of sweat.
Surely she could have made no irrevocable decisions in
so short a time? He hoped it would have taken
considerably more time for the abbess to receive her
back, even if she had been prepared to, considering
the circumstances of Janeta's departure, and convince
herself that Janeta was now truly repentant and prepared to enter the noviciate. He had prayed desperately throughout the journey that he would find the

words to convince Janeta that he was genuinely sorry for his seemingly callous reception of her avowed intention to leave the Countess's service. He knew now that nothing, not even a life of constant wandering the towns and villages of England and Normandy following the tournament circuit, would prevent him from giving up everything the Earl was prepared to offer so that he could be with Janeta.

He turned, startled, as the wooden shutter on the wicket gate was opened and the portress addressed him, her manner flurried and hasty.

'I will let you in, sir knight, since you say your business concerns Demoiselle Janeta Cobham. The abbess is eager to hear what you have to say.'

The door swung open and Bertrand stepped through hastily. He hesitated only a moment, concerned at thought of leaving his prized Saladin unattended. The portress peered beyond him and saw the destrier.

'Bring your horse inside, sir knight. A groom will see him fed and watered in our stable.'

He walked Saladin after her black-clad form and was relieved when an old man emerged from one of the barn-like buildings near the cloisters and took charge of Saladin. The man ran a caressing hand down the courser's satiny black neck and Bertrand knew his favourite would be safe in such admiring company.

He was so concerned for news of Janeta that he hardly noticed the convent buildings as the portress led him to the abbess's lodging and admitted him to the parlour after a soft voice from within bade him enter.

The stately woman who faced him from a padded chair near the fire, her hand on the head of a seated greyhound, was younger than he had expected.

He felt suddenly awkward in the presence of so serene and pious a lady, and shuffled clumsily after making a quick half-bow.

'My portress did not quite hear your name, sir knight.'

The abbess indicated a faldstool where he could seat himself. 'Please, do sit. You appear to have travelled some distance. I am told you have news of our dear Janeta.'

He halted in the action of sitting down, rose again, and the stool fell. He turned and, trembling agitatedly, righted it. When he faced the abbess again he had regained some measure of composure.

'Do I take it, Reverend Mother, that Janeta is not here with you?'

'Why, no, sir knight. She left us somewhat abruptly just before Christmas. Her father eventually informed us that she was safe in the household of the Countess of Pembroke.' At this point her expression became severe, and Bertrand realised that, already, the news of the broken vow had reached the nuns here. He sighed.

'I am Sir Bertrand D'Aubigny, Reverend Mother. I—I was instrumental in obtaining the position for Demoiselle Cobham, and later became her riding instructor. I—— We became close—that is——'

'I think I understand, sir,' the abbess said, her grey eyes twinkling slightly. 'We have not totally withdrawn ourselves from the knowledge of the world. I can see by your earnestness that you have become extremely fond of Janeta. I take it her father approves?'

'Yes—no.' Bertrand felt himself intimidated by this stately, calm lady then, determinedly, he composed himself, drew himself up to his full height and said crisply, 'I love Demoiselle Janeta, Reverend Mother, and I believe she loves me. We have done nothing together which either of us might be ashamed to confess before a priest. I make no bones about the matter. I think you will have heard of the situation in the new Countess of Leicester's household. This marriage has upset Janeta and she determined to leave.'

'As suddenly as she left us?' The abbess leaned forward anxiously in her seat and the dog at her feet moved restlessly as it sensed her alarm.

'Yes, Reverend Mother. The Earl and Countess are concerned for her welfare as we have no idea where she went. I was sent to speak with her.'

The veiled head moved from side to side slowly. 'As yet she has not reached us, Sir Bertrand. I doubt if she would come here. . .'

'She told me she intended to.'

'Ah.' The single word conveyed swift understanding of Janeta's state of mind.

'How long ago was this?'

'Six days, Reverend Mother. Time enough for her to have reached you.'

'She was travelling alone, to the best of your knowledge?'

'That is what alarms us.'

'Of course.' The abbess frowned in thought. 'She left—Westminster?'

'Yes, Reverend Mother.'

'Then she might have decided to travel even further south to her father, though——' she sighed heavily '—I would not have thought that likely—for several reasons.'

He nodded, distracted. 'I will ride on there. We can but hope she decided to beg him for his help.'

'We have a guest-chamber. You should rest for the night.'

'Thank you, Reverend Mother, but I will press on now my horse is rested.'

She eyed him thoughtfully and nodded. 'I understand your haste. If—if Janeta should come here, you wish me to inform her of your visit?'

He went scarlet under her assessing gaze, then grinned. 'Please, Reverend Mother, I would be grateful if you would do that, and. . .'

'I will not allow her to take any irrevocable step until she is fully aware of the consequences and——' she smiled sweetly '—the alternatives.'

The abbess rose and extended her hand to him. He knelt and kissed the abbatial ring, then rose and bowed.

As he reached the door she said quietly, 'Let us know she is safe, sir knight. I understood long ago that Janeta had no real vocation, but we all grew to love her dearly and will pray for her safety and happiness.'

Bertrand nodded his head, his lips twisting a trifle ruefully.

'Thank you, Reverend Mother. Your prayers will help me find her, I'm sure.'

As he emerged into the grassy enclosure near the stable a young novice rushed up to him, holding out a spotless white linen kerchief and a leather bottle.

'The portress said you had ridden far, sir knight. Sister Boniface instructed me to see you had sustenance for your journey.'

He was touched by the simple kindness of these women and understood now, in some measure, why Janeta had determined to return to them. Here she had received the love and nurturing she should have obtained in her own home. He would have kissed the girl's rosy cheek in gratitude, but knew he must not. He contented himself with touching her work-worn hands gently and taking the food and wine-bottle from her. Already the groom was leading out Saladin.

''E's been well fed and watered, sir, but I'd beg you not to ride him too hard and far tonight. By the looks of 'im 'e's done yer fair service. To treat him 'arsh now may be to lose 'im.'

Bertrand stored food and wine in a canvas side saddle-bag. He had not stopped to burden himself with a sumpter. 'Thank you kindly, gaffer. He's a prized animal. If he founders I'll be further delayed. I'll take care, be sure of it.'

He mounted and rode towards the gate. In readiness the portress had opened it and waved him through. He wondered, grimly, how the news that their former pupil was in some dire trouble had spread so quickly among these women, but blessed them for their love.

He stayed the night in Winchester, mindful of the old groom's advice and knowing it to be sound, then he was on his way again at first light, following the directions for the Cobham manor one of the Earl's men had given him before he had left Odiham.

The place was larger, more imposing than he had expected. A half-ruined keep stood to the right of the main building and Bertrand supposed the Cobhams had dwelt there formerly and then, probably after the dangers and depredations of Stephen's reign, had abandoned it for the more comfortable stone-built manor-house. He had ridden through the village which clustered round the stone church with its sturdy Norman tower and noted cots and fields well-tended. It seemed that Sir Hugh oversaw much of the work here and left little to a bailiff or, if he did so, the man must be eminently trustworthy.

He did not expect to be welcomed and was not surprised when a haughty-faced young man, clad in a plain but fine woven tunic and cloak, emerged from what appeared, from the sounds emanating from it, to be the mews. On hearing his name, and in whose service he was, he ordered him abruptly to take himself off.

'I'm Ralph Cobham, Sir Hugh's son. My father has only recently returned from Court. We've heard the news of the Earl of Leicester's fall from favour and cannot say we are surprised, only puzzled it's taken so long. I can't imagine what purpose you can have in seeking out my father. He'll take no part in any Court squabbles, I can tell you. . .'

'Sir, my business concerns your sister, the demoiselle Janeta.'

The man's greenish eyes widened in utter astonishment. 'Janeta? But she's not been here since she was a child. . .'

'What is this?' Sir Hugh's harsh voice made both men turn, startled, as he stepped out from the stables. Like his son he was plainly but well clad in homespun wool tunic, riding-boots and cloak, its hood pushed back to reveal his dark, grey-flecked hair, and Bertrand thought both men had just returned, possibly from overseeing work on the demesne.

'You're D'Aubigny, in de Montfort's service, the man injured in the Christmas tournament. What is this about Janeta?'

He strode up to his son and their unexpected visitor, his brows drawing together in a scowl, whether of anxiety or fury Bertrand could not determine. He called imperatively for a groom to take charge of Bertrand's mount and snapped at his son, 'What are you thinking of not to offer this man food and ale? You'd best come into the hall, sir.'

He led the way up the stairs to the door above the undercroft, past the screens and into the hall. As Bertrand had surmised from his examination of the outside of the property, the hall was smaller than in older buildings, but equipped with side-hearths, snug and comfortable. The rushes were fresh-strewn and the arras on the walls and the furniture had recently seen careful attention. Sir Hugh Cobham was well-served.

He seated himself at the long table near the hearth and indicated brusquely that Bertrand seat himself on the bench opposite. Ralph Cobham, obviously feeling the weight of his father's displeasure, set about summoning servants to bring food and ale.

A young wench came running and supplied what was needed. Under his father's frowning gaze, Ralph read dismissal, and took himself off, the rigidity of his departing back revealing his annoyance at being rebuked so plainly before a stranger.

Bertrand downed a tankard of ale and looked up anxiously at his host.

'Your son indicated that he had not seen his sister for some years, Sir Hugh. I had hoped to find her here with you.'

Sir Hugh's frown did not lessen but he showed no astonishment. 'Then she has left the new Countess of Leicester?'

Swiftly Bertrand informed him of the relevant facts and Sir Hugh grunted.

'You say she left no messge for the Countess? That is unlike her. Both here and at the nunnery she was instructed well in courteous behaviour.'

'I know, sir, and we are all alarmed for her wellbeing.'

'You did not offer to escort her to St Catherine's where she expressed a desire to go?'

Bertrand's cheeks were stained with angry and shamed colour. 'I was on an important errand for the Earl and was not convinced she would leave Westminster without leave from the Countess. The moment I returned to his side, at Odiham, I intended to—— Well, no matter. What concerns me now is the need to find her. Anything might have befallen her on the road.'

'You say L'Estrange showed her marked attention during the journey to Westminster and afterwards?'

Bertrand's chin jerked up at the abruptness of the question. The Earl had spoken uneasily about L'Estrange's interest in Janeta. Now her father revealed the same concern.

'Yes,' he said slowly. 'He rode with her part of the way, as you, yourself, saw. He spoke to her of her mother, she told me. Naturally that piqued her attention. She did not know her own mother, sir, as you know well, and that must have aroused curiosity.'

Sir Hugh's dark eyes flashed with sudden fire and he muttered a soldier's curse half under his breath. Bertrand stared at him, astonished.

Sir Hugh rose, pushing back the bench so that it grated on the tiled floor. 'You think it possible she might have sought his help?'

Bertrand's eyes widened. 'I had not thought—but—yes, I suppose she might have done. She had little money, no mount; he might have offered. . .'

'Aye, likely so, and she would have trusted him. Women do,' he snarled viciously.

'Sir?'

'He has a manor near Guildford. We go there, sir knight, at once, after I've summoned men-at-arms to ride with us. I take it you wish to accompany me?' The question was barked.

'Aye, sir, if you believe—— But I confess I cannot understand why he should take her there, unless. . .'

'Aye, if he keeps here there long enough, willing or no, she will be forced to wed him.'

The colour drained from Bertrand's face. 'I'll kill him first.'

'Not so easy. He is a formidable opponent in fair fight, but he rarely fights fairly.'

He was shouting for attention again and a steward

came running, listened to instructions, and left the hall to call together the escort Sir Hugh demanded.

'I will arm myself. You'd best get what rest you can and finish your meal. We ride within the hour.'

Bertrand nodded. He called as Sir Hugh made to leave the hall, 'Sir, can I enquire why you suspect Fulke L'Estrange of such foul intentions? You have had dealings with him in the past?'

'Aye, lad, and he scarce more than a boy. He has grown in malignity and cunning since then, and his appetite for power has never diminished. He did me great wrong and I cannot forgive him. There are reasons why he would wish to wed Janeta, and not entirely for her bright eyes, reasons which you should know, since you appear to have a fondness for her.'

Sir Hugh turned back to him and his smile was not pleasant.

'Reasons which you shall know, soon now. Prepare yourself to ride. If she has been missing seven days we could be too late to prevent his purpose.'

Bertrand watched his departing back, as rigid as his son's, and swallowed sharp bile. So de Montfort had been right. L'Estrange's intended victim in the tournament had been he, Bertrand, and, worse still, his real prey was Janeta.

Please God the abbess's prayers would aid them now in their bid to free her from that man's clutches. He had not told Sir Hugh he was prepared to die for his daughter. The man had known that.

Janeta woke feeling decidedly unwell. Her eyelids seemed gummed up and there was a dreadful throbbing in her head. She struggled up against the pillows, determined that this sudden malaise should not keep her from rising and dressing immediately. She must not delay the start of the final leg of their journey to St

Catherine's. Despite her brave attempt, she was forced
to lie back against the pillows again and could only
croak an answer when there came a knock at her
chamber door.

A young serving-maid entered and tiptoed to the
side of the bed.

'Mistress Spooner sent me to see if'n you was feelin'
better, mistress.'

'Better?' Janeta forced her eyes to open and sat up
again. She stared groggily round the chamber. Strong
light was streaming through the unshuttered window
and it hurt her eyes so that she winced sharply, but she
knew at once that the day was well advanced.

'What time is it? Why did no one wake me?'

The girl's dark eyes rounded and she backed from
the sharpness in Janeta's tone.

'Mistress, we did try to wake you, but Mistress
Spooner said it looked like you'd taken a chill and
should stay in bed today. You wouldn't eat a thing I
brought, but Mistress Spooner said it best if you didn't
try till you felt better. I come up to see, mistress.' At
Janeta's imperious frown she addressed herself to her
first question and turned to the window. 'It be well
past noon, mistress. Will you be fit to eat supper in
hall? If'n so, I'll bring hot water and tend 'e. . .'

'After noon?' Janeta frowned in concentration, but
the effort hurt. How bright the light seemed! Her
throat was dry and she felt dizzy and weak. 'But what
of Sir Fulke? We were to set out at first light for the
Winchester road.'

The girl shook her head. She wore a kirtle of
homespun undyed wool and, over it, a brownish-purple
belted short tunic that Janeta thought was dyed with
blackberry juice. Her dark hair was mostly concealed
beneath an unbleached linen kerchief. Compared with
the slatternly Gytha, Avice Spooner's servant, this girl

was neatly turned out and her manner deferential, almost nervous, rather than surly.

'I dun know about that, mistress, but Mistress Spooner said as 'ow you was too ill to mount an 'orse and must bide in bed today.'

Janeta blinked and strove to think. Her head felt muzzy still and her eyelids so heavy, almost as if she'd been drugged with poppy cordial, as she had once been when a tooth had given severe pain at St Catherine's and the infirmarian had dosed her.

How strange, when she had felt exhausted and aching but not unwell last night when she had retired to bed. Aching! Had she taken a bad chill? She had put down the aches and pains she had suffered to the unaccustomed riding but it was possible that those very pains might have been the harbingers of the chill she appeared to be suffering from now.

'I'll get up now,' she said confidently, and swung her legs sideways, but she had overestimated her recovery, for the floor appeared to rush to meet her as she put her head down and sudden sickness threatened. She forced back the sharp bile which rose in her throat and lay back again.

'It seems Mistress Spooner was right. I have taken a winter chill,' she said weakly. 'I'm sorry, but I think I must stay where I am for a while longer.'

'Aye, mistress, best do that.' The girl's voice, with its southern country burr, was warm with sympathy. 'I'll fetch warm water and towels and bathe your face, then I'll go tell Sir Fulke and Mistress Spooner ye'll bide where you be for a bit.'

Janeta was glad of the girl's ministrations and lay back exhausted again, too queasy to think of food when the girl offered to fetch her some refreshment.

'Just a drink, please, nothing more. Perhaps some cool ale.'

'Aye, mistress.'

The girl scurried off and Janeta lay drifting in and out of sleep. She woke, startled, to find Avice Spooner looming over her with a goblet in one hand.

'It's as I thought, Fulke. It will be several days before she's capable of coming downstairs, let alone sitting a horse. Demoiselle Janeta, try and drink some of this. I added herbs I've found beneficial in the past for severe chills like this.'

Janeta found herself half lifted in the bed and recognised Fulke L'Estrange's tall figure as he supported her shoulders while Avice Spooner held the cold rim of the metal goblet to her lips. The wine was sweet and cloying, to cover the taste of the bitter herbs, Janeta thought tiredly. She murmured what sounded a thick-voiced apology for the trouble she was giving everyone, but Sir Fulke hushed her soothingly and Avice Spooner continued to press her to drink down the draught. She tried to smile her thanks and drifted off to sleep again.

When she woke she found the serving-girl seated on a stool by the bed, stitching industriously at what looked like a homespun shirt. She jumped up at once when she saw Janeta's eyes flicker open.

Janeta stared at her, striving to make out where she was and where she had seen this girl before.

'It's Eadgyth, mistress. I've been tending you over the last few days,' the girl said quickly.

Janeta pushed herself up in the bed, her eyes roaming the chamber.

'This is Sir Fulke L'Estrange's manor, isn't it?' she asked.

'Aye, mistress.' The girl's plump cheeks flushed with pleasure. 'Ye really are feelin' better. Ye've been most out of yer head these past few days.'

A sharp pain seemed to lance through Janeta's head as she moved it against the pillow but, despite that, she felt much clearer than she had the last time she had woken in this bed.

'I've been ill?' she questioned, and the girl nodded slowly. 'Oh, yes, I can just remember Mistress Spooner saying I had taken a chill and she gave me a cooling draught.'

'Aye, mistress.' There was a curious note in the girl's voice and Janeta's eyes followed hers to a filled goblet standing on a chest by the bed. She reached out to take it, but hastily the girl's strong fingers fastened on her wrist.

'If'n you be thirsty I'll get you some ale, mistress. I'll throw this away. It's been standing all night.' Her eyes seemed to implore Janeta and she added, 'I didn't give it to you last night, mistress. Ye'll not tell Mistress Spooner that ye didn't drink it?'

Janeta drew a hard breath and her eyes continued to hold those of the girl.

'No, I swear I will not,' she said hoarsely, and watched as the girl crossed the room and emptied the goblet from the open window, after first leaning out to assure herself that no one was below. She turned and gave Janeta a lop-sided smile, then hastened from the chamber only to return in moments with a leathern jack of ale.

Janeta drank thirstily and wiped her hand across her mouth.

'The reason why I can think better this morning is because I didn't take Mistress Spooner's draught?' She spoke very softly and the girl gave a hunted glance over her shoulder, then turned back and nodded.

'I think so, mistress.'

Janeta moved fretfully. She still seemed very weak but the muzziness had retreated and she felt less sick.

'Perhaps Mistress Spooner thought it best for me to sleep,' she prompted gently. 'Though,' she added, 'I'm glad I did not take the stuff last night for I do feel much better.'

The girl's expression was becoming more frightened and Janeta leaned towards her and caught at her hand.

'I will repeat nothing you tell me, Eadgyth. Why were you so anxious I should take no more of it? Please, you must tell me, and quickly before someone else comes.'

'She—Mistress Spooner—tended my lady Maud.'

It was out, and so simple a remark, so bald a statement that Janeta felt the chill of it raising the hairs on the back of her neck. Her fingers tightened on the girl's.

'I loved 'er.' The words were stubbornly spoken.

Janeta said softly, 'I think I understand what you dare not say, Eadgyth. Thank you for trying to help me. I was ill, surely?'

The girl's sturdy shoulders were lifted in a shrug and her eyes now avoided those of Janeta.

'You are warning me that I was deliberately kept here?'

This time Eadgyth made no answer, but looked stolidly back at her.

'But why?' The words were whispered as Janeta tried desperately to find an answer to that question herself.

Suddenly she knew, as if some hidden truth had been revealed to her, that Fulke L'Estrange had had no intention from the beginning of taking her to St Catherine's. She had had a strange presentiment when they had crossed the ford at Guildford but she had put down the sudden warning fear to the tales of the terrible things which had happened there. Now she knew her feelings had been deepened on first sight of

L'Estrange's fortress. He had brought her here for his own purpose and she had foolishly put herself into his hands, so trustingly, because she had been so upset by her quarrel with Bertrand and her disappointment at the way the Lady Eleanor had used her. She had been vulnerable, and L'Estrange had recognised it and decided to turn that to his own advantage.

She lay back, gathering her strength, steadfastly determined to drink and eat nothing which Eadgyth did not herself prepare and serve to her. The terrible questioning went on within her mind. What purpose had Fulke L'Estrange for her? Her father had shown openly his detestation of the man. Had he been subtly warning her to be on her guard? But then she had nothing but gratitude for L'Estrange for his rescue of Bertrand and the Earl. Now the thought hit her with devastating realisation. Had L'Estrange in fact saved them? He had been in charge of that tournament from the beginning.

She saw Eadgyth start nervously and move from the bed as mailed feet could be heard ascending the tower stair. She motioned the girl to silence and pointed to the stool where she had originally been sitting.

The door was thrown open and Fulke stepped into the chamber, Avice Spooner behind him. Janeta caught that sudden glitter of light in his eyes as he saw that she was fully awake.

'Ah, Avice, our guest is herself again.'

Janeta said nothing, nor did she smile in welcome.

Avice Spooner came to the bedside and put a hand to Janeta's forehead. 'No fever,' she pronounced, then questioned, 'You are feeling better, Demoiselle Janeta?'

'Much better.' Deliberately Janeta kept any coldness from her tone, recognising the need for caution in her dealings with these two. 'So much so that I am sure I shall be fit to travel in the morning.'

Fulke L'Estrange said evenly, 'I should not be too venturesome. We should not overtax your strength too soon.' He was smiling, his lips stretched wide, but the geniality did not reach his eyes. Janeta felt a sudden revulsion against his presence in her chamber. Her flesh crawled. Carefully she did not look at Eadgyth, but she remembered the unspoken words which had hinted at a sinister purpose for his desire to have Avice Spooner tend his invalid wife. Was the woman his mistress? The idea jolted at her consciousness and she recalled the feeling she had had about Avice Spooner, that she was no true gentlewoman. The Lady Maud had failed to give L'Estrange an heir. Had he no longer had any need for her? Had she been an heiress, her dowry long spent, and his need for fresh funds pressing? He was always so elaborately dressed. An ailing, childless wife could no longer serve his purpose and he had had to be free again. Despite her inward resolution to show no sign of her altered attitude towards him, Janeta found herself shivering with dread.

She said determinedly, 'I think if I rest alone for the rest of today I shall be much stronger tomorrow.'

It was a decided dismissal, but if the pair resented it they said nothing. L'Estrange came to the bedside and gallantly lifted Janeta's hand to his lips. He bowed and nodded to Avice Spooner to precede him through the door.

'I look forward with delight to seeing you tomorrow, fully restored to health,' he said softly, and she avoided his gaze as he drew the heavy door to after him.

Once the steps had retreated down the stair again Janeta signalled to Eadgyth to come close.

'Is the tower door guarded?'

The girl looked round, as if she feared being overheard. 'Yes, mistress. At all times there are armed men in the bailey and on the leads of the house roof.'

Janeta nodded and chewed her nether lip thoughtfully.

'Well,' she said at last, 'we shall have to wait to see what tomorrow brings forth. Stay within my chamber for the night, Eadgyth, and see that you oversee what is dished up for me in the kitchens.'

Again the girl nodded, her eyes moving uncomfortably about the room, as if she was being constantly watched.

With Eadgyth sleeping contentedly beside her on the truckle-bed, Janeta felt more secure. She spent the early hours of the night considering what possible purpose Fulke L'Estrange had for detaining her here in his home by subterfuge. The morrow would show if he intended to continue his purpose by outright refusal to escort her further, or even force her, compel her to remain. She had seen the manor from their approach. She did not think it would be an easy matter to leave without his consent. It was a heart-stopping thought and she longed to be able to turn to Bertrand for assistance. By now he would have forgotten her existence, believing her immured within convent walls again, or, if he could not so easily forget her, he would be making new brave plans for his future in the de Montfort household. She felt the hard prick of tears and resolutely forced them back. By her own will she had cut all ties with Bertrand D'Aubigny. While she would love him till she died, she could no longer wish him to suffer the loss of their parting.

In the morning she woke early and requested that Eadgyth bring her food. She ate with relish for the first time since her arrival, knowing the food to be untainted by any herbal brew.

When Eadgyth offered to help her dress, Janeta

hesitated, then caught the girl's eye. In that instant she knew Eadgyth had tended her during her supposed illness and must, by now, have seen the secret mark on her breast and throat. She nodded her agreement and bit her lip as the girl finally adjusted the linen wimple around her throat.

Eadgyth made to speak, choked back the words, then said with a rush, 'There is nothing to be secretive about, mistress. I have seen more than one marked so. A lad in the village bears such a strawberry-coloured stain on his face.'

'And do the villagers avoid him?' Janeta questioned softly.

The girl bit her lip and nodded, embarrassed. 'Aye, that they do, mistress, but it's foolish. Wulf be a fair man and honest. I likes 'im well.'

'But would you consider marrying him, Eadgyth?'

The girl blinked rapidly. 'I don't know, mistress. He 'aint asked me, but I reckon I could do worse, that I do.'

Janeta smiled and caught the girl's chin between her two hands. 'You are a kind girl, Eadgyth. To your knowledge, has either Sir Fulke or Mistress Spooner seen the mark?'

'Sir Fulke, no. I doubt if 'e's bin near you when you was undressed; I don't know about Mistress Spooner.'

'Ah.' Janeta nodded and released the maid. 'If the tower door is open we'll search out Sir Fulke in the hall now.'

She descended the spiral stair without experiencing any weakness in her legs. Eadgyth opened the door at its foot and they passed into the bailey and were allowed to proceed without hindrance, though Janeta found the eyes of the four men-at-arms on duty there fixed upon her curiously.

Fulke L'Estrange sprawled at his ease in his chair at

the head of the long table. He was still enjoying breakfast. There was no sign of Avice Spooner.

He pushed the chair back and rose. 'Have you come to join me in the morning meal, demoiselle?'

She approached and shook her head. 'Thank you, I have already eaten. How soon, sir, can we set out for St Catherine's?'

He stood facing her, feet astride, one thumb thrust into his sword-belt.

'Not today, demoiselle. The weather will worsen after noon. It would be unwise to travel.'

'I have no fear of harsh weather, Sir Fulke,' she said quietly, 'and neither, I think, have you.'

He laughed. 'Well, then, let us say I am in no mood to travel.'

'When can I expect your mood to change?' It was a direct challenge now, and he chuckled in understanding.

'Who knows?' he shrugged.

'It would be an unknightly act to hold me here against my will, Sir Fulke.' There was no mistaking her knowledge now and he laughed again.

'I think you would be wise to return to your tower chamber, Janeta. There you can be tended carefully—and protected.'

He made an unmistakable gesture to one of the men-at-arms who stood on guard near the door. 'Escort my lady guest to her chamber.' Then he turned back to Janeta. 'I will come and see you, Janeta, when I have received news for which I have been waiting.'

Janeta shook off the hand of the man at her elbow. 'Explain yourself, sir. Have you sent to my father? I can tell you now, he will provide no ransom. He values me poorly.'

He shook his head, still smiling. 'I think you misjudge him, Janeta, but no, the man I have approached concerning you is not your father.'

'I don't understand—— Why, then—you cannot mean Sir Bertrand D'Aubigny. He has no gold. . .'

'Not D'Aubigny, though if he were aware of your presence here I fear he would be already making a nuisance of himself.' He sighed gustily. 'I have made one attempt to prevent him from interfering in my affairs. Sadly, I failed, but you yourself made a better job than I could ever have managed in making sure that he would not pursue us.' He was grinning broadly and Janeta was furiously aware of that dangerous yet charming twinkle in his eyes which gave the false appearance of joviality. She was seething with fury, so much so that the strength of it kept out fear.

'Then if you expect to gain by freeing me. . .'

'Not gain by freeing you, Janeta, but gain, inestimably, by holding you.'

'Holding me prisoner? But I am worthless. . .'

'Janeta, Janeta, have you not looked in a mirror since you left the convent? Did not Bertrand D'Aubigny convince you of your worth? Why should I wish to hold you against your will when it would suit both of us better if you were to accept my hand? You cannot really wish to bury yourself within the grey walls of St Catherine's?'

'Marry—you?' Janeta's voice was hoarse with astonishment and horror. 'I have told you, Sir Fulke, I intend to become a bride of Christ. Since I cannot give myself to Bertrand D'Aubigny how can you believe I would accept your hand?'

'Because you simply have no choice, my dear Janeta,' he said blandly. 'I have held you here now for several days. Your kinfolk will consider you totally compromised. Believe me, I shall obtain permission to wed you.'

'You are mad,' she whispered, between gritted teeth. 'I will never wed you or any man.'

He came very close to her now, so that she could breathe in the ale fumes and also some indefinable scent which clung to his tunic and mantle.

'Listen to me, Janeta. I want you. I've planned to wed you since I first set eyes on you. I will have you. I'm used to obtaining what I want. Now, go with my man willingly or he'll be forced to carry you back to your tower room kicking and screaming, which would not sit well on your dignity. Sit there alone and think what you will gain by this match—a household of your own, a strong lord to protect you, children. . .' His fair brows rose in amusement. 'The picture of our life together cannot be so unattractive compared with what you expect at St Catherine's. Once you are mine, and truly mine——' he lingered on the phrase, so that her cheeks flushed at the implication '—I'll not prove too demanding a husband. My word on it. I have——' he paused deliberately '—other ways of entertaining myself.'

She saw a clear picture of Fulke and Avice Spooner together and sharp bile rose in her throat at her own former gullibility.

There was nothing she could do. The man-at-arms was leering at her insolently and she knew if she refused to leave with him he would sweep her up and carry her. She would not grant Fulke L'Estrange that satisfaction. She turned and made for the screen door.

Before reaching Guildford Sir Hugh instructed his men to ride in pairs through the town, some ahead of him and Bertrand and the rest to follow.

'If I remember the terrain correctly there is a small thicket about a mile beyond the manor. We will meet there. See your men are well-concealed,' he ordered

his sergeant. He turned back to Bertrand. 'We don't
want to attract too much notice riding through the
town. We cannot hope to win Janeta's freedom by
force. I want you to have a good look at the village
before we decide what is best to be done.'

Bertrand nodded agreement. Sir Hugh knew the
terrain and he was content to abide by his judgement
at this stage. He rode in silence, still totally bemused
by the astounding information Sir Hugh had given him
earlier. They had spoken little on the road and
Bertrand was having difficulty in assessing the man's
character. Just what were Hugh Cobham's feelings for
Janeta? Could he really be depended on to do all in
his power to rescue her from Fulke L'Estrange's
clutches? Bertrand ground his teeth in fury at the mere
conjuring up of the man's person. With or without
Cobham's assistance, he was determined to have
Janeta out of that house before another night had
passed.

There had been no time to inform Simon de
Montfort of his intentions. Cobham had impressed on
him the urgency of his errand and he agreed that
Janeta must be rescued by strategy rather than force,
yet when he saw the place, as the two rode leisurely
through the village clustered round the manor, he
recognised that the business would be difficult in the
extreme. He had not expected Fulke L'Estrange's
manor to be, in reality, a fortress. It would take a siege
party to obtain Janeta's release by direct means.

In the designated thicket the two met up with the
men who had ridden ahead and waited to be joined by
the rest of their small force. Finally Sir Hugh instructed
his men to dismount within a clearing, secure their
horses and take the opportunity to eat the rations they
had brought with them. Apart, he conferred with
Bertrand.

'I see now what you meant about the house.' Bertrand munched on a manchet of bread and meat. 'It would be pointless just to ride up and demand Janeta's release. Within that house, had we twenty times our number, the fellow could still remain and defy us.'

Sir Hugh nodded. 'And most undoubtedly would do so.'

Bertrand said eagerly, 'I must get inside, swim the moat and. . .'

'Just so, and then what?' Cobham finished his own food and looked grimly ahead in the direction of Grimsdell. 'You would be one man against many, and however resourceful would be unlikely to accomplish what we desire. From what you have told me, L'Estrange has made one attempt on your life. If you are captured he would cut your throat with no compunction whatever. That would be no use to Janeta. We need to know far more about that house—where Janeta is, whether she is being held now against her will or whether she still trusts the man. We need to know just how many men-at-arms he has and how and where placed. That way we could at least plan our next move.'

Bertrand saw the sense of that. 'I'll go into the tavern we saw in the village and see if I can get any information from the villagers.'

'They are hardly like to trust a strange Norman knight who arrives suddenly and deliberately does not present himself at the manor. No, neither of us should go. My men are wearing cotes without device; I saw to that when we set out. I'll send my sergeant.'

Bertrand was about to argue. His one aim now was to have sight of Janeta by whatever means, and he felt he could not sit tamely in this clearing while others did the work for him, but he caught the obstinate jut of Cobham's jaw and, once again, deferred to his judgement. He sighed and nodded. Sir Hugh dispatched his sergeant, who grunted and appeared to have done such work before. Bertrand realised that the veteran had seen service with Sir Hugh in the unsettled days towards the end of King John's reign, when many a baron had defied his sovereign and it had been left to individuals to defend their own property or attack their neighbours if necessary.

It seemed hours before their man reported back. Bertrand could not settle and prowled the small wood, watching the road from time to time, though from cover. Hugh Cobham continued to sit on his haunches in the clearing and wait patiently. He had forbidden his men to light a camp-fire, cautious of arousing interest from the village by smoke spirals. Bertrand regarded him with scant patience. At length, after the fourth time the younger man had strode back to the clearing, Cobham gave a little wintry smile and gestured to Bertrand to come close.

'I understand your frustration. At this time of the year the sun will set early, but the night is the best time for action—if that is what we decide on.'

'We have to do something,' Bertrand blurted out. 'I know you think me an impetuous fool but I'll not allow Janeta to languish one more night in that creature's hold. If he hurts one hair of her head. . .'

'He'll not,' Sir Hugh returned shortly. 'That would not be to his advantage. I don't regard you as foolish. By no means. I know what she means to you.' He hesitated and avoided Bertrand's gaze. 'You think I have no real love for her. Well, that's as may be. I've seen little of her over these ten years. I thought that for the best. I still think it was so, but she's my Alice's child, and I'll give my life for her if need be.'

He turned and levelled a direct look at Bertrand, who shifted uncomfortably.

'I think I understand, sir.'

'God grant you are never placed in the situation I was.'

Bertrand's lips compressed and he turned away.

One of the men stood up and glanced towards his lord. So alerted, Sir Hugh rose as his sergeant strode into the camp.

'Well?'

The veteran shook his head. 'I couldn't find out much, sir. Sir Fulke hasn't allowed his men out of the manor-house, at least not recently. There was no one actually from the house I could question or overhear while gossiping. The villagers received me friendly, like. I think they thought me a mercenary seeking employment. It's a poor place, bush on a pole over the door of a hovel, and Sir Fulke is rarely at home. He provides few facilities for his villeins and the steward drives them hard so that he can despatch as much coin to the capital as possible. Sir Fulke has extravagant tastes.'

Sir Hugh grunted and Bertrand made an impatient gesture. All this they knew. What of Janeta's plight?

'The villagers saw him arrive with the maid. Since then they know nothing of her. No one's emerged except that Sir Fulke's squire rode out the following day in a great hurry, so I'm told, and took the Guildford road.'

'Heading for the King at Westminster or Windsor.' Sir Hugh nodded.

'He'd dare that?'

'Aye, Bertrand, Fulke L'Estrange would dare anything. He believes himself the devil's emissary, and he had the right master for it.' Cobham broke off and snapped at his sergeant, 'You know nothing, then, about the house?'

'Very little, sir. I could see there's a tower. It's likely

she'll be kept there. The villagers are admitted to the hall when called to pay their dues. About the rest of the house they know little or nothing. They all assured me there is a goodly troop of men-at-arms in service. I could see two on the leads.'

Sir Hugh eased his hauberk on his shoulder and stretched his knee.

'It looks as if someone will have to swim the moat tonight to spy out the possibilities. We are no further forward.'

He turned, irritated, as there was a sudden outcry from the group of his own men. A frown deepened on his brow. He'd given strict commands for quiet. It seemed there was a struggle in progress, and Bertrand strode over to investigate. They could afford no disputes now among the company.

A man was pulled to his feet and turned roughly to face Bertrand.

'An intruder, sir,' one of the men said breathlessly. 'I caught him spying while I went apart to—'

'Yes, yes.' Bertrand cut him off. Obviously this fellow had followed their sergeant from the tavern. If so, their presence here might well be known to the manor garrison by now. He surveyed the captive curiously.

He was big, gangling, probably about twenty years of age. His long, straggling brown hair hid most of his face, but when his head was jerked up by his captor the hair was flung back, and a long purplish-red stain extending from the left eye to the cheek was revealed. He stood docilely within the soldiers' grasp. The man wore no mail not even a leathern cote. He was clad in homespun tunic and braies and was hooded against the cold wind—a villein on this demesne, clearly.

'What are you doing in this wood, fellow?' Bertrand questioned sharply.

The man might have made the same request of them. After all he lived near here, but surprisingly he made no such demand, or even answered insolently, though he appeared to be undaunted by the sight of so many armed men.

Sir Hugh came up and eyed the man as curiously as Bertrand had done.

'You come from the village of Grimsdell?' He spoke in English.

'Aye, sir. I came after yonder man.' He indicated the sergeant, who started at the sight of him, having probably recognised him as one of the men in the tavern.

'If you are so curious about our presence here, why did you not report immediately to your lord?'

The man looked directly back at Sir Hugh. 'I wanted to 'ear what was said.'

'Oh?' Bertrand moved threateningly towards the fellow, but Sir Hugh held up one hand in warning.

'I wanted to 'ear if ye'd come for the maid.'

'Ah.' Sir Hugh gestured to his men to release the prisoner and the man came a little nearer to the two knights.

'My wench waits on the maid—in the tower room. I'm allowed in—by the cook—to see 'er, once in a while. My Eadgyth is the only one who doesn't fear this.' He indicated the livid mark and his lips set mutinously. 'She's fond of the maid. They've been drugging 'er.'

Bertrand started again in fury, but the man went on doggedly.

'She wants to be a nun but 'e keeps her in the tower—the Virgin knows why. He's the devil in this village, the lord knows, not me.' His dull, dark eyes took on a sudden defiant gleam. 'Eadgyth says they two did for the Lady Maud, Sir Fulke's wife, and Eadgyth loved her too.'

'They two?' Bertrand questioned, and the man turned back to him.

'Aye, 'e's a mistress 'e often brings to the manor, from Lunnon, they say.'

'And he wants to marry her, so he rid himself of his wife?'

The man gave a scornful laugh. 'I doubts if marriage be in 'is mind, sir, not for 'er, but she's in there with 'im, 'elping 'im 'old the maid.'

Bertrand let out a hiss of concentrated fury. 'Can you get me inside?'

'Aye, sir, that's why I come, to see if'n you were out to 'elp the maid, for my Eadgyth. Yesserday she tells me she wants to find a way for the maid to escape. . .'

'You know the house?'

The man shrugged. 'Well, enough, but it'll not be easy. There are men-at-arms in plenty.'

Bertrand shrugged. 'I know.'

'If'n ye'll trust yeself to me I'll tek ye to me cot and get ye a tunic and a hooded cote like mine.'

Bertrand turned to Sir Hugh, who nodded slowly. 'You'd best be the man to make the attempt. God knows, Janeta has little reason to trust me. Try to find her, and get a signal or message out by this fellow if you can't find a way of getting her out.'

'Could she swim the moat with me?'

Sir Hugh pursed his lips. 'I doubt that. All her young life has been spent at St Catherine's.'

'No matter, I could carry her with me. If I'm not out by morning with Janeta, do what you must—or can.'

He nodded to the villein to go before him, gave one quick glance back at the rescue party, raised one hand in farewell, and made for the road back to Grimsdell.

CHAPTER ELEVEN

JANETA wasn't too alarmed when the door abruptly opened later that afternoon. She had expected Eadgyth to return from the kitchens with some mulled ale, for the cold had intensified within the tower chamber and the brazier wasn't sufficient to dispel it completely. She closed her lips on a gasp as she recognised Fulke L'Estrange.

He closed the door behind him and leaned against it at his ease, arms folded. He was dressed in his most elegant attire; scarlet surcote over blue embroidered and furred under-tunic.

Janeta retreated to the wall beneath the one high lancet window and faced him with as much defiance as she could muster. It was clear that Avice Spooner had been ordered not to accompany him this time and Janeta's heart beat uncomfortably fast as she wondered why that was so. She could not hope for Eadgyth to return to her now. The serving-girl would not be able to approach the tower chamber while Grimsdell's lord had business there with the prisoner.

'What do you want, sir?' She framed the question bravely enough, though the answer must be so obvious as to make the question posed faintly ridiculous.

'You, of course.' His bearded lips parted in a smile but, for the moment, he did not move from the door.

'I have told you. I will never give my consent.'

'Let us say I expected you to show some degree of reluctance.'

'Do you dare suppose I am deliberately pretending to be coy?'

247

'No, Janeta, I do not believe that of you. That would be expected behaviour from your Bertrand's esteemed sister-in-law. She enjoys teasing men and, I think, she would not be too shocked either if they played her game too readily.'

Janeta gave another little shocked hiss of breath. 'Roesia spoke with you—about her detestation of me?'

'She spoke quite honestly of her jealousy. Oh, she would never have wed your Bertrand. He has no fortune, nor even a sizeable expectation of fortune, but she would have preferred him to remain in subjection to her charms. Your arrival on the scene spoiled that for her. I fear she will be your enemy forever, but that can matter little, once you are my wife. The petty jealousies of others can have little effect on us.'

'I will not marry you—or any man.'

His tone hardened and he straightened somewhat. 'The messenger I expected is tardy in arrival. No matter; if you are mine already, even should his answer be unfavourable, I think I shall be able to send him back with a more definite message. I doubt if I would be refused a second time.'

'I don't know what you are talking about,' Janeta said wearily. 'I have already made it plain to you that my father will provide no dowry for me, at least none that would make it worth your while to wed me.'

He gave a loud, braying laugh. 'Who spoke of your father, Janeta? It was to the King, your brother, I sent.'

At first the two unbelievable words did not register, but she opened her eyes wide and said wonderingly, 'The King? What makes you think the King could possibly care enough about my welfare to concern himself with what happened to me?'

'Perhaps not, but he still cares for the reputation of his father and, incidentally, yours.'

She stared at him, totally bemused. 'His father? But. . .'

'Yes, my dear Janeta, his father, I said, and yours. His Grace our late sovereign, King John.'

Had she not been leaning hard against the wall now, she would have fallen. His words were so astounding as to beggar belief, but he spoke them so coldly and with such confidence that she could only clutch at the roughness of the stone for further support.

He was leaning forward now, his tone pleasant, as if imparting some titbit of gossip that could only flatter or please her.

'Oh, yes, you are John's child right enough. I was there when you were conceived, or near enough as makes no difference. I slept across the outside of your mother's chamber door to guard the King's privacy. I told you how very beautiful your mother was, and John could never resist a beautiful woman.'

She was icy cold now, her body rigid against the stone, her eyes grown huge with wonder and horror.

He went on in bantering tone. 'Your father—I mean Sir Hugh Cobham, of course—was in high favour at Court in those days. He served the King loyally and I was not lying when I spoke of John's good points. He had many, you know, despite the criticism of the Church. John was never the Church's true child as Henry is. There was something of the pagan in John. Well, he came to the Cobham manor on two occasions to hunt, and saw your mother. He could be—very persuasive.'

'How dare you even mention my mother with your foul tongue?' Janeta forced out at last. 'You lie in your teeth. I know you do.'

'No, Janeta,' he said very gently. 'Already you are beginning to believe me. Things are falling into place. You know now why Sir Hugh placed you at St

Catherine's, beyond the reach of libellous tongues, why he could not have wed you to some poor knight of his choosing, whether he willed or no. You are the King's half-sister, and your future must be determined by him and none other.'

'My mother would not have betrayed my father.' It was a pitiable little cry of protest.

'I have said how persuasive John was, and he knew well how to charm women.' Fulke shrugged, smiling, as if in remembrance. 'I learned a great deal from him about the art of wooing women, to my advantage, I must say, and I am grateful for it. I don't know just how matters stood between Hugh Cobham and your mother. Like enough, she was wed to please her father and, though contented enough, found her blood quickening when John paid her courtesies. In all events he was the King and not to be denied—as your father was forced to accept in the end. He left Court, but he found swallowing his hurt pride cold fare, I'll warrant. Unfortunately John died before your birth and your mother lived only a short time after that. If one of the causes was shame for her situation, or even loss of her heart's love, I'll never know. My own fortunes changed then, of course. I wasn't considered a suitable companion for the boy King. My——' his smile broadened '—let us say my experiences of life did not sit well with a boy still under tutelage.' He sighed. 'It was a great loss. I had entertained great hopes of preferment under John. I was of considerable value to him in providing him with certain—necessities. But then the axe fell and I was forced to wait my time. The King knighted me at last—Pembroke knew well enough that my knowledge was dangerous and he kept me quiet—but, as you know, Janeta, I have an insatiable appetite for grandeur and greatness and you could provide me with those.'

She was silent. Her mind was grappling with the horrific implications of his revelations. He was right. Happenings were falling into place in her mind. Her father's coldness—her very existence reminded him of his wife's perfidy. And the mark, the devil's mark on her flesh at birth—did that, too, proclaim her relationship to the Plantagenet line, descent from the notorious witch, Melisande, who had refused to attend mass when urged by her husband, the Count of Anjou, and disappeared from his sight when he had attempted to compel her to remain within the Church?

As if to reinforce his words, and her growing belief, Fulke said softly, 'You resemble your mother, true, but there is a likeness to the Princess Eleanor. I saw it whenever you two stood close. Your hair is dark, like John's, but there are touches of the Plantagenet red within the tresses too.'

She had the Plantagenet temper too, ungovernable rages which had frightened her and also convinced her she had no vocation for the convent life. It was beginning to well up within her now. She must try to keep calm. Nothing could be gained by flying into a temper. Fulke L'Estrange had too many servants at his disposal and he was capable of dealing with a frightened and angry woman without even calling them. She must try to convince him that nothing could be gained by this fanciful notion of his to compel the young King to grant him her hand in marriage and, with it, considerable lands and property.

She said with dangerous quietness, 'I cannot see how the knowledge of some bastard child born to the late King could be dangerous or even inconvenient to King Henry. You will gain nothing but opprobrium by this unknightly behaviour. It was considered practical to consign me to a convent; surely nothing has changed?

If you let me go there I swear I will make no complaint.'

He had folded his arms and was smiling broadly again.

'You do not know the young King Henry as well as you think. He defers constantly to the priests who throng his Court chambers. He will be sensitive to further scandals concerning his late father, particularly one which accuses John of betraying the trust of a loyal subject. He will find it a simple matter to reward me well to keep silent, especially as——' he hesitated meaningfully '—you, his half-sister, will be compromised, irretrievably, by your stay here at Grimsdell.'

'Whatever the King decrees I will never give my consent. I will proclaim to the world at the marriage ceremony my intention to renounce the world and enter the noviciate at St Catherine's.'

The smile faded and that deadly cold gleam appeared in his eyes.

'But would they take you, my dear Janeta, if you are already despoiled?'

She gave another terrible gasp and flung out one hand, as if by this ineffectual gesture she could physically hold him off. He advanced now determinedly, and with a deepening sense of horror she realised his patience was exhausted. He had waited too long for a response from the King. Now he would act. If he bedded her, the King would have no choice but to accept with good grace the situation and repair the damage as best he could by a marriage—unless he intended to abandon her utterly. In either event she was doomed.

She gave a terrible cry of distress and outrage as he reached out his arms and took her shoulders in a hard grasp. She was against the wall. There was no way of retreat. The nearness of him aroused the half-con-

trolled rage and she let out a snarl of fury. How dared
he lay impious hands on her? Despite his attempt to
grip her arms, her hands were still free, and she went
for his cheeks and eyes. Startled, he released her
momentarily, one hand up to the torn flesh of his
cheek. She managed to evade him and make for the
door but he recollected himself immediately and tore
after her, seizing her bodily and throwing her across
the bed. She fought unrelentingly, but he was so much
bigger and stronger than she, and she knew he must
win in the end. He too had lost control now and
furiously angry, dark colour mottling his cheeks and
brow. His breathing was becoming laboured but he
was forcing her inexorably back against the bed. With
one strong arm he held her down and with his other he
tore at her clothing. The bodice of her gown ripped
and, with it, her wimple. She gave a little desperate
moan and still struggled against his onslaught. She
would not scream or cry. He should not have that
satisfaction.

Forced back against the pillows, she tried desperately to use her one free hand to cover her exposed
breast.

He gave a sudden animal howl and she prepared
herself for final subjection, then, astonishingly, she felt
his weight across her body withdrawn. Shrinking back,
she half raised her head to see him struggling back
against the bed-foot, releasing her. Her fascinated gaze
went to his distorted face. His mouth was open and he
was making a terrible choking noise. One hand was
pointing towards her throat and breast and she realised
he had exposed to view the wine-coloured stain. She
forced herself back against the bed-head, watching in
terrible concentration Fulke L'Estrange's frantic withdrawal. He raised himself from the bed, stood upright.
She could see the sinews of his neck standing out like

cords. He caught convulsively at his upper arms, reared backwards, then fell heavily, his head striking the small faldstool behind him. She leaned forward, watching, waiting for him to stir. It seemed for those deadly moments that time stood utterly still. Her own breath was coming raggedly in harsh gasps. Then, abruptly, before her frightened eyes, the door was thrust open. She tore her gaze from the supine body of Fulke and towards the opening. A man stepped through and closed it softly behind him. He was cloaked and hooded, dressed in homespun, and she looked unbelievingly at the unsheathed dagger in his right hand, then her terrified eyes sought his face as he thrust back his hood.

She gave a terrible anguished cry, then launched herself at him, half slithering across the sprawled form of the man lying between them. 'Bertrand, oh, Bertrand. . .' She was sobbing now uncontrollably, as yet unable to comprehend that he was really here with her, a miraculous answer to her tearful pleas to the Virgin.

Gently he put her aside as his eyes took in the situation. He knelt down briefly before the body of his enemy, feeling cautiously for the pulse at Fulke's throat, then bending to put his ear to the man's heart.

He looked up to meet her frightened eyes and shook his head very gently. 'He's dead, Janeta. You've nothing more to fear from him.'

She began to shake. Hysterically she murmured, 'I don't understand. He can't be dead. I didn't touch him. . . What could have happened?'

Bertrand said, 'I think he suffered some kind of fit, judging by his colour.' He took her firmly by the shoulders. 'You mustn't distress yourself. Don't look at him, Janeta.' The command was uttered sharply. 'I need you to hold up just now.'

'What do you mean, "fit"? You mean he died of shock?' She covered her mouth with her hand. 'Sweet Virgin, I killed him.'

Bertrand's tone was sharp again, recalling her to her senses. 'Nonsense. The man died of his own excesses.'

'But he was quite young. . .'

'He over-indulged himself. We all saw it at Court and commented on it. This is no fault of yours.'

'We struggled—he—he——' she gulped frantically '—he tried. . .'

'I don't doubt it.' Bertrand's comment was pithy. 'Clearly he brought on his own death. Now listen, Janeta, you must not think of that now. We still have to get out of here. That will not be easy.' He led her gently back to the bed and seated her down on it. 'Where are your clothes—in this chest?'

She nodded, her eyes moving fearfully from Fulke L'Estrange's curiously sprawled form to the chamber door. She was still shaking, but with an effort she forced her limbs to obey her and, standing up, went to help Bertrand find a cloak.

'How did you come here, find me?' she whispered as he placed it round her shoulders. Already she had managed to find a wimple-pin to fasten together the rents in her gown. He could feel her trembling against him and held her close.

'Sweetheart,' he chided, 'trust me. I'll manage to get you clear but you will need all your courage.' He tilted up her chin with one finger and she managed a watery smile to reassure him of her determination to prove no burden to him. 'Your father guessed L'Estrange would hold you when we knew you had been talking with him at Westminster. He brought me here but we thought it best I should be the one to find an entry into the manor-house. He feared you might not trust yourself so readily to him.'

'My father? Sir Hugh?' She gazed back at him wonderingly. 'He is here, at Grimsdell? He came after me?'

'Yes, he waits in a wood near here with a small company of men. You will be quite safe once we have managed to leave the manor.' He glanced significantly down at Fulke L'Estrange's body. 'But that might prove difficult. I hear he has his mistress with him and she'll not take his death as philosophically as we do. She has a goodly force at her beck and call.'

Janeta gave a little shudder of loathing. The very thought of Avice Spooner and the woman's ministrations to the late Lady Maud made her flesh crawl. Sharp bile rose in her throat as she recalled how she herself had been drugged. Later, when she had served her purpose, would she have suffered a like fate?

Bertrand was watching her reaction closely. 'I see you know the lady well.' He grinned mirthlessly. 'Wulf, Eadgyth's man, followed our sergeant to the wood. He told us how anxious Eadgyth was to help you to freedom. It was his notion to get me into the manor dressed in his clothes. He brought me into the kitchens and through into the bailey. Apparently he has entry into the house to see Eadgyth on occasions. Of course,' he added succinctly, 'it was left to me to gain entrance into the tower.'

The remark was chillingly uttered. Janeta glanced down hurriedly at his dagger, sheathed now, and lying snug against his hip, suspended from his leather belt. He had killed at least one man-at-arms. It might prove necessary to kill others before they won free.

'Wulf is the man with the birthmark?'

He looked at her quickly. 'Yes, but a good man for all that. He has nothing but contempt for L'Estrange. Like Eadgyth, he loved the Lady Maud, and believed

L'Estrange brought about her death with the help of his mistress.'

'Yes,' Janeta said tonelessly, 'Eadgyth holds the same opinion. Bertrand, we cannot leave them here.' She glanced shudderingly down at L'Estrange. 'They could be held responsible, both for our escape, should we manage it, and—and for—his death.' The last words were ground out through gritted teeth.

'I thought of that. I instructed Wulf to find Eadgyth and take her to the wood. You will need an attendant for the journey and your father will find work for Wulf, I'm sure, or I will. I doubt any having claim to the manor will demand his return to serfdom here.'

Janeta thought that, in the circumstances, the new owner might well be glad to be rid of him. She said questioningly, 'My father came to save me? I find that hard to believe. L'Estrange told me——' she bit back the lump forming in her throat '—he said. . .'

'I think I can guess what he told you and why he wanted you.'

'My father told you—that—that I—am a bastard?' The word was so low that he had to bend to catch it.

'He told me you are of royal Plantagenet blood.'

Her blue-grey eyes met his brown ones squarely. 'Can that make any difference to—to the circumstances of betrayal?'

'Perhaps not, to your father.' His lips tightened. 'Your parentage means nothing to me, except—— No matter. For the present we must put all that behind us and concentrate on means of escape. Are you ready?'

She nodded. Her mouth was dry. She was suddenly very afraid, more for Bertrand than for herself.

'I'll open the door. Keep well behind me. Leave me to deal with the guards outside. Judging by the lack of hue and cry they'll not have missed their comrade yet,' he said grimly. 'I dragged him into the tower below the first stair rungs.'

Janeta pulled up the hood of her cloak and prepared to keep close behind him as he moved to the door. Before he could touch the latch they both froze as light feet ran pattering up the stair and a voice called, 'Fulke? It is I, Avice. You have been so long gone that. . .' Her voice sounded breathless, a little plaintive, as if she feared her master's anger.

Janeta started and half stumbled, but Bertrand signalled with finger on his lip that she must stay silent. He tiptoed to the door and quietly turned the key, then took his place where he would be behind the door when Avice Spooner entered. He waved Janeta back towards the bed. Frightened eyes on him, she obeyed.

'Fulke?' Avice Spooner was beginning to sound openly impatient now. The irony of the situation was not lost on Janeta, who wondered how Avice Spooner actually dared to intrude, when she must know the reason why Fulke L'Estrange had come to the tower chamber.

There was a hesitant rattle on the latch, then, just as cautiously, the door was pushed half-open. It was growing gloomy now within the room and for moments Avice Spooner stood on the threshold, trying to focus upon the occupants. Clearly she had expected Fulke to answer angrily or actually forbid her entry. She was puzzled and only advanced very slowly.

The moment she had cleared the doorway Bertrand was upon her, grasping her from behind, a hand over her mouth lest she cry out and alert the guards just outside the tower. The woman struggled frantically in his hold as Janeta tore the bed-sheet into two broad strips, gritting her teeth at the strength required to part the cloth. Triumphant at last, she dashed up to the struggling pair and, reaching behind Bertrand, managed to secure one strip over Avice Spooner's mouth and tie the ends securely behind her head. She had very little compunction for her task and watched stolidly while Bertrand took the other strip from her and tied the woman's wrists behind her back. Only then did he release her and allow her to slide forward upon her knees. The desperate struggle over, Avice Spooner was able to grasp the situation. Her horrified eyes took in Fulke's sprawled body and she gave a cry, suppressed by the gag, and on her knees painfully started towards him.

'He's dead,' Bertrand informed her coldly. 'No, it was no fault of either the demoiselle Janeta or I. He suffered a seizure.'

Avice Spooner managed to lie alongside Fulke, hampered though she was by her pinioned wrists, and Janeta closed her eyes as she saw the woman's tears splash down on to Fulke's silken tunic. At least one person mourned his passing. He had been cruel and venal and had used Avice Spooner shamefully, as he had used other women, but it seemed she had truly loved him. Possibly he had persuaded her by her very passion for him to assist him in the work of freeing himself from the wife who had no longer been useful for his purposes.

Bertrand came to Janeta, his mouth very close to her ear.

'The men-at-arms will have noted her entrance and expect her to emerge very soon. We shall have to move very quickly now.'

She nodded, averting her gaze from the woman's evident sorrow. They had little chance of avoiding notice now. Her limbs were beginning to tremble again but she forced her spine to remain rigid and controlled them. She must not fail Bertrand now.

His raised eyebrows were asking her if she was

ready, and she lifted her chin in silent acquiescence.
He glanced back briefly at the pair on the floor and
moved to the door. Janeta crept up close behind him.
She felt very cold and sick, yet, for the first time since
she had awoken from her drugged sleep and realised
Fulke L'Estrange's intentions, she knew hope. Despite
the dangerous nature of their plight Bertrand was here
by her side, and she had confidence that he would
overcome the difficulties. The landing was shrouded in
dark shadows now and she could see nothing below.
The very air seemed to be palpitating, and she understood she was hearing her own agitated heartbeat.

Bertrand turned once and touched her shoulder
reassuringly. 'Remember, keep very close behind me.'

It was then that all hell seemed to break loose in the
bailey below. There came the sounds of running feet
and men shouting commands.

Bertrand gave a muffled oath and put out a hand to
prevent Janeta advancing further.

'We must return to the chamber. Something is
definitely wrong.' He pushed her within and stood with
his back again to the closed door.

It was becoming so dark in the room now that she
could hardly discern his features, let alone read his
expression.

Avice Spooner was huddled near her dead love,
apparently blind and deaf to all outside influences,
sunken within her own misery.

'What can the disturbance be about?' Janeta
mouthed. 'Avice Spooner is here. No one can know
yet that Fulke is dead.'

He shook his head grimly. 'Possibly your father has
become impatient and decided to demand your release.
In all events the captain of the guard will soon be
requesting a reply to the challenge from Sir Fulke.

God damn Hugh. Why could he not have given me more time?'

Janeta said nervously, 'When Sir Fulke is discovered, surely it will be in the garrison's best interest to surrender us?'

'Aye, so long as we are both living when they do so. Sir Hugh has few men. The guard captain might consider it best, even without Sir Fulke's acquiescence, to hurl back defiance. The manor has stout defences.'

Janeta slumped back against the door-frame. She knew their danger only too well. Sir Fulke had held her against her will, aided by his garrison. It might be considered best if she were dispatched, so that she might not be capable of accusing her gaoler. The blame could be put squarely upon Sir Fulke, and he unable to defend himself. Bertrand, of course, would be silenced with her. She moved very near to him and he gathered her into his arms, his hands gentling her, his chin nuzzling her hair beneath its veil.

Feet ascended the stair. She recognised the fact that they were not mailed. Not the captain of the guard, then, no strike of iron spur on stone.

'Sir—Sir Bertrand? Are you in there, sir?' The challenge was muffled and Bertrand gave a great relieved sigh.

'It's all right. That's Wulf. Wait a moment, man. I'll let you in.' He left Janeta inside the chamber and went outside on to the landing, where he engaged in a quick explanation of the state of affairs inside. The man entered with him. As he crossed to the wall below the window Janeta's fascinated eyes took in the dark wine-stain which marred his features. 'There's a force besieging the manor, sir. I was tekking my Eadgyth to the wood as you ordered and saw this army approaching. I could 'ardly believe me eyes—mounted knights and armed men and carts. I should say there's at least

a 'undred men and some siege equipment being
dragged up from Guildford. I dashed on with Eadgyth
and told Sir Hugh, sir, and he brought up 'is company
to join the force. It seems the King 'as sent the Earl of
Leicester to demand the release of the maid.'

His eyes went warily to Janeta, whom he recognised
for the first time.

'I managed to get across the moat unseen in all the
commotion and climb in through one of the windows
near the back kitchen. The guard captain be well
engaged, sir, so while he was I thought it best to let
you know 'ow matters were. All the men in the bailey
and near the tower are drawn up on the ramparts to
view the attackers. Nobody bothered about me.' He
looked down ruefully at his dripping tunic and
chausses.

'Eadgyth—is she safe?' Janeta pressed him.

'Oh, aye, mistress, she be with Sir Hugh.'

'Thank the Virgin.'

The noise below was continuing. Hoarse comments
were shouted from the highway. There was renewed
shuffling of feet and the unmistakable sound of arrows
finding their targets, sudden cries of alarm and the
ominous booming sound of an approaching siege-tower
being wheeled along on its platform.

'Wulf, it's time we took a hand to prevent any more
bloodshed,' Bertrand ordered. 'If that tower is moved
into position the whole situation could worsen. Wulf!'
he snapped as he saw that the man was staring down
at the two figures on the floor. At first the gloom in the
chamber had hidden them from him. Possibly his foot
had caught the body of his lord and he was now aware
of his presence in the chamber.

'You—you killed 'im, sir?'

'No. He was dead when I broke in.'

Wulf's enquiring gaze passed to Janeta, and

Bertrand said hastily, 'The demoiselle had no part in Sir Fulke's death. He collapsed and died.'

'Then the devil 'as 'is own at last. There'll be few tears for 'is passin' in the village, I'm telling you, sir.'

Bertrand sighed. 'I imagine not. Now, Wulf, I take it there's a way up to the leads on this tower?'

'Aye, sir.'

'Right, then let's get up there and see if we can parley with the Earl.' Bertrand held out a hand to Janeta. 'I will not hide from you that up there, in full view of both attacking force and garrison, you could be in danger, but once the Earl has seen you are unharmed I believe the guard captain will surrender. There will be no more reason for him to continue to resist. If the fighting continues and the tower is attacked you could as easily be killed here as up there. Will you risk showing yourself with me?'

'Of course. I will do whatever you consider best,' she said quietly.

Bertrand signalled to Wulf to precede him through the door. 'We'll follow in moments. See if you can find a lighted torch.'

Wulf left them and Bertrand turned to Janeta. 'Sweetheart, let me hold you in my arms. Will you forgive me for so foolishly dismissing your distress at Westminster? I could not understand how important the matter of Eleanor's marriage was. I came hurrying back, determined to give up my place in the household, but you'd already left. I sought you at St Catherine's and then. . .'

Her lips were trembling and tears rolling down her cheeks. She was thankful that it was almost too dark now in the chamber for him to see the marks of her shamed sorrow.

She came very close to him and reached out a tentative finger to touch his face. 'Don't, Bertrand, don't. We were both at fault. I should have fully understood how dear your post in Simon's household was to you. I have spent long hours in this chamber thinking about what was said—and unsaid. Don't you think I've regretted my foolish, girlish posturing?' She broke down then and he could hear her openly crying. 'I prayed to the Virgin—and—and she sent you to me. It cannot be wrong for me to love you. I know that now.'

'Hush, my love. No more regrets. My lord Simon is here. He and the Lady Eleanor were as anxious about your welfare as I was. All will be well when he sees you.'

Wulf appeared in the doorway, illuminated by the smoky glare of a lighted torch he had taken from the landing sconce below. Tinder and flint had been laid near it and he held it high to light their steps upwards to the castellated roof of the tower. Bertrand took Janeta's hand and watched closely as she warily climbed upwards, holding her skirts high. Wulf stood on the top landing and held the torch while Bertrand wrestled with the refractory door-latch. He hesitated for a moment, wondering if men-at-arms were stationed here on the leads, but there was no sound nor light. He concluded that if there had been they had joined their comrades on the battlements below when the attacking force had been first sighted. He stepped out cautiously on to the roof, saw that all was clear, and called to Janeta.

'Come now, close to me, slowly, and stay well behind us until I have been seen from below and identified myself.'

He advanced to the battlements and peered down. Limned against the wavering torchlight he must have made a commanding figure to those below. There were shouts of recognition, and Bertrand could just distinguish hands pointing upwards. Torches were lit on the battlements and below, in front of the gatehouse. Beyond, near the village, he could see camp-fires indicating that already the Earl's force was in command of the surrounding countryside and prepared to remain for some time.

He cupped a hand to his mouth and shouted to the guard whose upraised faces were now fixed on him.

'You there, summon your captain and request a parley with the Earl of Leicester. Tell him Bertrand D'Aubigny has the demoiselle Janeta Cobham safe and that she will be returned to the care of her father immediately.'

A sullen voice called back, 'And who in the devil's name are you? I answer only to Sir Fulke, my own lord.'

'Then you'll need to journey to hell itself to speak with him. Sir Fulke is dead of a seizure, as this man will testify. I'll bring up Mistress Avice Spooner as further witness if necessary. She is my prisoner, securely tied in the tower sleeping-chamber near the body of Sir Fulke. Man, there's no further need for loss of life. I have here the reason for the attack on Grimsdell. Demoiselle Cobham, will you show yourself?'

His heart swelled with pride as he saw how confidently she came forward to join him at the battlements, the torchlight illumining her slim form. Her hand reached out and took his and he held up both to reveal her trust in him. There was a great roar from below, more than likely from the Earl's men, whether signifying triumph or fury at her earlier abduction he could not tell. The men of the garrison grouped together, their attention now fixed on their captain. Bertrand waited until a trumpet sounded and Simon de Montfort's voice reached him from the gatehouse.

'I see you both, Bertrand. I command Grimsdell garrison to keep these two people safe or suffer death for it to a man. Now throw open your gate in the King's name and allow my escort free entry. After investigation of this affair at the King's insistence, all blameless men will go free. I swear it on my knightly oath.'

Bertrand felt Janeta's tension as she swayed slightly towards him and he drew her back from the crenellations.

'Bear up, my love. There will be no resistance. It would be pointless and the guard captain knows that. It will be over soon and you reunited with your father.'

Her fingers clung to his convulsively. He could see her slender, loved form so tight and rigidly held lest she reveal her fear. Her skirts were ruffled in the wind as her head-veil swept across her face, and he longed to lift her into his arms before them all and show her and them how dear she was to him—but he knew now who she was, and he ground his teeth in helpless fury as he realised how much further now than ever she was beyond his reach.

The captain's voice came at last, hoarse with effort and still as sulky.

'You demand our surrender in the King's name, my lord, and cannot be denied, especially as my own lord is no longer by my side to countermand that order. The bridge shall be lowered and the portcullis lifted. My men will throw down their weapons within the bailey as you enter.'

Bertrand sighed his relief and drew Janeta and Wulf towards the tower steps.

Janeta sat on her bed in the little chamber which had been Lady Maud's. Her concern that Fulke's wife had died here had been less than her revulsion at using the master bedchamber, where she was sure he had slept with Avice Spooner; nor could she have borne to return to the tower chamber. She had no idea where Avice Spooner had been bestowed. More than likely the woman would be carried with them, a prisoner, when they left Grimsdell. Certainly she had helped Fulke L'Estrange in his forcible imprisonment of Janeta, though it was doubtful that any charge could be laid against the woman now of having any hand in Lady Maud's death.

Eadgyth had brought warm water and helped Janeta bathe and wash her hair. She had felt an instinctive desire to wash away all trace of her encounter with Grimsdell's master. She had had no suitable clean gown in which to appear before Simon de Montfort and Sir Hugh Cobham so Eadgyth had provided her with one of Lady Maud's.

'The gown will be short, my lady—you're a good bit taller than she was, and it's out of fashion, I dare say. Sir Fulke never cared 'ow she were dressed, but that creature never wore 'er gowns, ye can be sure o'.that. For one thing they was too small for 'er and for another she didn't think 'em fine enough.'

The gown was clean, smelling sweetly of the lavender and rosemary which had been placed within its folds when laid away in a chest in this chamber. It was simply cut in soft brown homespun wool, home-dyed, more than likely, but Janeta was glad of it. Eadgyth had also provided her with fresh linen for wimple and veil, coarser than she had worn at Court but highly suitable for her needs.

She had dined earlier with the Earl and Sir Hugh in the great hall. Bertrand had been placed near her and, though she had felt the food would choke her, she had met his encouraging gaze several times during the meal and had forced herself to eat for his sake. It was too

late for them to travel and the Earl had been glad
when Eadgyth had provided attendance and the clean-
swept lodging for Janeta.

Bertrand had told most of the tale for her and the
Earl had listened gravely.

'I cannot believe it possible that any man who had
taken knightly vows could have treated a lady so,' he
pronounced. 'My Eleanor will be horrified to think of
your suffering, and relieved when I deliver you safe
into her care at Odiham.' He looked at her intently
then and she coloured hotly. So he knew why she had
run from Westminster.

'Yes, my lord,' she murmured, shamed. 'I shall be
grateful for my lady Eleanor's care and relieved that
she will take me back into her household—after all
that has happened.'

He gave her a wintry little smile. 'I think Eleanor
will be glad of the company of a true friend.' They
were closeted with Sir Hugh, and there was no one
else in the Earl's company to hear what was said. He
looked towards Sir Hugh and said softly, 'I hear I have
a new sister.'

Janeta crimsoned again and Sir Hugh reached out a
hand and captured hers.

'Child, it will take time to come to terms with what
you have discovered here. I regret that in the past I
have appeared unloving, but you must understand. . .'

'I do understand,' she said vehemently. 'I know now
why you placed me where you did. There must have
been times when you could not have borne to look at
me.'

He turned away slightly and his voice was hoarse
with emotion.

'You must not judge your mother, Janeta. She did
not marry me in love and, difficult as it is for you to
understand now, the late King—well, he appealed to

her sense of romance.' He smiled bleakly. 'I imagine the songs of the trouvères were her comfort when I was busy about the manor or away at Court. I loved her—in my way. She gave me my son and I shall always revere her for that—but I could not show my love in the way she wanted and needed to know. It is all over now, long ago, but for her sake I will protect you, not only with my name but in all ways needful for your welfare. I shall be grateful if you will continue to consider me your father.'

'You came for me,' she said breathlessly. 'You have fulfilled the true office of a father and I will be proud to call you so.'

Now she sat and considered her future. She knew there was no place for her at St Catherine's. The Lady Eleanor was, in truth, her half-sister, and in her household there would be a refuge, but what of Bertrand? During those hectic moments in the tower chamber, following Fulke L'Estrange's death, she had had no time to realise the implications of her true identity. Now they hit her like a blow to the heart. Eleanor had sought refuge in an oath of celibacy when she had been determined to avoid a loveless marriage and had bitterly regretted it. Now she, Janeta, could be in a like position. Only too well she understood Eleanor's plight and could no longer judge her. Whether she liked it or not she was the King's half-sister, and he might well decide to marry her to some knight of his choice—and she could lose Bertrand forever.

Eadgyth was busy making up the truckle-bed. Janeta leaned forward eagerly. 'Do you know where Sir Bertrand is lodged for the night?'

The maid's eyes met hers uneasily. 'I could find out, mistress.'

'I have to see him—here—now. Can you bring him here, none knowing?'

Eadgyth rose from her knees where she was tucking in a sheet. 'Aye, mistress, if that be your wish, but. . .'

'I know, but please, Eadgyth. I must see him, and tonight.'

The maid nodded and left, but Janeta could see she was alarmed at the prospect of their being discovered.

It seemed a long time before she returned, though Janeta knew it was actually only a matter of minutes. Bertrand hurried past her into the chamber and Eadgyth said nervously, 'I'll stay outside the door, here, mistress, and let you know quick if anyone comes.'

Bertrand enfolded Janeta in his arms as the door closed.

He said shakily, 'It seems days instead of hours that we've been parted. Oh, my love, I resent every second I am not with you.'

She lifted her face for his kiss. 'I love you so dearly,' she said tearfully. 'I don't know how I could ever have left you. Oh, Bertrand, what have I done?'

'Nothing that cannot be remedied, sweetheart. We shall all soon be back safely at Odiham and, soon after that, ensconced at Kenilworth. Nothing will part us then.' He cupped her chin within his hands. 'You're trembling, my love. What is it? You've nothing to fear now.'

'Except being parted from you.'

He frowned slightly. 'You are not still thinking of entering the nunnery?'

'No, no, but I am in the King's hands now. He will decide my future. We cannot rely on the Earl to speak for us, especially now he is no longer in favour.'

She could see that he was considering carefully what

she said. 'I doubt that the King will interfere in matters which concern only members of the Earl's household.'

'I am his half-sister,' she said softly. 'He, and he only, can decide whom I wed. King John wed his bastard daughter Joan to Prince Llewelyen of Wales and there has been talk that that marriage has foundered. . .'

'But the King had long recognised the Lady Joan. The situation is not comparable.'

'Bertrand,' she whispered fiercely, 'if you love me, you must take me away from here now, out of this house. Take me to Normandy. Become a mercenary where no one will know us. I will follow you with the baggage wagons, go anywhere, suffer any hardship, so long as I will be with you. There must be a way for us to leave this house.'

'Sweetheart, the house teems with the Earl's men and those of your father. The portcullis is down and the drawbridge up. L'Estrange kept this place as a fortress.'

She clung to him desperately. 'Sweet Virgin, if we wait we'll be lost. There must be a way.'

He drew her head down to his shoulder as he sat beside her now on the bed. 'I'll speak to the Earl in the morning. You must be brave, my love. You have been through such a lot, I think you fear misfortune before it can strike.'

He was so close she could smell the familiar scent of weapon-oil and leather. The old longings rose in her to be his, completely, the thoughts she had deliberately submerged within her being, feelings she hardly dared to admit to herself. Her flesh had crawled when Fulke L'Estrange had touched her but she wanted Bertrand's hands on her body, his lips touching the sensitive, intimate places, her ears, her breasts. . .

Her tears were soaking the shoulder of his tunic and he could hear the frantic beating of her heart.

She murmured piteously, 'If I were to be yours, Bertrand, yours completely, no one would separate us. Fulke L'Estrange dared to—to force himself on me because then—then I would have been so compromised that the King would have been only too willing to wed me to him. If you and I. . .'

'If you and Bertrand were to do anything so patently foolish it could cost you his life.' A coldly quiet voice spoke from the doorway.

Bertrand turned defiantly, cradling Janeta against his heart to face his lord. In his need to comfort Janeta's distress he had not heeded any warning sound from the corridor. If Eadgyth had attempted to alert them to their danger neither of them had heard it, being too intent on their own needs. The Earl quietly closed the door and advanced to face the seated pair.

Janeta looked up at him pleadingly. 'You must not think ill of Bertrand. It was I who sent for him. I wanted—needed to know. . .'

He shrugged lightly. 'I understand, Demoiselle Janeta. I, of all people, *must* understand, but when I saw Bertrand had left my side in the hall I knew instinctively where he had gone and in what peril he had placed himself. Bertrand, my friend, to touch her without the King's sanction will doom you. Don't you realise that?'

'But Fulke L'Estrange thought——'

'Demoiselle, Fulke L'Estrange did not know his sovereign. He judged Henry to be weak, easily lead, easily threatened. He was wrong. I know the King. Yes, he is young and needs to be counselled, but he is stubborn and, like his late sire, he can be ruthless and cruel when it suits him. He thought you sufficiently important to send me after you with an army, Janeta.

You are his kin and he'll not have you sullied.
L'Estrange made the mistake of his life in underesti-
mating the ability of Henry to hold a grudge.' He gave
a faint sigh. 'Haven't I had evidence of that recently
myself? He gave me leave to wed Eleanor in the teeth
of clerical opposition but he regrets it now, and I doubt
if I'll ever have the power to influence him fully again.
I have sacrificed his favour to obtain my heart's desire,
and I'll not shirk the price I must pay, but I beg you
take warning. If you wed Bertrand without the King's
consent he could render you a widow within hours.'

Janeta gave a great shuddering breath and gently
extricated herself from Bertrand's arms. 'Then we are
lost? Bertrand is landless, has no fortune nor standing
in the land.'

Simon de Montfort shook his head gently. 'Do not
give up hope yet, Janeta. I have been ordered to take
you to Odiham. I will send a message to the King,
begging him to give consent to your marriage to
Bertrand, and your father will add his pleading to that
request, but for the moment, for his sake, you must
keep your distance from Bertrand. There must be no
more secret trysts during the journey or when we have
arrived. Swear to me now, both of you, that you will
obey me, or I shall be forced to send Bertrand to one
of my manors under armed guard, to be held there.'

Bertrand rose to his feet, his face suffused with
angry colour, but Simon put a restraining hand on his
arm. 'It is for your own good, Bertrand.' He turned to
Janeta. 'Will you swear to me that you will speak to
each other only in the presence of either your father or
myself?'

She buried her face in her hands. 'Yes, my lord, for
Bertrand's sake I must.'

Before Bertrand could try to hold her again the Earl
drew him from the chamber. He turned in the doorway

to say soberly, 'Believe I have your interests to heart, demoiselle. I will do whatever I can for you.'

The door closed on them, and on all her hopes and dreams. When Eadgyth came in moments later, Janeta was sobbing despairingly.

On arrival at Odiham the Earl was greeted by the Countess's steward in a distinct state of agitation.

'My lord, your presence, and that of Sir Bertrand D'Aubigny and Sir Hugh Cobham, is required in the great hall on a matter of some urgency. I am instructed by my lady countess to conduct the demoiselle Janeta to her chamber immediately. Your advance messenger arrived very early this morning, my lord.'

Simon paused with Bertrand and Sir Hugh as their horses were led away to the stables to glance round the courtyard, a puzzled frown darkening his brow.

'It seems my messenger was not the only arrival today. There appears to be considerable activity within the stables. I presume my lady Eleanor has received couriers from Westminster.' He turned to Janeta, who was standing awkwardly with Eadgyth waiting for the Earl to dismiss her. 'Go quickly, demoiselle. You will find the Lady Eleanor delighted to have you safe home.'

Couriers from Westminster? Janeta's face blanched. Already it seemed that the King had decided her fate. The Earl had dispatched a courier instantly to Westminster the night the Grimsdell garrison had surrendered, so King Henry knew the Earl would bring her straight here to Odiham. She curtsied and nodded to Eadgyth to attend her and follow the Odiham steward, who set off at quite a pace, somewhat at odds with his age and dignity. She told herself fiercely that her surmise was probably incorrect. More than likely messengers from Court had business with the Earl, and for this reason he had been requested to present himself in the hall in haste. Set against matters of State, she, Janeta, was of slight importance. More than likely, now that her safety was assured, the King would forget about her, or at least allow her to resume her life in the Countess of Leicester's household without further concerning himself about her.

Eleanor received Janeta warmly and dismissed her ladies in attendance, ordering only Martha and Eadgyth to remain in her bedchamber. She signalled to Martha to take Eadgyth into the adjoining room and, after the doors had closed on her attendant, took Janeta by both hands and pulled her hastily into an affectionate embrace.

'Janeta, how thankful I am to see you. Let me look at you.'

Janeta attempted a respectful curtsy but Eleanor forestalled her.

'At least, in private, let me call you sister.'

Janeta flushed darkly. 'My lady, I fear you must be distressed by this news. . .'

'I certainly am not,' Eleanor laughed. 'I felt an affinity with you from the first.' As she saw Janeta's eyes fill with sudden tears she drew her close again. 'What is it, Janeta? You were not—touched?' Her eyes conveyed a grave anxiety and Janeta shook her head vehemently.

'No, no, my lady. Fulke tried—he wanted to be sure of me—but—but he suffered this terrible fit and—and before I could summon assistance he—he died.' She burst into a storm of weeping, the relief at her kindly reception allowing her to give way, at last, to the remembered horror of that dreadful moment.

The Countess drew her to a chair and gently pushed her into it.

'Child, I am sorry I had to pose such a question

but—but it was necessary for me to know exactly what happened. Let us be blunt. You are still a virgin?'

Janeta's lips trembled but she nodded again, tilting her chin in determination to hold her ground.

'Good.' Eleanor rose and paced slowly away for a moment. 'I am sorry once again that I must hurry you—I know you need rest after the journey and your ordeal—but—but we have a very important visitor here who requests to see you. Martha and your new maid will help prepare you.'

Janeta sat rigid in the chair, all her fears returning instantly. Then the messenger from Court was here on business concerning her future. She drew a little rasping breath and the Countess turned back to her with a little smile, but Janeta was aware that there was tension behind that smile. She had gone over and over in her mind what possibilities might lie ahead. She was a royal bastard, but not of noble birth. Though her supposed father had served the late King loyally he had no considerable fortune. Sir Hugh had told her bluntly from the first that he could not provide her with a dowry. Why should the King wish to do that? It would be much simpler to confine her to a nunnery where her true identity would remain a secret.

Her limbs trembled while Martha and Eadgyth completed her toilet and clothed her in a gown of softest pink velvet cinched in tightly at the waist with a gilded leathern girdle, jewelled at the hanging ends. Eleanor sat in her chair and watched the work critically. Janeta was too bemused and wearied to protest that the velvet gown was far too splendid for her to appear in before the King's messenger, especially if he was here to inform her that she must eschew splendour such as this forever and don the habit of a bride of Christ. When Martha made to comb out her long dark hair to hang loose upon her shoulders she put up a hand to prevent her.

'No, I must wear veil and wimple. I should feel undressed without them.'

Eleanor rose and crossed to her, her head a little on one side. 'A barbette and veil should suffice. Martha, bring me the fillet covered in cloth of gold—yes, and my crimson mantle, fur-lined. It will be chilly in the hall.'

When the work was completed she held up her own ivory-backed mirror for Janeta to assess their work. Janeta's lips parted in a soundless little gasp as she saw now how, standing side by side, she and the Princess Eleanor did indeed resemble each other. Eleanor's lips curved in a smile of satisfaction.

'Yes, it is evident—when you know. How strange that I did not see it clearly before.'

'I think Fulke L'Estrange did,' Janeta murmured through stiffened lips.

Eleanor nodded and waved away the two women. 'Take the Lady Janeta's new attendant to the kitchens and see her fed and find a place to bestow her bundles, Martha. I will take the Lady Janeta to the hall myself.'

The two women curtsied and backed from the chamber.

Janeta said haltingly, 'My lady, will you forgive me that I thought wrong of your—your decision?'

Eleanor's blue eyes clouded with doubt. 'I do so love him, Janeta. I am prepared to risk anything for him—even my immortal soul.' The last words were whispered. She touched her belly fleetingly, 'I think I already carry his child, so—so the Curia must listen and grant my plea to be absolved from my oath.' Her lip trembled. 'Sometimes, when I lie on my bed after—after he has left me, I feel a terrible apprehension I could not share with him, as if—as if the price I must pay for breaking my sworn oath will doom him—and my unborn children.' She gave a nervous little laugh. 'There, I know that is fanciful, and in the light of full day I am able to put it aside. At all events it is a penance I am willing to pay for the joy I have in him.'

Janeta was silent, tongue-tied by the revelation of the abiding love of these two who had taken her to their hearts. She swallowed the pitying lump which had formed in her own throat, reached out, and, taking Eleanor's hand, raised it to her lips.

Smiling through their tears, the two women, hand in hand, descended the stair to the great hall.

The steward hastened forward to conduct them to the raised dais where the Countess's chair of state stood. Eleanor drew Janeta along briskly and, for a moment, she did not see that the Earl and Bertrand were standing side by side near the chair. Behind it stood Sir Hugh Cobham. Then she saw who was seated within it. Janeta half stumbled, recollected herself, and bent in a deep curtsy.

Henry Plantagenet was dressed quite plainly in a fine wool green tunic and, over it, a fur-lined brown mantle clasped with a gold enamelled brooch, its only ornament. He wore no coronet for this very private visit to his sister's manor. He waved his hand genially to the two women to rise and nodded dismissively to the steward. The Earl, Sir Hugh, Bertrand, Janeta and the Countess were now alone in the hall with their sovereign. He looked round for Simon, who drew Bertrand forward to stand before the King's chair.

King Henry looked very young, almost vulnerable, but Janeta recalled Simon's warning that he could be both obstinate and ruthless and noticed the hard set of the youthful bearded lips. She also noted the drooping eye which was the only mar to her royal half-brother's handsome face. His eyes were blue, like Eleanor's, and his hair bore that sheen of red which Fulke had glimpsed in her own tresses. She waited in trepidation for his royal decree concerning her future.

He smiled suddenly, and it was as if the sun had appeared after a heavy shower. He held out one ringed hand graciously. 'So, little half-sister, for so I must call you now, I see you are unharmed and fully recovered.'

'I am, Your Grace.' She feared her limbs would let her down but she made her voice steady. 'I thank you for your concern. Know, Your Grace, that I would never reveal anything about my birth which would cause you embarrassment.'

'That is good to know. Nevertheless I find it is my duty now to provide for your future. Your father—I mean Sir Hugh here—had meant you to enter St Catherine's nunnery. I understand you opposed his wish.'

Janeta controlled her rising panic and nodded. 'I felt I had no vocation, sire.'

'Well, well,' he sighed. 'We do not wish any other member of our family to make an irrevocable oath which she would later regret. So, it appears I must arrange a marriage for you.'

Janeta could find no words to object. She waited, her eyes wide with terror.

'Sir Bertrand D'Aubigny, you were instrumental in freeing the demoiselle from a compromising and dangerous situation. I take it you would have no objection to receiving her hand in marriage and thus silencing all scurrilous talk which might arise after this disgraceful affair?'

Bertrand's voice was level and very clear. 'I would deem it a signal honour, Your Grace.'

'Good, good. The Earl and Sir Hugh are in agreement that it would be in the demoiselle Janeta's best interests. I will put it in hand that a manor be found for you in Warwickshire, as I am informed you wish to remain in the Earl of Leicester's household.' He looked intently at Janeta. 'You will accept my choice?'

Janeta's heart was hammering so loudly within her breast that she could not hear her own answer. 'Yes, Your Grace, with all my heart.'

He turned smilingly to Eleanor. 'I think arrangements have been made in your private chapel to conclude this business, and then we can all refresh ourselves in your private solar. I am hungry as a hunter, as I am sure all the travellers are.'

Eleanor nodded. 'My chaplain is waiting, sire. Is it your intention to be present?'

'Indeed. Why else should I travel from Westminster?' He rose, stepped down from the dais, and gallantly offered his arm to Janeta.

'Allow me, sister, to escort you to your bridal and give you to your bridegroom.'

She was deadly afraid. Not of the pain; the lady Eleanor had warned her of what to expect, and that there might be pain at first—but there would be delight later, she had said. Janeta had been too young for her nurse to prepare her for her bridal and the nuns, of course, had never mentioned the subject. The Countess had tacitly understood that and had taken Janeta aside from her maid and dismissed her own attendants while she had patiently explained what she felt the young bride needed to know.

No, she was not afraid that Bertrand would not treat her with gentle consideration—she knew him too well to fear him—but she had not been honest with him. She should have told him that she was disfigured, set aside from all other women, told him long before this when he would not have been placed in a position when he could not openly reject her. She had had the opportunity but had always shied from the revulsion she might see in his eyes, the superstitious dread she had seen in others when she had been a young child at home.

Eadgyth had left her alone. The Lady Eleanor had helped undress her, kissed her and wished her well. Bertrand was still below with the King, the Earl and Sir Hugh. He could not leave the King's presence until Henry rose to retire himself or graciously dismissed the young bridegroom. Eadgyth was most likely with Wulf. Janeta smiled in the half-darkness. Those two formed their miniature household, and she supposed Bertrand would see to it that they were wed soon, for she was sure that they were already bedded.

The marriage ceremony had seemed unreal to her, conducted in the beautiful private chapel of Odiham Manor. The King himself had placed her hand in Bertrand's and she had felt the heavy weight of Bertrand's seal-ring upon her finger. The private banquet which followed the ceremony had seemed equally strange, distant, as if she were not taking part in it. She had shared plate and loving-cup with Bertrand, had felt Sir Hugh's gaze upon her and wondered, almost hysterically, how Ralph would take the account of how the King himself had honoured the wedding of his despised sister. Afterwards, when Lady Eleanor had risen from the table, indicating that it was time for the bride to retire, Sir Hugh had excused himself to the King, risen and accompanied them to the door.

As the Lady Eleanor had stood back he had stooped and kissed Janeta very gently in blessing. 'Your mother would be truly proud of her daughter this day, as I believe your father would too. I regret I did not give myself time to truly know you. I wish you all happiness, Janeta.'

She had reached up impulsively, flung her arms

round his neck and kissed him soundly upon the cheek, then she had run hastily to join the Countess.

She turned nervously from the fireplace now as the door opened quietly and Bertrand slipped into the chamber. The King was a pious man, fond of his family, and he valued dignity. He would have allowed no riotous behaviour for the bedding and she was glad of it.

Her husband stood for a moment, hesitating, then came to join her near the fire, undoing his sword-belt.

How lovely she was, he thought, standing tall and straight, in that almost transparent shift, drawn tightly up to her throat with the firelight moulding and gilding her body beneath. There was a sudden catch in his throat and for moments he was bereft of speech. He could not believe she was truly his. Her glorious hair cascaded on to her shoulders and almost to her waist, the flickering flames highlighting those subtle red glints which he had admired so long ago, it seemed now, in the hut near Winchester.

She moved slightly, her hand to her throat. 'Has— has the King retired?'

'No, he recollected himself at last and sent me up— to you.'

'Oh.'

He put out a hand to touch her hair. 'I shall not hurt you, Janeta. I am a patient man. I suppose they kept you ignorant. . .'

'No, the Lady Eleanor has been talking with me. I. . .'

'That was good of her. I was prepared to be both teacher and husband.'

She backed a little from him as, again, he put up a hand to touch her cheek.

'I just want to look at you now, my Janeta, without that confining shift.'

'No,' she whispered piteously, 'please, when we are in bed—when the candles are out. . .'

'Janeta,' he said chidingly, 'there is naught for us to be ashamed of now. The priest has made us one. Our bodies must be joined and then our souls will be, I swear it.'

'I know,' she said breathlessly. 'I am not afraid. I love you, Bertrand, I do, with all my heart and soul, but I cannot bear you to look at me.'

He checked her move towards the bed and firmly began to undo the drawstring which fastened her shift.

She did not resist. It would be useless, she knew, and so she stood docile, while the tears began to rain down her cheeks.

'I should have told you,' she sobbed. 'You had the right to know.'

Her shift fell to the floor and she stood, gloriously revealed to him, high, firm young breasts standing proudly, small waist and taut, flat belly.

He bent and put his lips to the crimson mark, traced it gently from her throat to her breast, arousing her so that she gasped in sudden shock.

'This,' he murmured hoarsely, 'is this what is causing all the trouble, what you fear to show to me? My darling, I saw it the night we met. It was so cold but you had thrown off your blanket in sleep. I came over to tuck it more firmly round you My borrowed tunic had slipped from your shoulder. Even in the dim light of the hut, when our camp-fire burned low, I saw the birthmark clearly.'

'You are not afraid? It is the devil's mark. Melisande, my witch ancestor, bestowed it on me. The sight of it killed Fulke L'Estrange. He tore my gown and wimple and—and when he saw—he made choking noises and he fell. . .'

'Sweetheart, how can you, convent-bred, continue

to believe such superstitious nonsense? Fulke L'Estrange suffered some shock. He was John's squire. It is possible John himself bore such a mark. I don't know. L'Estrange was likely with him when he died. There was talk of poison, you know, though I think the late King died of an excess of wine and overripe peaches. L'Estrange was unlikely to have been in any plot to kill his master. John's continued existence meant preferment for him. Who knows what went through his mind, my love? It is even possible he suffered a sudden pang of conscience in so misusing his former master's daughter. The mark is but a birth defect, not even that to me. It sets you apart, an adjunct to your beauty.' He kissed it again, so that she sighed with acute pleasure. 'Now, we have talked too much. Let me take you to bed, sweet love.'

She lay within his arms and Eleanor's promise came true. Bertrand, her gallant knight, was considerate and skilful. Now that she was no longer afraid of rejection, she allowed herself to be wooed. His hands and lips awakened desires which she knew had been stirring within her, longings she had tried to repress. When he took her, at last, there was pain, but it dissolved in ecstasy. Afterwards, as they lay close and she bent to kiss his hair, slick with the sweat of exertion, she knew fulfilment at last. At little half-smile played about her lips. Bertrand, her landless knight, had a royal bride, but few would know it and she would always be truly content to be called simply my lady D'Aubigny.

LEGACY of LOVE

Coming next month

GINNIE COME LATELY
Carola Dunn

Regency

When Justin, Lord Amis, returned from abroad, he found that in his absence his father had married a penniless widow—and taken on her brood of unruly children! Justin felt the family were unprincipled upstarts, and he was sure the eldest daughter Ginnie was masterminding the irritating attacks upon him by her siblings, but every time he was confronted by her beauty he seemed incapable of routing her. Reinforcements were needed, and he summoned his fianceé, Lady Amabel, and all her tonnish friends to a house party...

CHEVALIER'S PAWN
Sarah Westleigh

Wales 1406/7
Book Four—D'Evreux Family Saga

Chevalier Raoul de Chalais had grown up vowing revenge against the d'Evreux family for the way they had treated his grandfather Stephen. He hoped that serving Henry IV would give him an opening against them.

Then fate took a hand. Besieging a Welsh castle brought him hostage Lady Katrine Lawtye, who was intended for Lionel d'Evreux, the Earl's heir. Five years captive, and she was still a gallant soul—could she be the instrument of his revenge? Better marriage to him than delivered up to the hated d'Evreux!

LEGACY of LOVE

Coming next month

RACHEL
Lynda Trent
England 1850

Rachel Pennington was fast approaching spinsterhood, but she simply refused to marry a man who wasn't dashing and mysterious. And no man in her sleepy village so far from London fit the bill—until handsome and *very* mysterious Jared Prescott moved into the neighbouring estate. Jared had come to the country seeking privacy, and he couldn't risk coming clean with his suspicious neighbours when there was a killer on the loose. But he hadn't counted on meeting pretty, persistent Rachel, much less wanting to court her! Suddenly, his reputation as a hermit was a damned nuisance…

THE PRISONER
Cheryl Reavis
North Carolina, USA, 1865

Union Captain John Howe escaped a living hell when he tunnelled his way out of a Confederate prison camp. Now he was saddled with his own prisoner, the sad, stubborn Amanda Douglas. Even her previous spartan existence had not prepared Amanda for the dangerous trek she was now making, entirely against her will.

But when John gazed at her through his beautiful, haunted eyes, bright with fever, she was lost. Could a priviliged Yankee son and a poor, proud Rebel girl keep their love safe from the world?

SPRING FLOWER COMPETITION

How would you like a years supply of Temptation books ABSOLUTELY FREE? Well, you can win them all! All you have to do is complete the word puzzle below and send it in to us by 31st December 1995. The first 5 correct entries picked out of the bag after that date will win a years supply of Temptation books (*four books every month - worth over £90*). What could be easier?

COWSLIP									
	L	L	E	B	E	U	L	B	Q
BLUEBELL	P	R	I	M	R	O	S	E	A
PRIMROSE	I	D	O	D	Y	U	I	P	R
DAFFODIL	L	O	X	G	O	R	S	E	Y
ANEMONE	S	T	H	R	I	F	T	M	S
DAISY	W	P	I	L	U	T	F	K	I
GORSE	O	E	N	O	M	E	N	A	A
TULIP	C	H	O	N	E	S	T	Y	D
HONESTY									
THRIFT									

PLEASE TURN OVER FOR DETAILS OF HOW TO ENTER ➡

HOW TO ENTER

Hidden in the grid are various British flowers that bloom in the Spring. You'll find the list next to the word puzzle overleaf and they can be read backwards, forwards, up, down, or diagonally. When you find a word, circle it or put a line through it.

After you have completed your word search, don't forget to fill in your name and address in the space provided and pop this page in an envelope (you don't need a stamp) and post it today. Hurry - competition ends 31st December 1995.

Mills & Boon Spring Flower Competition,
FREEPOST,
P.O. Box 344,
Croydon,
Surrey. CR9 9EL

Are you a Reader Service Subscriber?   Yes ❑   No ❑

Ms/Mrs/Miss/Mr _____

Address _____

_____

_____ Postcode _____

One application per household.   F

You may be mailed with other offers from other reputable companies as a result of this application. If you would prefer not to receive such offers, please tick box. ❑

COMP395